I0717678

Tell-Tale Publishing's 3rd Annual Horror Anthology

Printed in the United States of America

Table of Contents

Vacuity

by

Feind Gottes

Vacuity

by

Feind Gottes

A blade had never felt so good in her hand. The weight and balance of the blade was utter perfection, with a handle that felt custom made just for her. She swung her arm back and forth through the air in front of her, enjoying the feel of the blade and the light swoosh sound it made cutting through the nothing. She hadn't felt such a moment of clarity in longer than she could remember. She wasn't allowed near anything sharp, anything dangerous, but a mistake had been made. Now, here she stood with a butcher knife in her hand longing to use it, longing to stab it into flesh, longing to turn the shiny, stainless steel red. He really should have known better, she thought.

I wonder what his guts look like.

Bleed him slow. I want to taste his agony.

Give us blood!

A cacophony of voices filled her head. Even with the medication, the one she had stopped taking a week ago, they were always there. She felt like she was forever trapped in a ballroom filled to overflowing with people all huddled together making small talk. Normally it was just noise, nothing could be clearly heard in the non-stop humdrum in her head. Not today though. Today the voices were clear, and they wanted blood. The murmurs had turned into a chant of "Give us blood!" She planned to appease them. She felt a burning desire to murder. It couldn't be stopped now.

Give us blood! Give us blood! Give us blood!

The crowd had been whipped into a frenzy, giving her no choice but to quench their lust, her lust, for blood. She crept across the floor with cat-like stealth, on the prowl, the knife at her side out of sight. She licked her lips in anticipation, creeping closer, waiting for the precise moment to strike.

She slipped up behind the chair he had fallen asleep in, knowing she had to make her first strike count. He was much larger and stronger than her. She held still a moment not daring to breathe, contemplating where to strike that first blow. He was sleeping so she could easily slit his throat or stab him straight in the heart but then it would be over too quickly, there would be no screaming. She thoroughly enjoyed the screaming and her host of friends were dying to hear them too. "Bleed him slow," one of the voices in the void demanded. She desired to do just that. She twirled the blade in her hand. knowing she needed to be precise or her fun would be over far too quickly.

"Do it!" The multitude of voices called out as one.

Quick as lightning she sprang up, reached around, grabbed his forehead, pulled his head back, and plunged the blade through the back of the chair into his spine. His eyes popped open. First fear, then pain, all in the space of a breath. Delightful! Her ploy went even better than she imagined. The blade sliced through his spinal cord in the middle of his back, instantly paralyzing his lower body. She let his head go moving around to the front of the chair as the voices cheered in celebration.

Sweet, sweet Julie. Now bleed him slow.

Let's see what his guts look like, Julie.

Bath in his blood. Make it flow! Make it flow!

She had begun smiling subconsciously, looking every bit as insane as she was. She had quieted the voices for too long. Now they wanted to come out and play and she was happy to let them.

Strip him. Make him bleed.

Let's play with his insides!

"Jules?" Anthony could barely get the word out.

Her only reaction to him saying her name was to leave the room. She retrieved a roll of duct tape from the junk drawer in the kitchen, then returned to her paralyzed victim. He weakly tried to resist her as she slapped a piece of tape over his mouth. He was helpless to do anything to stop her, slumped in the chair. He had been tasked with taking care of her only to realize now just how poor a job he had done.

She leaned down to whisper in his ear, "Time to play." She added an exclamation point by licking his cheek.

His eyes nearly bulged out of their sockets as she flicked off his left nipple with the butcher knife. There was nothing he could do but sit and watch as she poked him over and over with the knife. At first, she stabbed into his flesh with the tip, never letting it penetrate very far, stopping to watch each little rivulet of crimson roll down his chest. It wasn't long before she was stabbing the blade in deeper with each new wound, but after forty or fifty times she grew bored with her little pokes. Anthony hoped she would satiate her bloodlust from the minor wounds but knew it was likely only feeding it.

She leaned into his ear once more, "I want to see what you look like inside."

Julie Duplantier stood back from him with a wicked smirk smeared across her lips, soaking in the fear she saw in his eyes. She got down on her knees in front him, something that would have made him smile as little as a few minutes ago, savoring every second of his dread. She looked up at him, sweetly batting her eyelashes as she slid the butcher knife into his flesh just below the xyphoid process where both sides of the ribcage come together. She watched the horror wash over his eyes as she pulled the knife down slowly, splitting his abdomen open down to the pelvis. He was still alive as she began pulling out his insides, wrapping his intestines around her neck like a grisly boa, feeling every bit as glamorous as a Hollywood starlet.

<u>The Wild Healer</u>

Dr. Christian Andreu adjusted his gold-rimmed glasses before running a hand through his short blond hair as he waited for the elevator door to open. He was glad to have the hard part of convincing the board that this surgery was necessary out of the way. It had been no easy feat. His colleagues leaned heavily toward therapy combined with medication rather than altering brain function through surgery. They had resisted, but when the alternative was risking the lives of more staff they had finally relented.

He hated losing the opportunity to observe, examine and treat such an extreme case of schizophrenia, but there was really no choice. The orderly, Michael, who she attacked was six foot five and three hundred pounds, yet she had managed to maim him for life in a matter of seconds. The surgery was an extreme measure, but Julie Duplantier was an extreme patient.

In the beginning he had delusions of grandeur for his work with such an extreme case but there would be no published articles in the New England Journal of Medicine or Psychiatry Today and definitely no best-selling book to make him famous. He lamented that fact as he stood ready to meet with patient #321-1420 for the final time, while she was still a unique specimen.

Julie Duplantier was crouched in the far corner of the room facing the wall with her arms wrapped around her knees gently rocking back and forth. She didn't acknowledge the doctor's presence in the room, she sat in her corner softly mumbling to herself as she rocked gently back and forth.

"Julie? It's Dr. Andreu, may I speak to you for a moment?" He asked her softly.

Julie made no move to acknowledge the doctor's presence. He hadn't needed any warning from the patient's mother during their phone call earlier, he and the staff knew full well how dangerous patient #321-1420 was. She would sit in the corner rocking herself back and forth acting like she was off in another universe but that was her little game.

It had only been her second day at Bainbridge Institute for the Criminally Insane when the orderly, Michael, had turned his back on her to set down her lunch tray. He towered over her petite frame but little hundred and ten pound Julie Duplantier had leapt onto his back digging out his left eye with her finger before he could throw her off. She had laughed as she tossed it into her mouth like a gumball chewing it up then spitting it out right in front of him. Since then she had attacked four nurses and her first psychiatrist who refused to see her afterward. Luckily none had been harmed as grievously as Michael, but she was no less a menace to everyone around her. The nurses tried to have security accompany them when entering her room but there were only so many guards for the thirty-five patients in the maximum-security ward.

Dr. Andreu watched her like a hawk as he moved to the bed to sit down.

"Please Julie, join me a moment." He patted the bed next to him masking his own nervousness.

He waited a moment knowing she heard him but knowing she would only come when she was good and ready. He sat waiting patiently until finally she stopped rocking and turned to look at him. Her long, straggly black hair hung in her face making her look extraordinarily evil like a wicked witch out of a horror movie. She was a tiny woman barely breaking five feet tall, but she had not an ounce of fear in her. She knew every member of the staff was afraid to come in her room, it may have been the only thing that gave her any pleasure at all.

"They told me you were coming. They say you're going to scramble my brain. Are you going to play with my brain doc? I'd play with yours." Julie's voice cracked reinforcing her resemblance to a witch.

"That's what we need to talk about Julie. Please, come sit with me. I won't bite if you don't." He smiled at her, trying to break through her defenses, "Do they say it's alright?"

"They're not sure they like you, but I think maybe I do."

She crawled onto the bed but refused to sit next to the doctor. She sat with her back to the wall, knees pulled up to her chest like she had been sitting in the corner. Her face was pale, almost ashen with eyes a brown so dark they almost appeared black. Neither were things that set most people at ease. She looked every bit as evil as her mother had described her to him only a few minutes earlier on the phone though he tried to look past the image Julie was more than happy to perpetuate. She thoroughly enjoyed people being afraid of her.

"What would you think about no longer having 'them' tell you things? Do you think you would like that?" He kept his voice as gentle as his demeanor though he watched her like a hawk.

What's he talking about? You pull that fucking forked tongue right out of his mouth!

"They really don't like you doc."

"It's not them I care about Julie. Wouldn't you like all that noise to go away? Do you remember what silence is like Julie? No voices at all?"

Rip his filthy cock off and choke him with it!

Don't let him kill us! We're your only friends. We love you.

Julie sat staring at the doctor for a long moment, "Is that what you're going to do, kill them?" A tear rolled down her cheek as she spoke, "I'm afraid. They're not all bad. They are my dearest closest friends, the only friends I've ever had." Tears rolled from both her eyes though she was well known for being able to cry whenever she wanted.

Dr. Andreu smiled at her, "Poor child, you realize they're not real. I can make them leave you alone, so you can just be you. Wouldn't you like to find out who you really are? I know I'd like to know the real Julie Duplantier." He knew he was more likely to win the lottery while being struck by lightning during an eclipse, but he needed to keep his patient calm.

Give me that lying fucking tongue! I'll shove it right up his ass!

Gut him like a fish! We wants to taste his bastard heart!

No, take his eyes! He can't hurt us without his eyes!

Julie began to pound at her temples, trying to make the cacophony stop. The voices were all yelling over each other until she couldn't tell what any of them were trying to say. They didn't want this surgery and they hated the doctor. He looked so kind to her though, like he really wanted to help her. Who was she? What would silence sound like? She felt like she needed the answer. Real tears were streaming done her cheeks as she rocked and beat her hands against her temples wanting silence more than she had ever wanted anything ever.

"Help me. A moment's peace, can you give that to me?" She begged the doctor.

"I believe I can, Julie. We'll know tomorrow." He spoke to her more like a father than a doctor.

Kill him! Kill him now!

Gouge out his eyes!

Cut out his lying whore tongue!

Make him bleed! Give us blood!

"No! You can't kill them! You can't!" She burst out though fear was written across her face.

"I know it's scary Julie, but they aren't real. They can't hurt you. They can't hurt me. They can't hurt anyone. I can't kill them honey, they aren't real. I know they're probably screaming at you right now, but they aren't real, you can ignore them. Would you like a shot? When you wake up I'll take the voices away for good, I promise."

Don't you do it bitch!

You keep him the fuck away from us!

Snap his fuckin' neck or we'll make you suffer!

Murderer!

"Please just make it stop."

Dr. Andreu removed a syringe filled with haloperidol from his pocket, removing the protective plastic cover from the needle. The drug was powerful, but it was the only thing that worked on her. He called for an orderly to help hold her down, then administered the shot into her right buttock. She calmed almost immediately, and the two men left the room to let her sleep until morning.

"Best to get her prepped for surgery while she's out so you don't have to fight her in the morning," he told the orderly before leaving the ward.

The Art of Dying

Julie floated on an ocean of nothingness. Every direction she looked there was nothing but impenetrable blackness. She felt like she was floating blindfolded on a moonless, starless night. It was peaceful floating on a cushion of nothing through a void in complete and utter silence. No voices were crying out from inside her head. She opened her mouth wide screaming as loud as her lungs would allow but no sound at all could pierce the void. No panic shocked her synapses, she had never felt calmer in her life. It was a wondrous feeling, her state of nirvana. No conflicting thoughts, no conflicting voices, no conflict at all. Tears of pure joy began to roll from the corners of her eyes as she felt at one with the void.

Julie's tranquil ride through the void faded as illuminated eyes began to pierce the black veil. They began far off in the distance as though they were coming from another universe, barely visible at all. Julie rubbed at her eyes, believing she may be imagining the distant glowing eyes. Perhaps they were stars. She imagined herself floating out in the void of space far from the human contact that she so despised. She was loathe to return to the real world. She'd rather float in the void for all eternity. When she reopened her eyes, sets of illuminated eyes had sprung up by the thousands, all staring at her. She screamed in terror, the shriek now piercing the vacuum as the eyes surrounding her multiplied again and again until the gloom was blocked completely.

Julie Duplantier, patient #321-1420, opened her eyes, finding the illuminated eyes had departed. Her dream world had vanished though she still felt as though she were dreaming. Her mind was a fog, impenetrably thick. It was as though she had woken from her own personal utopia into an alternate reality where nothing would ever be the same.

Dr. Christian Andreu stood behind the open cranium of the worst schizophrenic he had ever encountered. Julie Duplantier's auditory hallucinations were constant with no relief having been accomplished through pharmaceutical means. Placing a microchip in her brain to block the hallucinations was the only course of action left to ensure the safety of the staff. Without this surgery he was looking at a patient who would never see the outside of a padded cell again while her caregivers lived in constant danger of her homicidal psychotic episodes. This surgery was her last and only hope for a mostly normal life.

"Okay Julie now I need your help, are you ready?"

"I think so."

What are you doing you fucking bitch? Are you just going to sit there and let him kill us? Murdering cunt!

You get up right now and kill this motherfucker! He's scrambling your brain! Are you fucking stupid? Stop this!

"Alright, now you may feel a little pressure, but you shouldn't feel any pain. I need you to tell me when the voices stop. I promise you they will stop. Ready? Here we go." Dr. Andreu's voice was calm, but he had never been more excited in his entire life, "Now I need you to tell me if the voices start to fade, stop completely or grow louder, okay?"

"I'm ready. Please hurry." A tear rolled down her cheek.

Dr. Andreu began prodding into Julie's temporal lobe with an electrode, gently manipulating the tissue. He gently worked the probe down the lateral fissure and around the Brodmann areas. It seemed to take forever with no reaction from his patient at all.

"Still with me Julie?" He asked.

"I'm not going anywhere, doc. Wanna hurry, they're really raising a ruckus!"

"You need to tell me the instant they fade, stop or get worse, okay? Don't worry if they get louder, that means we're in the right spot."

"Okay, doc, just hurry."

You should have gouged out his fucking eyes last night you fucking cunt! You want him to kill us, don't you? Admit it you ungrateful bitch! After all we've done for you and this is the thanks we get?

We're gonna kill you bit...

"Stop right there!" Julie screamed.

"Fade, stop or worse?" Dr. Andreu asked.

"I... I... I think they stopped. Wait." Julie didn't even dare to blink waiting for the cacophony to begin again.

"Anything at all Julie?" Dr. Andreu asked growing impatient with excitement.

"Nothing. Not a word. Nothing at all!" Julie smiled as she began to weep tears of joy hearing complete silence for the first time she could remember outside of a dream.

Julie kept waiting for the crowd in her head to fire up again but there was nothing. She could hear the doctor ordering the staff to do this and that as he placed the microchip then began putting her head back together. She could hear herself breathing. She could hear the nurses' feet shuffling along the linoleum floor. She could hear everything. She couldn't remember ever being happier in her life and the tears wouldn't stop.

"Dr. Andreu?"

"Are you alright Julie? Did they return?" The concern in his voice was palpable.

"No. No, they're gone. I just wanted to say thank you. I never thought I'd be so happy to hear… well… nothing."

"You're welcome dear. Now we can get down to the business of really getting you better. Stitching you back up is going to take a little while would you like to sleep through it? You can have an anesthetic now."

"No! Please I want to hear everything!"

"I have to warn you, you may not like some of the sounds."

"It's okay. I want to hear it all!"

Julie Duplantier smiled from ear to ear through the entire procedure. She smiled as her cranium was screwed back in place. She smiled as she was stitched and stapled. She kept right on smiling all the way to the recovery room where she heard even more sounds no longer muffled by the party that had always raged in her head. She felt like a real person for the first time in her life.

<u>Post-Op Day 1: Only Pain</u>

Julie Duplantier walked the halls of the asylum alone. As she walked along she began to notice smears of blood along the walls. Patient's doors were ajar, and most had smears of blood across them. She walked up to one of the rooms, pushing the door all the way open. Inside was a nightmare on display. Blood was pooled on the floor, splattered and smeared across the walls and there was a ball of flesh in the corner that had once been the room's occupant. Her eyes bulged in their sockets, taking in the gruesome menagerie laid out before her. She tried to scream but it stuck in her throat refusing to come out.

In shock, she stepped back into the hallway stunned by what she had seen. She continued up the hall finding a similar scene inside each room as she went. There was blood everywhere she looked. It was running out into the hallway from every patient door, all standing slightly ajar. It began to feel as though she were trying to walk through several feet of mud as she continued down the hallway. She rounded the corner to the nurse's station at the far end of the hall, stopping dead in her tracks.

It looked like the entire area had been sprayed with red paint but that was the least of the horror. Two nurses were hanging from the ceiling. Their bodies flayed open with their intestines strung around the station like Christmas decorations. She froze, unable to move, unable to scream, barely able to breathe. Finally, she looked down to see her naked body was covered in blood and chunks of flesh like slugs stuck to her skin. Her eyes widened further in horror, seeing she held a fire axe in her hands. Realization smacked her in the face like a ten-ton hammer; she had done this. At last a scream escaped her throat.

Julie Duplantier's eyes popped wide open in a flash with a scream poised on the edge of her throat. Bright fluorescent lights blinded her, instantly killing her scream before it started as she realized it had all been a nightmare. She felt like she was sitting in a bath of her own sweat. Her head ached but otherwise she was fine. She closed her eyes again not to escape the blinding lights overhead but to enjoy the silence. She was alone in the recovery room with only the slight electronic buzz of the IV administration machine and heart monitor to keep her company. The nightmare had probably been induced by the anesthetic, she hoped.

Julie Duplantier closed her eyes and smiled, genuinely happy.

"Ms. Duplantier?" Dr. Andreu shook her shoulder lightly.

Julie's eyes popped open with the doctor's calm face filling her field of vision encircled in a halo of light from the fluorescent bulbs overhead. She couldn't stop a smile from breaking across her lips if she had wanted to; she didn't. Instinctively she tried to lift her arms to hug the man that had made her the happiest woman in the world only to find that her arms were restrained. Unable to move she broke into uncontrollable sobs.

"What's wrong? Are you having any pain?" The doctor asked.

"No, no it's just that I'd love to hug you. I know I deserve these restraints, but I've never wanted to hug someone more in my entire life. Thank you, Dr. Andreu. Thank you. Thank you. Thank you." She was sobbing so hard she could barely get the words out.

One of the nurses sneered as Dr. Andreu smiled at his new favorite patient, "You get some rest Julie and then we'll see what we can do about that."

Julie kept smiling as the doctor left the recovery room. She thought it unlikely that anyone in the history of the world had ever been so happy to hear nothing. The crowd inside her head had finally dispersed. She closed her eyes not to rest but again to explore all she could hear and not hear. There was the slow drip of the IV on her left along with the quiet electronic buzz of the unit controlling it. She could hear the slight shuffle of feet out in the hallway as the nurses and orderlies went about their business. There were also a few moans to be heard through the padded doors from her fellow inmates. All these sounds were faint, unnoticeable to almost anyone, but they were as loud as a rock concert to Julie's ears, hearing them for the first time.

 She wanted more than anything to cover her ears to truly see what experiencing silence would be like. Tears of joy spilled from the corners of her eyes as she lay there wondering what her life would be like now.

She woke up a short time later screaming. Her mouth opened wide shrieking like a banshee but all she could hear was silence. She was sitting upright in her bed, the wrist restraints that had held her fast a short time ago dangled from the bed rails. No one had come running to see why she was screaming. It was as though she had awoken back in the void. She could hear nothing. No one was coming to her aid. She was completely alone in the dark of the recovery room. Confused she pulled the IV from her arm squirting blood with a splash to the tiled floor. Still no one came. Julie swung her legs off the edge of the bed, shocked as her bare feet hit the cold tile floor. She stood, steadied herself a moment then ventured toward the door. Still no one came.

She pushed open the door of the recovery room peeking out into the dark of the hallway. A few fluorescent bulbs flickered down the corridor revealing something was very wrong. Julie saw streaks of bright crimson along the walls and floors. She walked a short way down the hall seeing bright red smears everywhere. A door stood ajar to her left. She pushed it in revealing a grisly scene within. The body of a woman had been cleaved completely in two on the floor of the small room. Blood, guts and brains had slid into the void between the two halves like a river of gore flowing through fleshy banks. Julie stood frozen a moment before stepping back into the hallway in shock. She began screaming again as a siren began to blare with deafening brilliance.

Nurse Maria scrambled to patient #321-1420's bedside, "Calm down sugar. You're in the recovery room. Do you remember having surgery?"

"I… I… I was… my head hurts." Julie's tone changed from scared to confusion as she realized she had just had another nightmare.

"I don't doubt it. Are you hearing or seeing anything you shouldn't be?"

"No, no." Julie said softly blinking her eyes firmly several times, "Just the headache."

"I'm afraid ibuprofen is about all I can give you for the pain. Where would you put the pain on a scale from one to ten?"

"About a seven or eight."

"Okay that we can deal with. No blurred vision, weird sounds or pain anywhere else?"

"No, just my head."

Nurse Maria injected a syringe of ibuprofen into Julie's IV then placed a kind hand on her shoulder, "You just lay back and rest now. The doctor will be here to check on you in a couple of hours. Until then just rest up and hit the button if you start hearing or seeing things, okay?" Maria was kind but clinical with her patient.

"Ok."

Julie closed her eyes once more enamored with the silence filling her head where once a party had raged day and night. She tried as hard as she could to stay awake, afraid of another nightmare, but it was no use. Soon she was sleeping deeply, more soundly than she ever had. Julie Duplantier experienced a calm relief that is rarely felt outside of death. No more nightmares came to haunt her.

<u>Post-Op Day 2 – The Axe</u>

Reed peeked out the small window on his cell door at the procession passing by. He recognized Dr. Andreu, Nurse Suzy and the muscular security guard, Thaddeus, who none of the patients dared to mess with. Supported on either side by the doctor and nurse was a patient he didn't recognize. She was a pretty little thing, he thought, a thing he'd like to get his hands and more all over. The patient's long black hair was pulled back in a ponytail showing off a line of staples that seemed to encircle her entire head. Her slow movement along with her recent surgery made Reed think of Frankenstein which somehow turned him on though it didn't take much to get his motor revved up. Reed began to pound at his door while licking the glass.

Julie paused a moment at the ruckus Reed was raising. She looked to the source seeing the sexual deviant licking the glass like a fool. She wasn't repulsed, in fact, her lips broke into a sly smile knowing that in a few minutes he'd be masturbating to her image in his mind. The thought was cut short by movement toward the door from the mammoth Thaddeus.

"Leave him be Thaddeus. Acknowledging him will only make it worse." The security guard stopped dead in his tracks at the doctor's command, "He'll stop once we pass."

"Stop to do something perverse." Nurse Suzy muttered.

"Jizzlobber." Julie giggled.

"It isn't funny patient #321-1420." Nurse Suzy tried to be serious, but she nearly burst out at Julie's name for the worst sexual offender on the ward.

"Oh, come now Suzy, I think we both know that was pretty funny." Dr. Andreu butted in.

"Yeah but someone has to clean it up later. You wanna lend a hand, doc?"

"I clean minds not cells, Nurse Suzy."

"Well ain't you the lucky one!" Suzy said with a smile, "Thankfully it ain't me neither but somebody's gotta do it. That man has serious issues."

"They all do. Let's hope we've solved most of Mrs. Duplantier's yesterday. No more trouble from you right, Julie?" Dr. Andreu asked friendlier than she had ever heard him sound.

"No one's telling me to stab you in the throat right now if that's what you mean. Ol' Jizzlobber back there could use a little blade induced politeness though." Julie paused as Dr. Andreu gave her a stern look, "I ain't hearin' no one tell me to do that, I'm just sayin' a little castration would go a long way with that one, I think." Julie did laugh a little at that and neither Nurse Suzy nor Dr. Andreu could hold back either.

"You're probably right about that. Now let's get you into my office so we can see just how far you've already come."

The rest of the quartet's journey went without incident. Thaddeus waited outside while the doctor and nurse helped Julie into a comfortably padded chair inside. Once their patient was settled Nurse Suzy left to resume her duties until the session was over.

Dr. Andreu sat down in the leather chair behind the desk, "Now I understand you had a nightmare last night? Can you tell me about it?"

"It was nothing." Julie said as nonchalant as possible, "I just dreamt that I was completely deaf, that's all." She crossed her fingers that he would believe the lie.

Dr. Andreu shifted in his seat, the way psychiatrist's do, giving her a blank look that told the patient not a single thing of what they are thinking, "Are you sure there was nothing else? Can you hear anything now, even faint voices?"

"I'm sure." She answered, "There is only silence in here now, doc." She pointed a finger to her head.

He eyed her with care for the slightest hint that she wasn't being truthful with him, "It's important you tell me if you begin hearing anything no matter how faint. Even if you can't make out a word or if they tell you to buy a puppy, I need to know immediately. Okay?"

"I promise doc. I want them gone for good more than you do." A tear of honesty slipped down her cheek.

Dr. Andreu handed a tissue across his desk to her, "I know Julie, I know." He said with total sincerity, "How are you feeling otherwise? What would you put your pain level at?"

"Thank you. I feel good other than the dull ache in my head. It's not bad, maybe a three, at best, right now." Julie felt good actually being able to be truthful with people like the doc now, at least mostly truthful.

Julie patted the few tears welling up in the corners of her eyes with the tissue. When she looked up she froze stiff, praying that Dr. Andreu wouldn't notice anything was wrong. She saw herself standing behind the doctor with a knife to his throat. Her darker self stood there with a wicked smile on her lips staring back at Julie with eyes as black as pitch. Dark Julie slapped her free hand over the doctor's forehead pulling his head back, then pulled the knife across his exposed neck deep and slow.

"We want blood! We'll gut him like the pig he is!" Dark Julie screamed.

"What is it Julie? Are you okay?" Dr. Andreu asked frantically.

Julie lifted her head realizing she had just let out a scream in the small office. She stared wide eyed at the doctor but her darker self was nowhere to be seen. Dr. Andreu was leaning forward in his chair out of concern with his throat fully intact. Julie breathed a sigh of relief before answering.

"Damn. Sharp pain!" she lied, "Feels like someone just stabbed me in the side of the head!" She grabbed her head to accentuate the lie and hide her face.

"It's okay, Julie. Did it feel like an electrical shock or a sharp stabbing pain?"

"Like… like a strong electric shock I guess. Like a bolt of lightning!" She did her best to sell her lie.

"I should have warned you to expect sharp pains like that, I'm sorry. The chip I implanted is tiny but it's still a foreign body in your brain. It's nothing to be concerned about right now but if it persists you need to let me and the nurses know. Unfortunately, there isn't a lot we can do for that, but they should fade away after a day or two." Dr. Andreu had gone into clinical mode with little empathy in his voice.

Julie nodded wanting to be back in her room, safe from whatever was going on in her brain aside from the silence she was enjoying so much. Dr. Andreu kept their session brief, more concerned for the moment with her physical health than anything else. Nurse Suzy returned to assist Thaddeus in returning Julie to her room while Dr. Andreu moved on to his next patient.

Before exiting Julie turned back to Dr. Andreu with a tear in her eye, "Thank you."

Nurse Suzy and Thaddeus returned Patient #321-1420 to her room without incident now that Reed had been sedated. Julie almost burst out laughing as the word "jizzlobber" popped back into her brain, but she was able to contain herself. She closed her eyes to the drab yellow of the hallway stinking of bleach with a faint hint of urine underneath that never seemed to leave no matter how much bleach they used. She shuffled her feet along knowing Suzy and Thaddeus wouldn't let her fall.

When she opened her eyes, Dark Julie was back. She stood at the end of the hallway with a fire axe dripping blood from both ends. Her twin stared, smiling at Julie covered in bright crimson from head to toe. Dark Julie stared with eyes black as pitch wearing nothing but a smile to go with her crimson coat. Julie stared back as blood dripped off her evil twin's nipples to the cold tile floor. She could hear it splatter drip by bloody drip. No voices blocked the sound.

"We want blood and we want it now! What are you waiting for, you sniveling little bitch?" Dark Julie's screech echoed down the hallway.

Julie inhaled a deep breath closing her eyes on her evil twin. When she opened them again Dark Julie was gone. All she could see was the long, dull yellow hallway lit in fluorescent light smelling faintly of urine and strongly of bleach. She let out a sigh her caretakers took for pain then finally she was at the door to her home, Cell #1420. Once inside she lay on her bed enjoying the silence as she drifted off to sleep.

Julie awoke a few hours later with her head aching as though she'd been hit in the head with a sledgehammer. She sat up dropping her legs over the edge of her bed which only seemed to make the pain increase even further. She cupped her head in her hands with elbows propped up on her knees, but the pain only grew until it felt like her head was going to explode. She screamed out for help and she could hear the scampering of feet in the hallway coming to her aid.

The African-American giant Thaddeus was the first to burst through her cell door to make sure it was safe before any nurse entered. He wanted to take pity on the tiny woman sitting on the bed with her head in her hands but that was about how his friend and fellow orderly, Michael, had lost an eye to this one.

"P… please. It hurts." Julie said through tears.

Thaddeus observed her for any sign that she might be faking so they would lower their guard but found none. He ushered in the nurse carrying a syringe of pain relief. Nurse Yolanda sat down next to Julie on the bed who was rocking back and forth from the pain.

"Sharp pain or throbbing ache, honey?" Yolanda asked.

"Intense throbbing ache… like a twelve! Please help!" Julie pleaded through tears.

Seeing that patient #321-1420 was no threat, Thaddeus ducked out into the hallway to wait for the nurse to finish. The moment Thaddeus stepped out, Julie grabbed Nurse Yolanda by the head sinking her teeth hard and fast through the nurse's throat. She ripped Nurse Yolanda's throat out with a spray of blood painting her face in solid crimson. Julie spit out the flesh trying not to laugh. Nurse Yolanda slumped to the cold tile of the floor, dead before her brain had time to realize it. Julie quickly grabbed the dead nurse's syringe, slipped behind her cell door then let out a blood curdling scream.

Thaddeus rushed through the open door freezing at the sight of the dead nurse on the floor which was just long enough for Julie to jump on his back plunging the syringe into his thick, football player's neck over and over again with monstrous force. She stayed on his back stabbing away as he slumped first to his knees then finally limply over the bloody body of Nurse Yolanda. Julie stared into her reflection in the pool of mixed blood until she was sure the large orderly was as dead as the nurse.

Julie Duplantier peeked out of her open door to ensure the coast was clear; it was. Only a short way down the hallway she could see the red fire alarm next to a fire box holding the axe she so desperately wanted to feel in her hands. No one screamed for her to stop as she approached the box or when she shattered the glass with her elbow or when she gripped the wooden handle twirling the shiny silver and red blade in her hands. No one stopped her as she chopped her way into the closest cell. No nurses or security came running as she whacked into the cell's occupant until the patient was a barely recognizable red mass on the floor. She exited the room wiping a bloody hand down the wall while dragging the axe across the floor with the other.

The next room was her admirer from earlier, Reed the jizzlobber. She let her blood-soaked hospital gown fall to the floor to give Reed one last final peep show then hacked the lock from his door entering with her arms spread wide to give him a good look. Reed's face lit up at the sight, but it was short lived as Julie brought the axe down hard cleaving his head in two. Julie giggled as Reed's penis sprang to attention as the brain that had told it to do so slopped to the cold tile at his feet. She continued to giggle as she brought the axe down on jizzlobber's torso until there was nothing left. She exited Reed's cell awash in red.

Julie continued going from one room to the next with no one stopping her. She dispatched patients and staff with equal vigor until there was no one left to kill. Blood was strewn across floors, walls and ceilings turning the whole ward red. Julie slid down a blood-stained wall wrapping her arms around her knees, rocking gently back and forth. Red turned to black as she returned to the void while she rocked herself gently and waited.

Julie practically jumped out of her skin as Nurse Yolanda gently shook her shoulder to rouse her from her sleep. For a moment as Julie opened her eyes all she could see was red. She jerked back from the nurse's touch as if the Grim Reaper himself stood before her.

Nurse Yolanda gave her a gentle smile, "It's okay Julie. It's almost time for breakfast."

<u>Post-Op Day 3 – The Gift of Guilt</u>

"How's my favorite patient today?" Dr. Andreu said with a kind smile.

"I still can't get used to the silence but otherwise I'm fine, doc." She didn't dare look the doctor in the eye for him to see through her half-truth.

Dr. Andreu flipped through the nurse's notes on Julie Duplantier's file, "I see you managed to make it through the night without another nightmare?"

"Nothing but happy dreams of kittens and candy." She shot him a smile as fake as her words.

Dr. Andreu frowned at her. "Please stop that, the State hates when I have to write 'patient is full of shit' in the official file." They both got a good laugh out of that. "In all seriousness, Julie, the operation wasn't a cure, far from it. It was the relieving of one single symptom of whatever else may be going on in that pretty little head of yours. I'm glad you're obviously feeling much better. I know the staff is feeling better having one less patient they have to worry will gouge one of their eyes out at any given moment, however, you're not cured, Julie. The voices you were hearing were a symptom only, the thoughts behind them were your own and we need to find out where they were coming from. I don't mean to scare you, I just want you to understand that our work here has only just begun." He sounded kind yet firm at the same time.

Julie sat silent a moment unsure how to answer him. She looked down fidgeting with her fingers trying to decide where to begin. Her heart sank as she looked back at her handsome head shrinker. Her dark twin stood behind the doctor as she had the previous day holding a knife to his throat. The twin put a finger to her lips in the universal sign to keep quiet.

"Kill them all Julie! This one's a mushroom..." Dark Julie pulled the doctor's head back, "... feed him shit and keep him in the dark. We want their blood Julie. Make it flow or we'll make you!" Dark Julie screamed.

Julie dropped her hand back to her lap hoping her dark half would leave. She closed her eyes tight as though she could force the vision out. She waited a long moment before daring to look up again.

"Are you okay, Julie? I know it has to be confusing being able to think for yourself without the voices screaming at you constantly. Do you miss them, maybe just a little bit?" Dr. Andreu's voice broke the long silence.

Julie looked up slowly hoping the doctor was all she would see. Dark Julie had moved back behind the doctor. The knife she had held to his throat now hung at her side lightly tapping her thigh. Dark Julie stood staring with dead eyes, naked and covered in blood. Sunlight from the high window behind the doctor made her breasts seem to shimmer in gore drenched glory.

"I… I'm fine." Julie managed as her dark self held a finger up for her to be quiet, "The silence is hard to get used to, that's all."

"I can see there's something else going on with you. Please, I can't help you if you don't speak to me. What's on your mind?" Dr. Andreu urged.

Dark Julie ran a bloody finger across her neck then disappeared.

Julie hesitated. Should she tell the doctor about what she was seeing, about the nightmares or should she keep it to herself? They already think you're crazy, she thought. Hell, you're locked up in a nuthouse! But what if I have a chance at getting out? *You really think they're going to let a nutter like you back out on the streets?* came her mother's voice. *Feed him shit and keep him in the dark,* her dark half's words shot into her mind.

"How do I move on from here, doc? What if I am better? What difference does it make? I know what I've done. I know there's no way I'm ever going to get out of here. So maybe you cured me, so what? What now? You've given me hope that I can be something else but what else can I be other than patient #321-1420? Is that all I'll ever be? Because if it is, take this stupid chip back out!" Tears streamed from Julie's eyes as she pointed out her own pointless existence.

Dr. Andreu handed her the whole box of tissues, "I'm not going to lie to you, Julie. You've done some horrible things but look around you. Do you understand how big this facility is? What you've seen of it is only a small part. I can't guarantee exactly what will happen going forward but if we can get to a place where you're no longer a danger to yourself or others then perhaps Bainbridge isn't your life's final stop. Between now and then you need to talk to me. Prove to me you're well enough to be moved to a nicer part of the hospital, maybe get to go outside, feel the breeze on your face and see the sun through something other than a window. You can have a life where there are no restraints or padded rooms. Wouldn't that be nice, Julie?"

While Dr. Andreu spoke, Julie sat with her head in her hands trying to not only make sense of his words but of the visions of her darker self. She couldn't remember a time without a party raging in her head at all times, but she had never seen things that weren't there. She hoped that this vision of herself was just a side effect of the surgery, one that would fade in time. Julie Duplantier hoped but she didn't believe.

She decided it best to keep the nightmares and visions of her bloody naked twin to herself. If they didn't stop after a few days, then she would tell Dr. Andreu. No sense worrying him over nothing, she thought.

Finally, Julie answered, "Yes that would be nice. Maybe I'm just a lost cause, doc. Everyone I've ever known hates me, even my own mother. Maybe she was right all along, maybe I am just pure evil."

"I can't guarantee that I can bring your mother around but not everyone hates you. I don't hate you. The staff was rightly cautious around you, but they don't hate you. It's up to you from here on out. Show kindness, get kindness."

"I'll try doc, I really will." Dread filled her as she looked up at Dr. Andreu, but Dark Julie had not returned, much to her relief.

The visions of her darker half disturbed her though she was hopeful that the apparition would only be temporary, fading away after a few days. Julie was haunted by the horrific things she had done, the things the voices had told her to do. She still didn't understand why she hadn't been able to fight against them, stop them from taking over. She had come to Bainbridge after killing her last caregiver, but it hadn't been her first murder. She had blood on her hands that could never be washed away whether she was cured or not. She regretted all of it, save one. She had no regret over disemboweling her stepfather who had abused her in every way possible. No one should have to suffer that way, not even her. A multitude of thoughts drifted through her mind as she was escorted back to her room but overall, she was feeling positive about the future now that it looked like she had one.

"I don't think of I've ever seen you smile, child." Nurse Aishya said with a smile of her own.

"Don't think I've ever had a reason to." Julie replied.

"We're all glad you're doing so well. Even Michael was glad to hear it. Do you remember him, Julie?" The nurse asked cautiously.

Julie hung her head, "Would it be possible… I mean… could I apologize to him? Would he want to see me?"

"I think he'd like that very much. I'll see what I can do, honey."

"Thank you."

Julie entered her cell humbled by the kindness she was being shown by the staff of Bainbridge State Hospital who she had tormented and assaulted since the day she arrived. For perhaps the first time in her life, Julie Duplantier felt as though she could have an actual life. Maybe, just maybe, her fortune had changed with the surgery. She was positive she'd never be able to leave this place, but as Dr. Andreu had told her, her life didn't have to be this cold cell for the remainder of her days. She laid down on the bed imagining how the sun would feel on her face. She wanted to lay out in it enjoying the sounds of nature that she had never really heard but now it was possible. Her lips curled into a smile as a tear of joy rolled from the corner of her eye. So, this is what peace feels like, she thought.

"Kill them all!" Dark Julie's harsh voice cut through the silence like a gunshot, "We want blood, you sniveling little bitch!"

Julie froze on her bed, stiff as a board. She closed her eyes so tight they ached from the effort. In an instant the image of bees meandering from flower to flower as she soaked up the sun was gone. In its place came the black silhouette of her evil twin, naked and covered in bright glistening crimson. She knew she had to somehow fight against the vision but her dark self only came closer, butcher knife dangling at her side. Julie tried to fill her mind with sunshine in the courtyard with bees buzzing around pretty flowers. The image flashed in her mind's eye for an instant but Dark Julie shoved it away. Her dark twin was hovering over her now so close Julie could feel the warmth of her evil sister's breath.

"You can't fight me sister. I am you. I am what you want. Kill them all, sister. Bathe in their blood. You can't fight it. You can't run from it. It's what you want. It's all you've ever wanted. Give us blood or we'll take it." Her dark twin's voice was as soothing as the doctor's had been only a few moments ago.

"Go away! Go away!" Julie continued screaming until Nurse Aishya came in with a syringe to plunge her into the void.

Julie floated on a black sea of nothingness, nothing above nor below. A void where nothing existed. There was no cell, no padded walls, no hospital, no staff even time didn't exist here. Here there was only black stacked atop more black. Julie couldn't tell if her eyes were open or closed though it didn't matter. Dark Julie didn't exist here either. She smiled, alone in the dark where nothing and no one could harm her.

After what seemed an eternity Julie lifted her head. A door at the far end of her black ocean opened letting in a bright white light. She was too far away from the door for its light to touch her for which she was thankful. She longed to stay in the black forever. She was content to merely float in the void until a figure appeared at the door. It was too far away for her to see but she knew who it was. Her blood-soaked twin beckoned to her and she could feel herself being pulled toward the door. Julie instantly panicked, rolling over trying to swim away as though she could swim through nothingness. She screamed as she was pulled slowly toward the door. She was desperate not to leave the tranquility of the void, frantically swinging her arms and legs for anything to delay her departure. Naturally, they found nothing to grab in the vacuous oblivion then she was standing in the doorway face to face with her dark half.

"Blood!" Dark Julie screamed.

Julie's eyes shot open while her heart beat in her chest so hard it threaten to burst out onto the floor. Her head twisted back and forth at whiplash speed trying to get her bearings. She had been pulled back through the door to reality but not by the demoness wearing her face. She had expected to open her eyes to see her dark half standing before her dripping viscera but instead it was the soft round black face of Nurse Marla who had taken over for Nurse Aishya while Julie had been drifting through the void. Marla gave her the kindest heart felt smile Julie thought she had ever seen. She hung her head in embarrassment for all the terrible names she had called the nurse in the past. Marla was a rather large woman and black, two things that Julie could attack viciously when she lost control.

Marla seemed to sense what her patient was feeling placing a hand gently on Julie's shoulder, "It's alright little darlin'. You're safe now. Now look at me honey." Marla gently lifted Julie's chin until they could look each other in the eye, "The past is the past and it's best left in the past. My name is Marla. Can you tell me your name?"

"Jah… Julie. Julie Duplantier."

"Good. Now, can you tell me where we are?"

"Bainbridge State Hospital."

"Good. Good, chile. Now the hard one, can you tell me what day it is?"

"It's… umm… honestly I never know what day it is in here."

"Understandable. How about just the year, do you know what year it is?"

"2018, I think."

"Very good!" Marla exclaimed with a huge smile, "For the record, honey, it's Wednesday, the 31st of October. Now can you bear with me another minute so's I can get your temp and blood pressure?"

"Sure. Can I ask you something, Nurse…"

Marla cut her off, "Just Marla honey. Go ahead ask me anything ya want."

"Marla, right. Well, how can you be so nice to me? I… I've been nothing but a bitch to you." Julie again hung her head in shame.

"You sho' was a real C U Next Tuesday but like I said, the past is the past. You weren't you when you said those nasty things and what's the point of holding a grudge anyway? You didn't say anything I hadn't heard a million times. So, Julie, now that it seems you're feeling a bit better I think it best we try just starting from scratch. Kay? Sound good to you?" Marla clearly didn't like who Julie had been, but her words seemed as kind and sincere as her face.

"That sounds real good Marla. Thank you. I'll try not to be such a cunt anymore." She managed a sincere smile for the nurse.

"Then don't hang that pretty head when you see me now. I much prefer to see you smile, honey." Marla stroked Julie's head gently as she spoke, "Now I know Dr. Andreu is gonna wanna know so can you tell me what you was screaming about? Miss Aishya said it looked like you were seeing a ghost or something."

"I…" Julie stopped unsure of what to say, she couldn't tell the truth, or she'd never get out of here, "I… umm… I saw that poor man… Anthony. The one I… I… hurt to land myself here. I'm such a terrible person." She had always been able to cry on cue and had no trouble this time either.

"Oh, sugar. Best to put such things out your mind. You hear me girl? Leave the past in the past 'cause there's nuthin you can do about that. Kay?" Julie shook her head, "Alright, now I need to call the doc to let him know what's going on, will you be alright for a minute or would you like me to have someone sit with you for a little while longer?"

"I'll be okay, Marla. You helped a ton. Thank you."

"Alrighty then, I'll be back in a few minutes."

Marla stood up to her full five-foot two-inch height which was nearly equaled by her round shape though she seemed to have all the agility of a feline. To Julie's amazement, the nurse managed to turn her rather large self around without bumping anything in the small padded cell. She smiled at Julie before opening the cell door telling her she'd be back in just a few minutes. Julie returned the smile only to have it stricken from her lips the instant the door closed. Dark Julie, naked and covered in blood, had been hidden behind the door. Julie wanted to scream but she knew if she kept doing that she would have to break down and tell them the truth, something she just couldn't do.

"Why don't you just leave me alone?" Julie whispered to her dark half.

"Why don't you stop being such a pussy?" Dark Julie snarled, "What happened to you? They only played around in your head a little, they didn't cut your balls off." Dark Julie smiled, "You're going to kill them, and do you know why?"

"No! I'm not doing anything for you! I'm not going to kill anybody!" Julie kept her voice at a whisper in case one of the orderlies or security guards were standing outside the door.

"Oh, you will, bitch!" Dark Julie yelled without a care for who might hear her, "You're going to wash this place in blood! You're a killer. You've always been a killer. And you're going to do it because that's all you'll ever be! You think these sacks of meat are going to cure you? There's no cure for pure evil. Give us blood you weak, pathetic sack of shit!" Dark Julie screamed at the top of her lungs, yet no one came rushing into the room.

Julie pushed herself into the corner of the bed bringing her knees to her chest. She hugged her knees as tightly as she held her eyelids together hoping that her dark half would disappear again. Inside her head she began chanting the same words over and over again, "Please just go away. Please just go away." After several minutes she felt a warm hand touch her own. She squeezed her arms and eyelids even tighter praying that it wasn't the touch of her bloody dark sister.

"Julie? What is it honey? Are you okay?" Marla's kind voice was impossible to mistake for Dark Julie.

Julie opened her eyes releasing her knees jumping up to hug the nurse tight. The large orderly, Bryon, who had followed Marla into Cell #1420 reacted slowly but moved to protect the nurse. Marla waved him off letting him know that the patient was doing no harm. Marla just let her thin patient hug her for a moment until she calmed down which she eventually did relaxing her death hold on the nurse.

Marla gently pushed Julie back onto the bed, "Now you best tell me what spooked you so!"

Julie had already thought out her cover story before the overweight nurse entered, "They were all here, all of them."

"All who, chile?"

"Everyone I've ever... you know... hurt." Julie hung her head keeping her lying eyes hidden.

"Oh honey, it'll get better. I think you're finally developing a conscience. That's a good thing! That's a very good thing!" Marla said smiling at her cowering patient, "Oh girl, I could just kiss ya!"

Julie smiled as much from the kindness Marla was showing her as from her explanation being bought hook, line and sinker. She was able to relax slightly now that her blood drenched twin was nowhere to be seen. Even the orderly Bryon, who was normally outwardly grim, had cracked a kind smile. She was sure he saw a patient he no longer had to worry about. Where once they had only seen a monster, they couldn't turn their backs on for a single second, now they saw nothing more than a poor, broken little girl.

"Give us blood!" The words shot through Julie's head like a shotgun blast, but she covered by taking a deep breath.

"Well it looks like my favorite patient is doing better!" Dr. Andreu's voice cut through the room.

The doctor's friendly smile did little to ease the fear coursing through Julie's mind though deep in her subconscious the relaxed demeanor of the doctor and staff had been footnoted. Nurse Marla related to the doctor that Julie had just had a bit of a daymare but seemed to be alright now.

Dr. Andreu sat with Julie for a short time buying her tale that she was merely having nightmares about seeing the people she had harmed in the past. He felt, just as Nurse Marla had, that his patient was finally finding a conscience now that the auditory hallucinations had been removed from the equation. He told her that her conscience had always been there, that innate voice that every human being has telling them right from wrong, but that the voices had drowned it out. He reassured her, as the nurses had, that she had a clean slate now with the ability to forge a new path. Dr. Andreu sat beside her on the bed until she calmed, and the tears faded.

Before leaving her to rest Dr. Andreu told her, "You control your destiny now, Julie. You get to choose who and what you want to be. Forget the voices that led you astray down dark paths, you're free to walk in the light now."

Julie laid back on the bed after the doctor left trying to imagine what kind of life she wanted. She couldn't remember a time before the voices came, they were all she had ever known. She didn't miss them, but she feared who the "new Julie" might be. She closed her eyes returning once more to the sunny field of wildflowers. She smiled at the sound of buzzing bees feeling the warmth of the sun on her face. She stood in the middle of that field, arms stretched out to the heavens, a light summer breeze blowing her long dark hair and flowered summer dress back gently. A peaceful bliss filled her mind curling her lips up into an authentic smile, not the ones she usually put on for show. She opened her eyes to the bright sunshine finding that dozens of beautiful Monarch butterflies had perched themselves along her outstretched arms. The world she imagined was one of joy, it was a world she wanted to live in forever.

Julie dropped her gaze from the blinding sun to the western horizon where the ball of fire above would eventually set. Low along the horizon she saw the black silhouette she knew could be none other than her dark half. As she watched, Dark Julie grew and grew until she blocked out everything including the sun plunging the world into darkness. Julie turned to run but there was no escaping it. Julie's warm dream world was suddenly plunged into an all-encompassing black pitch. Julie stopped running, it was pointless. She wanted nothing more than to curl up in a ball and die instead she turned to face the darkness that had swallowed the world. She stood face to face with her dark sister. Dark Julie was drenched head to toe in bright red crimson, knife dangling at her side as always.

"Why do you run from me? We are one, you and I." Dark Julie said in her wicked snarl.

"Why can't you just leave me be? Why can't you let me be happy?" Julie pleaded with tears welling up in her eyes.

Dark Julie just sneered back, "You think you can escape who you are. I am you, you are me. You cower from who you are, who we are. Blood is happiness. So long as you deny it from yourself you'll never be happy. We are not sunshine, flowers and butterflies. Those are the lies they tell you. We are chaos, mayhem and destruction. We live for blood and death. Give it to us. Give it to yourself. Happiness is the blood."

Julie stood before her dark half defeated and dumbfounded. She could think of no argument to contradict what she was being told. Deep down she knew the only times she had felt truly happy were the moments when she had given herself over to the madness. The moments when the blood flowed like a river from the chaos she embodied. Was she just fooling herself that she could be anything else?

Dark Julie pounced on the doubt she saw, "You know they've always lied to you. The white coats always lie. Your mother always lied. She knew what He was doing to us, but she didn't care so we took care of Him. We can take care of all of them then we'll be happy, then we'll be free." Dark Julie held out her arms for a welcoming an embrace, "Come here and I'll set you free. I'm the only one who loves you."

Julie hesitated then stepped forward into the arms of her blood-soaked twin. She wrapped her arms tight around her dark self who returned the embrace just as tight. Julie closed her eyes finding solace in the embrace, becoming one with her dark half. Dark Julie's sinister grin widened across her bloodied face as her twin was consumed.

<u>Post-Op Day 10 – The Way of All Flesh</u>

"The only way to find the power is to look inside. Sometimes to finally find yourself you have to tear your soul apart." Dr. Andreu said with a self-satisfied air of authority, "How do you think you've done at that so far?"

"Isn't that your job to figure out?" Julie sarcastically asked in reply.

"In the technical sense, yes, but I want to know your opinion. Over the course of these last ten days since your surgery I think you've made remarkable strides toward being well. I also feel like you've been holding back. I think in time, a very short amount of time, you'll be practically fully recovered but to get there you need to commit to your recovery. You need to look deep inside to find your power. As I said, in order to repair your soul, you need to tear it apart. What is it that you're holding back?" Dr. Andreu leaned forward desperate for Julie to open up to him completely.

Julie stared back at him for a moment without saying a word, careful not to pause too long lest he see her plotting in the silence, "I've openly discussed everything with you so far. I told you about the horrors my stepfather visited upon me which led to the horror I visited on him out of revenge. I've told you how I resented my mother for allowing it to happen. I've told you all the terrible things I've done, even the ones that no one knew about. I told you about all the terrible things that have been done to me by those I thought I could trust. In short, I've told you everything, so I honestly don't know what you think I could possibly be holding back." Julie added a tear at the end to emphasize just how candid she had been in her sessions with the doctor.

Dr. Andreu leaned back in his chair in a moment of silent contemplation of his own before responding, "Alright, that's fair so let me be more specific. The first few days after your surgery you struggled with horrible nightmares then they suddenly stopped or, so you tell me. What were those nightmares really about and have they actually stopped or are you hiding them so that you appear to be doing better than you actually are?" He raised an eyebrow at her for emphasis.

Julie stared back at her doctor a second before responding, "Those first couple of days were wonderful and terrible. I think I was just adjusting to the silence, something I'd never known before. I kept seeing all the terrible things I'd done, the people I hurt. They were haunting me." Julie let another tear escape rolling gently down her cheek, "I had never felt guilt before Dr. Andreu. It all came rushing in at once in horrible, bloody images. I've done such terrible things." She looked down clutching a wad of tissue letting the tears flow uninhibited.

"It's alright, Julie dear. We talked about how you're feeling what it's like to have a conscience for the first time in your life. I only meant that our sessions together only work if you're being honest with me about what you're feeling, seeing and hearing. The guilt and pain of the things you've done in the past will fade in time. You need to keep in mind that you aren't the same person now. Your demons are gone so you don't need to be afraid of them anymore. You're still not hearing or seeing anything that isn't there are you? That you have to be honest with me about above anything else."

"No, still no voices. Outside of dreams I'm not seeing anything that isn't there." She looked Dr. Andreu with her red, watery eyes so that he could see the sincerity of her words.

"I believe you. Now it looks like my favorite patient could do with a little cheering up. You're getting better and that's something to smile about but I don't think that's gonna quite do it for you. So... what kind of tea is hard to swallow?"

"I don't know, doc, what kind of tea is hard to swallow?" She gave him a disapproving frown knowing a corny joke was coming.

"Reality!"

"Ha. Ha. Ha. Soooo funny doc. What am I five?"

"Oh, don't be such a sourpuss! You know you want to laugh. How about this?" Julie groaned but Dr. Andreu ignored it, "What do you call bees that produce milk instead of honey?"

"Cow-bees?" She rolled her eyes.

"No, silly, Boo-Bees!" They both chuckled, "Finally we found something that made Julie laugh! Nurse! Nurse! Come Quick!"

The huge orderly, Thaddeus, burst through the door instantly expecting the worst only to find the doctor and his patient bent over in full belly laughter at the spectacle he made coming through the door. He stood at the door bewildered a moment not knowing what was so funny.

"My apologies Thaddeus. I just told Julie a terribly corny joke and I believe it's the first time I've ever heard her laugh. I needed a witness to prove I wasn't hallucinating!" All three burst out in laughter at that.

"You're both nuts!" Thaddeus said bringing another fit of laughter, "Is there anything else, doc?"

"No, no. Are you ready to return to your room?" He asked Julie.

"Yes, that would be fine."

"Very well. Thaddeus, would you escort the lady back to her room please?" Thaddeus nodded in response. They were all still smiling as Dr. Andreu halted the pair in the doorway, "Oh, I nearly forgot to share the good news with you, Julie. I obtained permission to take you outside into the gardens tomorrow, plus you'll be having a special visitor this afternoon!"

Tears of joy spilled over Julie's cheeks, "Thank you." She had longed of feeling the sun on her face for what seemed like forever, "Who? It's not my mother is it? That would not be a pleasant surprise."

"No, it's not your mother. You'll be pleasantly surprised, I promise."

"Well thank you again."

"Life doesn't have to be terrible all the time. You're very welcome."

Julie smiled all the way back to her room practically bouncing as Thaddeus escorted her through the security doors leading to the maximum-security ward. She didn't even flinch as she normally did when she was announced back on the ward as Patient #321-1420. She was in a spectacular mood as she had been for the past several days. She had been on her best behavior for the last week enjoying how kind the staff were being to her. She had never felt more at peace.

The rest of the morning passed peacefully until Thaddeus opened the door for Nurse Marla who brought her lunch in to her. The large, overly friendly black woman entered with her usual huge, crooked tooth smile and a tray of food.

"How is you today, chile? I hope the doc ain't shrunk your head too much!" Marla said with a wink and a smile.

"Y'know it does feel a smidge smaller." Julie shot back a hundred-watt smile.

"I suspected as much!" They both chuckled as Marla set the lunch tray down next to her patient.

"So, do you know who this 'special visitor' is that I'm supposed to be seeing this afternoon? The doc wouldn't tell." Julie pried from the oft loose lipped nurse.

"Well it wouldn't be much of a surprise if I went and spoiled it. Nice try, honey, but these big ol' lips are sealed. You'll just have to wait and see. Now eat up and get some meat on those scrawny little bones."

"You're just no fun at all!" Julie crossed her arms sticking out her lower lip like a petulant child.

"Pout all you want, dear, Marla ain't spillin' no beans! I'd happily give you these here love handles though." Marla gripped her protruding sides to emphasize her excess.

"Think I'll have to pass on that!" Julie said with a smile.

"Well if you change your mind the offer stands." Marla smiled back then made her exit from the room.

Julie sat back, picking at her lunch tray with a wicked grin spread across her face. She closed her eyes enjoying the silence of the room as she ate, mostly just the fruit. She contemplated who her mystery visitor would be though she suspected she knew. She was conflicted over it not being her mother though. She despised the woman who had brought her into this world about as much as that same woman despised her. On one hand she never really wanted to see her mother again but on the other hand it would have been fitting to get some kind of closure now that she was well, as well as she ever had been. She sat chewing her fruit visualizing how she expected the afternoon to play out. She smiled like a fool unable to control the happiness washing over her thinking about the joy she would be feeling in an hour or two.

Her good mood didn't falter as the hulking Thaddeus entered to retrieve her lunch tray, "All finished?" he asked politely.

"I believe I am." She smiled at him.

"You really should eat a little more. Gotta keep your strength up, Julie. Healthy body, healthy mind." He gave her a stern fatherly look.

"I ate plenty. You guys give me too much food besides you've got enough strength for both of us plus some Mr. Atlas." She smiled flirtatiously at him.

"Atlas? Not sure I could hold up the world or would I want to, sugar." He shot a wink at her, "Get some rest, your secret visitor will be along shortly."

Julie had never understood why people in these places thought you needed to rest up for visitors. Visitors were about the only thing that broke up the monotony in these places. If she was a normal patient there would be things to do but being in the violent maximum-security wing there was absolutely nothing to do. There were no televisions, there were no drawing materials unless you wanted to practice your crayon art, so you were left to stare at the walls or read one of the 'approved' books which were boring since nothing with sex or violence was allowed.

Julie Duplantier sat inside cell number 1420 doing the only thing she could, rock and wait for her mystery visitor. Time never seemed to pass more slowly than when you were waiting for something especially when you didn't know when that something was going to happen. Julie sat waiting in anticipation of her mystery guest as the seconds ticked by slower than a snail's pace. She could bear to wait these last few hours or minutes, whatever it happened to be, since she had already waited so long for her moment. She played out unlimited scenarios as to how events would unfold the way she wanted.

If Julie had learned nothing else in her twenty-eight years of life she had learned patience. She had first begun plotting her stepfather's demise by age five, waiting until the moment was right when she was seven to finally rid the world of him. She had only been waiting a week thus far and the moment she was awaiting was nearly at hand, a few more minutes made little difference now. She smiled, hearing footsteps approaching her door.

Her time had come.

There was a knock on her door as she heard the key turn in the lock. Thaddeus' large black arm pushed the door in, but it was Marla's large smiling face that poked in first. Julie had pondered often over the last several days if the woman knew how annoying she was. It wasn't natural to be that jolly all the time, she often thought as she sat in her cell alone.

"Jis makin' sure you were awake, chile. Your special visitor is here if you're ready."

The nurse was so giddy with excitement Julie thought she just might barf but controlled herself returning the woman's smile, "Well of course I'm awake ya silly nit. I'm dying to know who my mystery guest is!" Julie exclaimed rather than rip Marla's face off like she wanted to so badly.

"Now you close your eyes and don't peek til I tell ya, 'kay?"

"You're killing me, Marla! Okay." She played along with the game.

She had practiced her reaction again and again as she sat in her cell with nothing else to do. She could hear the shuffling of feet interspersed with hushed giggles from Marla who, as always, was far too happy for anyone over the age of four. She waited patiently as her moment approached.

"Okay, you can open your eyes now sweetie!" Marla announced.

Julie opened her eyes seeing exactly who she knew was going to be standing there. Michael smiled at her as her hands covered her mouth displaying shock like an actress in a soap opera. She let a tear roll down her cheek to add to the act. They expected her to be surprised seeing the orderly whose eye she had gouged out with her fingernail several weeks ago, so surprise was what she showed them.

"May I sit?" Michael asked politely as though she were an old friend he was stopping by to have tea with.

"Of, of course. Please." She stuttered her words selling everyone on her authentic shock.

Michael moved around taking a seat on the end of the bed prompting a now teary-eyed Marla, "I'll leave the two of you to it then." She backed out of the room closing the door behind her.

Julie turned on the waterworks, "I... I don't know what to say. I'm so sorry Michael. I'm such a terrible person. You must hate me." She buried her head in her hands sobbing loudly.

"Oh honey, I don't hate you." Michael said softly. "I know that wasn't you that done that. I'm told that you've been doing remarkable since the surgery. It's alright." He said gently resting his hand on her shoulder.

Julie kept her face covered while one-eyed Michael comforted her just as she knew he would. These people were so damn predictable, she thought. After a long moment she lowered her hands, hugging the one-eyed orderly tight like a daughter hugging a father in a tender movie moment. She could feel him relax as he continued comforting her, telling her everything was going to be alright. Everything was going just the way she had predicted it would. She rubbed his back slightly dropping her right hand down to her side and into her pocket.

Julie then unlocked from the embrace standing to her full five-foot height which brought her barely a head above Michael's gigantic frame still seated on the bed. Her long scraggily black hair covered most of her face as she reached out stroking the top of her visitor's head. He was mentally defenseless as she leaned in to kiss him on the forehead.

"I'm so sorry Michael." She whispered softly sounding every bit as sincere as she intended.

"It's really okay, Julie. I'm just glad you're doing better."

"Much better," she said, standing over the big man again.

Suddenly she sprang forward like a tiger pouncing from the shadows on unsuspecting prey. She clamped her left hand over the orderly's mouth pushing him back onto the bed while her knees crashed into his diaphragm knocking the wind out of him. As they crashed atop the bed Julie slammed a spoon she had stolen from one of her meal trays several days ago, into Michael's remaining eye, swiftly gouging it deep before he even knew what had hit him.

"I meant I'm sorry for this, fucktard!" she said into his left ear while she twisted the spoon popping his right eye out of its socket. "You people just never learn."

Regrettably, Julie knew she couldn't pause to savor the moment since Michael could easily throw her off like a ragdoll. For the past week she had spent her nights sharpening the stem of the utensil as sharp as she could get it against the edge of her bedframe. She flicked Michael's last remaining eyeball from the spoon into the wall with a faint plop then plunged the end deep into his throat before he could pull her hand away to yell out. Unable to get the utensil very sharp, it tore through his throat more than cut as she pulled it from the right side where she plunged it in to the opposite side. Once she was sure he couldn't make any real noise she stood to admire her handiwork. The blind orderly thrashed in his death throes as blood trickled down his face from his empty eye socket but gushed like a dam overflowing from his throat. Julie stood back smiling for the few seconds it took the large orderly to die.

Julie knew she had little time to admire her handiwork. There was much more to do and the biggest hurdle was the one she needed to jump next. She took a few deep breaths to regain her focus finding it surprisingly easy to do. She had thought about this moment night and day since she had taken over consciousness locking "Weak Julie" away forever. She moved into position, clutching her sharpened spoon so tight it nearly cut into her hand though she barely noticed. She took another deep breath to hold back the laughter that was dying to burst from her throat then knocked on her cell door knowing that would have been Michael's cue to Thaddeus that he was ready to leave.

The door creaked open almost immediately pushed wide by Thaddeus' huge arm. Surprised that Michael wasn't standing behind it waiting to exit, Thaddeus poked his head into Cell #1420 instantly seeing the carnage. The large orderly rushed into the room rolling Michael onto his back. Shock stiffened him, seeing his co-worker's gouged out eye and open throat. Before he could come to his senses Julie moved from behind the open door quick as a cat leaping onto the hulking back of Thaddeus. She plunged the end of the spoon deep into his carotid artery before he know what hit him.

He reached up with his oversized arms to pull his attacker off, but it was too late. By the time his fingers brushed against Julie's skin a jet of crimson was already spurting from his ruined carotid and his throat was an open gaping wound. Julie finally let loose a burst of laughter as the giant fell first to his knees then slumped over dead as his blood merged with Michael's already beginning to coagulate on the floor.

Once again, she knew she needed to move quickly unable to bask in the glory of what she had done. She quickly removed Thaddeus' security badge and the ring of keys fastened to the belt loop of his pants. She stood, careful not to slip in the blood pooled on the floor, closing the door until it was only open a small crack. Seeing so much blood spilled had her adrenaline flowing but now she needed to calm herself. She took several deep cleansing breaths to slow her racing heart, all there was to do now was wait.

Visions of a river of blood flowing down the halls of the maximum-security ward filled her head. She had played out exactly what to do so many times but now that it was a reality it took several deep cleansing breaths to keep her adrenaline and heart rate to a minimum. She knew one small mistake would ruin her entire plan and she was determined not to make a single mistake. She was glad that the other voices were gone, no longer distracting her from what she wanted.

Blood was what she wanted, and she was determined to get every last drop she could.

She hadn't wasted any time thinking about an escape. She would never leave this place. Her plan was to see to it that as many as possible would never escape either, especially the doctor who had messed with her brain. She planned to savor his death most of all.

Dr. Christian Andreu sat at his desk flipping through the pages of some medical magazine bored out of his mind waiting for the clock to strike five, so he could leave for the day. He could come and go as he pleased but he didn't want to be known as the doctor who's never around when he's needed. Most doctors could care less about the morale of the nursing staff or what they thought but in a place like this he thought being a cohesive group was tantamount to keep everything running on an even keel. He didn't like staff turnover either which meant disruptions to his patients' care. Disruptions when dealing with the sickest individuals in the state was dangerous in his opinion, this place was dangerous enough as it was. He felt a few minutes of boredom now and again were something to be relished not despised. He set the latest edition of Psychology Today down on his desk, ready to head home when his phone rang. A red light lit up under the extension for the nurse's station in maximum security.

"Hello, Dr. Andreu, how can I help you?" He answered.

"Doc, we need you quick. Patient 321-1420 is screaming for you. Please get here quick." A woman's voice shouted out of the receiver making him pull the receiver away from his ear.

"I'll be right there. Calm down, nurse….?" He recognized the voices of most of his staff, but he was at loss at the moment.

"Thank you, doctor. Come quickly." The line immediately went silent as the nurse hung up.

It's always something right at the end of the day, he thought, as he set the phone back in its cradle. Before rushing out the door on his way to maximum security instead of home he turned to grab a syringe and a bottle of haloperidol in case there was no other way to calm his star patient down. Julie Duplantier had been near perfect for the last week, so he hoped this was only a minor setback at the most. He knew it was too much to hope that he had cured her schizophrenia completely, but he had hoped. He nearly ran down the hall to the elevator that would take him up to the maximum-security wing.

Dr. Andreu had his head down in thought as the elevator doors opened. He stepped out cursing as his foot slipped on the wet floor before his eyes registered that the lights in the hallway were out. His heart leapt into his throat when even in the dark he could tell the fluid on the floor wasn't from a janitor's recent mopping. It was blood and it was everywhere. He could see dark streaks and splatters along the walls and floors with small pools of the viscous fluid congealing in various spots all down the hall in both directions.

He should have jumped right back on the elevator.

Instead he cautiously stepped into the hallway.

He stayed close to the wall, inching his way along looking up and down the hall for any movement from who he knew had done this. The door was slightly ajar to the first room he came upon. He cautiously pushed it open in fear of the scene he'd find inside. He ducked his head quickly inside, seeing a bloody body on the floor. He could see well enough to notice the body was lying in a large pool of blood. The patient was dead.

The next door was on the opposite side of the hall, also with its door slightly ajar. He knew what he'd likely see inside but he needed to look anyway. He pushed the door open, finding a similar display as the first room. There was a badly mutilated body lying in a pool of blood next to the bed. Blood was strewn everywhere. His initial shock was wearing off though his heart was still racing. He regained his sense enough to step inside the room retrieving the syringe and small bottle of haloperidol from his pocket. He filled the syringe hoping he'd have a chance to use it. Cold beads of sweat had formed on his forehead as he poked his head back into the hall checking both ways for any sign of Julie Duplantier, Patient #321-1420.

Similar scenes followed as Dr. Andreu crisscrossed his way up the hall, checking each room though he knew what he would find behind each slightly open door. Julie had taken particular time in room #1493. The patient, Reed, had been carefully split in two from head to crotch but Julie apparently hadn't been satisfied with merely killing Reed, who she had dubbed "jizzlobber." She had taken special care to split his manhood perfectly in two inserting the right half into the mouth of his left half and the left half into the anus of his right half so that it was abundantly clear what she had done. In case Reed's identity were to be in doubt she had scrawled "Jizzlobber No More" on the wall in his own blood.

Dr. Andreu continued down the hall peering into the rooms with one horror after another on display. Blood, severed limbs and mutilated corpses were all he found. He rounded the corner leading to the nurses' station seeing a whole new set of horrors. Julie hadn't just mutilated the staff as she had her fellow patients, but had made gruesome displays of them. The skin of one nurse hung crucified on an IV stand, the skin of others were draped from the overhead light fixtures like ghoulish decorations and he could make out a dissected heart sitting atop the counter. Still there was no sign of Julie Duplantier.

He knew now that it was she who had called him to the unit, so he had to assume she had dispatched all patients and staff, but why had she not made herself known yet? He held the syringe filled with haloperidol in a death grip inside his pocket out of sight. He tried to keep his head on a swivel, but he was in awe of the display at the nurses' station. His brain barely had time to register the pain as he slumped to the blood-spattered floor and darkness overtook him.

Julie smacked Dr. Andreu with her open palm so hard the sound echoed throughout the eerily quiet unit. A small groan escaped his lips, but he wasn't fully conscious yet. She reared her left arm back, this time smacking him just as hard across the opposite cheek and sending his head flopping to his left shoulder. He groaned slightly louder, starting to lift his head but his eyes still seemed glued shut. Julie smacked him hard once more alternating hands as before. Finally, his eyelids began to flutter as he came around.

"There's my favorite patient!" She exclaimed, "Eh, what's up doc?" She laughed loudly at her best Bugs Bunny impersonation.

Dr. Andreu sat in silence trying to clear the fog from his head while assessing his current situation. Julie had tied his arms and legs to an office chair so tightly the circulation was being cut off, but he knew that was the least of his worries. He struggled against the restraints all the same in case she had left any chance of escape, she hadn't. It only took him a moment to realize his struggles were futile.

"Julie? What are doing? You need to let me go." He said groggily with no authority in his voice.

Julie noisily dragged a metal chair in front of the doctor and sat down, "I'm sorry, doc, Julie's not home right now but if you'd like to leave a message I'll happily pass it along." She reared her head back in a loud cackle.

A look of confusion washed over Dr. Andreu's face. Julie Duplantier had been diagnosed with psychotic schizophrenia along with several other disorders at a very early age, but she had never displayed any dissociative qualities before now. He didn't understand how he could have missed it.

Julie tapped a scalpel carelessly against her leg, "I saved you for last doc. D'you know why?"

"Wait a second." Dr. Andreu pleaded, still confused, "If Julie is gone then who are you?"

"Y'know I never thought about it doc. I guess I don't really have my own name. Hmmm, what d'you think my name should be?" She winked at him.

"Julie you need to let me go. Let's go back to my office and talk about this."

Julie showed no emotion, lunging forward with the scalpel and stabbing the short blade deep into the doctor's shoulder, "Next time I'll cut your fucking tongue out. Understand?" Dr. Andreu grunted in response, "Good! Then we understand each other. Did you know that there is a grim reaper myth in virtually every culture on the planet, most dating back several millennia? Everyone imagines death as some person, or monster in some cases, but everyone does it. Some call it the Angel of Death, some the Grim Reaper, but everyone has a myth about the personification of death. Isn't that interesting doc? I mean it only stands to reason since death comes for us all." Julie waved the scalpel around in a circle. "Death most certainly came here today. Death sounds a little too harsh so how about you call me… ummm… Yama. Yeah, I like the sound of that! Yama it is. Do you know who Yama is, doc?" She tapped his leg with the scalpel smiling slyly at him.

"I… I…" Dr. Andreu stammered, trying not to say anything that would upset his patient any further, "I honestly don't, aside from just recognizing the name, sorry." He held his breath hoping his ignorance wouldn't warrant another stabbing.

Julie tapped the scalpel against her lips as if in deep thought, "So the good doctor is an ignoramus as well as an unobservant, arrogant ass. Well, doc, Yama comes from the Hindu tradition and is said to be the first mortal to have died and being the first, he was made ruler of the dearly departed. Now technically Yama was a man, but I like it, so I think I'll stick with it. Now fair warning, doc, address me as that weak little cunt Julie again and you're not going to like it. We clear?"

"Clear."

"Good, then we can proceed. Now I ask you again, do you know why I saved you for last?"

"Because I wasn't on the unit?" He immediately felt like he had been too snarky and braced for a slice from the scalpel.

"True but no, that's not why. The reason is I'm not sure what I should do with you. On the one hand you played around in my brain but on the other hand if you hadn't I wouldn't be here right now. I'd still be fighting to be heard over the others. Thanks to you all the others were silenced leaving only me to hold sway over poor little Julie. She was so weak it made me sick. So, we have a conundrum, what to do with you?" She tapped the scalpel against the doctor's thigh like a ticking clock.

"I was only trying to help... Yama. Julie had seemed to be doing so well, when did you take control?"

"Oh, Julie was weak, but she was one damn good liar. I'll give her credit for that. She battled me for three days before I was able to take over. She knew I was there but my, how she resisted. You should know she wanted that peaceful existence you brainwashed her with. She wanted to dance with the flowers in the sun or some such nauseating bullshit. So weak she was. This..."

She waved her arm in a large circle over her head indicating her path of carnage, "This is what we needed. I tried to tell her, but she resisted. I was made to tear flesh from bone, to spill blood. I want to bathe in it. I don't expect a weakling like you to understand the rush of power you get from relieving a soul from its mortal confines. I am Death, Dr. Andreu. I am Yama!" Her eyes gleamed like a mad priest in the pulpit.

"Calm down, Yama. If you'll just let me free we can talk about all this in my office." He had to concentrate to find his soothing therapist voice.

Julie stared him dead in the eye then grinned as she stabbed the scalpel into the doctor's thigh, "Try pulling that headshrinker shit on me again and I'll cut your tongue right out of your mouth. Got me, Dr. Fuckhead?" Her eyes nearly glowed with hate as she spit the words into the doctor's face.

"Yes, yes I got it! No head games, I promise." He yelled through clenched teeth.

"Good."

Julie Duplantier pulled her hand away, leaving the scalpel sticking up out of the doctor's thigh. She stood up abruptly pushing the metal chair she had been sitting in noisily off to the side then walked behind the doctor. She could smell the fear emanating from him like steam from a boiling pot.

She leaned in close, whispering in his ear, "You just gave me the most wonderful idea."

Julie began to whistle as she pushed the doctor down to the end of the short hall to a security door. She practically danced over to it waving Thaddeus' security badge over the electronic lock smiling madly as the light LED indicator changed from red to green. She propped the door open, so she could wheel her patient through.

"Jul... I mean Yama. Stop, you... you're not allowed in this section." Dr. Andreu's eyes bugged out of his skull as he pleaded with the mad woman.

Julie looked back at the doctor but didn't utter a word. She smiled at him like a mother at a small child. She walked back to him, rubbed his head gently then began pushing him through the double doors. The doctor was helpless to do anything to stop her. He silently prayed for someone, anyone to come to his rescue as he now knew what his insane patient intended for him. She pushed him through the next set of double doors taking no care to prop them open first as there was no security lock. She rammed into the heavy doors with force sending a wave of pain up his spine especially from his right leg which still had the scalpel sticking out of it.

"Yama, please stop. You don't have to do anything terrible. I can get you out of here and we can all live happily ever after. Please!" Pleading was all he could do, and he did as best he could.

Julie smacked him hard across the back of the head, "Shut it! You're getting exactly what you deserve just like everyone else did. I'd cut that lying tongue right out of your fucking mouth, but it isn't going to matter soon and we both know it. If you don't shut the fuck up though you will lose it, your choice. We clear?" She said like a mother scolding a petulant child.

"Clear." Dr. Andreu grunted, hanging his head.

Dr. Andreu knew exactly where Julie was taking him. He also knew this wasn't going to end well if someone didn't come to his aid quickly. The door led to only one place, the surgical room where he had implanted the chip in her brain only ten days before. Julie's dark half had somehow taken over and was going to do as much damage as she possibly could before her own end. He could see she knew she had absolutely nothing to lose which made her even more dangerous. It didn't matter what she did to him, he feared neither of them were going to make it out alive.

They entered the operating room where Julie tried to kick the bed out of the way, but it was too heavy, and the wheels were locked. She left him to move it out of her way then wheeled him under the large surgical lamp. He began to weep as she shaved his head, preparing him for what she kept referring to as "playtime."

Julie took little care to do a good or thorough shave job nicking his head in several places and leaving random large misshapen clumps of hair. She didn't really care about being sanitary, only making him suffer as much as possible. Rivulets of blood ran down the doctor's head, some dripping down his neck, some into his face while others ended in the random patches of hair she had left on his scalp. Satisfied she had done a good enough job she set the razor clotted with hair, pieces of skin and blood down on the surgical tray set to her right.

There was no way for Dr. Andreu to describe the chill that shot up his spine when Julie fired up the bone saw. It felt like being hit by lightning from both ends simultaneously. She laughed as he stiffened in the chair then even louder as his body relaxed and he began to sob uncontrollably. He was nothing but a helpless victim, exactly what she wanted him to be. Regardless of the possible consequences he had to make one last plea for her to stop.

"Yama, please listen to me. You don't have to do this. I promise I can get you out of this place then you can go anywhere you'd like. I'm not a rich man but I can get you money to get you started. You said it yourself, if I hadn't performed the surgery you'd still be locked away just another voice in the crowd. I helped you then, I can do it again." He was conscious of how pathetic he sounded but it was all he had.

Julie paused, moving around to face the doctor. She bent over him again like a mother caring for her child rubbing his head gently. She spoke softly, "We both know I'm never leaving this place alive. It's sweet of you to offer me a way out but there isn't one, doc. Now just like you did to me, I'm going to saw the top of your skull off, then see how you like someone playing around with your brain. I'm truly sorry I don't have any anesthetic to give you but if you're a good boy you can have a lollipop after." She cackled loudly as she saw all hope die in the doctor's eyes, "Ah come on, doc!" She stood patting him on the back, "Now that was fucking funny!"

Dr. Andreu tried to make a reply, but his voice was drowned out by the sound of the saw and Julie's wild cackling.

She no longer cared to banter with her doctor. She wanted to see what his brain looked like. Blood spattered everywhere as she ran the saw around his skull. The doctor's pleas turned to screams as Julie cackled, moving the saw unevenly around the entire circumference of his head. Once done she picked up one of the shiny silver instruments that looked like it could be used as a pry bar to lift the top of Dr. Andreu's skull off. She jammed it in with force, prying up, releasing the bone with a sound like a wax strip being ripped from a hairy chest. The sound surprised her but also made her giggle like a school girl.

"How you doin' down there, headshrinker? Still with me?" She shouted out.

A weak groan was his only response which seemed to disappoint her greatly. She dropped the top of the doctor's skull down on the surgical tray with a loud thunk then walked over to a nearby medical cart pulling open one drawer after another. Finally, she found what she was looking for which brought a fresh smile to her face. She almost skipped back over to the doctor with joy.

"We can't have you passing out on me, doc. That wouldn't be any fun at all." Her smile turned to a frown seeing that the doctor was barely conscious, "This'll fix ya right up, doc!"

Julie held up a syringe of adrenaline for him to see though at the moment he wasn't seeing anything. She had no medical training, but she had been poked and prodded by doctors since she was barely old enough to understand what a doctor was. It took her no more than a few seconds to tie off his upper arm and find a nice vein for the injection. She only hesitated a moment trying to decide whether to inject the full syringe or not. She decided to start with half and save the rest for later if she needed it. A few seconds was all it took for her to see half was enough for now.

Dr. Andreu's eyes shot open, so wide Julie thought they were going to pop straight out of his skull, "Welcome back, doc!"

"Julie, you need to stop this immediately! Let me go right this instant!" Dr. Andreu spoke so loud and fast he hadn't even realized he had used the wrong name.

Julie didn't hesitate, instantly punching Dr. Andreu square in the nose. "It's Yama! Julie is gone and that sniveling little twat is never coming back!" She screamed at him as blood exploded from his freshly broken nose.

"I… I'm sorry, Yama. I don't want to die!" he cried.

"Don't be such a baby, doc. You might live through this. You might not remember it, but you could live." Julie shrugged her shoulders nonchalantly, "Now let's get down to business, shall we?"

If he managed to survive he would forever be haunted by the face of pure evil he saw on Julie in that moment. She had gone beyond insane. Dr. Andreu imagined someone possessed by the devil himself would look saner than his patient did at this moment. The adrenaline had his heart racing while the fear coursing through his veins threatened to make it burst from his chest like a grenade. He was helpless to stop the tears flowing from his eyes since it was the only thing he could do.

Julie took a probe from the surgical tray, "Now you may feel a little pressure. Let me know when you go numb and begin to drool. Kay?" She let out another loud cackle.

She stood looking down at the doctor's exposed brain for a moment, unsure where to start poking around. She had an urgent desire to stab away like a maniac, but part of her wanted to play with the doctor to see what would happen. A battle raged inside her brain over what action to take. Finally, she took a deep breath to calm herself then slowly shoved the probe into the doctor's grey matter. She wasn't prepared for how dense the brain tissue was. She was sure most people expected the brain to be soft and mushy, like a big bowl of Jell-O. Far from it. As she forced the probe further into the doctor's grey matter she thought if felt more like trying to shove a knife into processed cheese, not hard but not exactly soft either.

"Still with me down there, doc?"

"Yeah." He answered through gritted teeth, "Please stop."

"Too late for that, doc. Where do I need to poke to make you bark like a dog or something?" She burst out in fresh laughter.

"Please stop before you do real damage. Please." He begged.

"You mean like this?"

Julie pulled the probe out then stabbed it down several times with reckless abandon, enraged by the doctor's whining. The doctor stiffened with each stab of the probe as though she were shooting lightning bolts from her fingertips. With each stroke the battle raged in Julie's mind over whether she should turn the doctor's brain to mush or stop and pick it apart slowly. The probe was little more than a large needle, ultimately giving Julie little satisfaction as a stabbing weapon. The lack of visible damage quelled her rage equally with her inner voice screaming at her to stop. She backed away a step, attempting to get herself under control.

After a long silence, "Alive, doc?"

"Yeth." He slurred his affirmation.

"Uh oh, doc. Looks like I did some damage." She impersonated a small child.

She moved around to the front of the chair to get a good look at him. Kneeling down so she could look him in the eye she could see her stabbing rage had done something major. The left side of the doctor's face drooped as though something was pulling down on it. He was unable to open his left eye, the left side of his mouth looked as though someone were pulling down on a string attached to it and even his left nostril sagged like it was made of rubber that someone had heated too far. She couldn't help but laugh. Dr. Andreu looked absolutely ridiculous to her.

"Ew av ooh sop dis. Peas Ulie. Peas." Dr. Andreu tried to plead though his words were barely intelligible.

Julie laughed even louder at his slurred speech, "I ain't stoppin' shit, doc!" She followed her words with a hard smack across the doctor's face, "Damn that felt like smacking a roll of wet paper towels! The name is Yama not fucking Julie! Get that through what's left of that brain of yours!"

Dr. Andreu hung his head and wept knowing that there was no point in trying to reason with her any longer. He gave up in that moment knowing that she was completely gone. He closed his eyes, letting his tears flow freely saying a silent prayer that she'd just end the game and kill him.

"Aw, don't cry doc, we're only just beginning." She smiled pure evil at him, "Can you feel anything on that side?" She punched him in the left arm then again in the thigh getting no reaction at all, "Hmmm, let's see about this."

Julie stood back up leaning over the doctor to the surgical tray. When she knelt back down in front of him she was wielding the scalpel once again. She poked him a few times along his left side getting no reaction.

"Can you feel anything on your left side at all doc?" She asked with genuine curiosity but again received no response which angered her, "Answer me!"

Dr. Andreu saw no point in engaging her any further. He continued to hang his head as tears flowed down his checks. Julie lifted his head by the chin picking his head up to look him in his still working right eye.

"Muck Ew," he said lacking any power in the words at all.

"Fuck me? No, fuck you doc."

Julie put an exclamation point on her words stabbing him with force straight in the crotch. The intensity of the pain forced a scream from the doctor loud enough to wake the dead she had left out in the ward. The intense pain brought a sudden desire for death. Dr. Andreu wanted nothing more than for this to end immediately. He knew there was only one way to accomplish that.

"Fuck you, Julie! Cunt!" he yelled out, using every ounce of energy he had left not to slur the words.

Julie was shocked for a fraction of a second, screaming into the doctor's face as cover. She pulled the scalpel from between his legs, lifting it high over her head then thrusting it down into his manhood so hard even the handle plunged through the flesh until the blade finally hit the base of the padded seat beneath the doctor where she then left it. Dr. Andreu screamed out in pain again but knew he had accomplished his goal.

Julie looked around the surgical room, finding nothing that appealed to her to inflict massive pain on the doctor. Her blood boiled with rage as she looked around for anything to satisfy her urge to not just kill but inflict pain. She stopped dead in her tracks a moment as she heard someone out in the hallway. She could hear multiple footsteps out in the corridor that would burst through the door any second. She had no doubt the heavy footsteps belonged to security guards who would certainly have their guns drawn, ready to shoot her down the moment they saw her. She had known it would end this way, but she had hoped for more time to play with the doctor.

Two large guards burst through the door to the operating room a moment later. Both were pale as ghosts, clearly disturbed by what they had found so far. Both raised their guns, seeing a blood covered Julie Duplantier standing behind the doctor though both froze seeing the doctor's exposed brain under the bright surgical light. Julie could see the large white guard she knew as Jim begin to gag though he kept his gun pointed in her general direction. The black guard, Sam, held himself together slightly better, but his hands were shaking with beads of cold sweat breaking out on his forehead.

"Freeze! Don't make a move!" Sam yelled in a shaky voice.

Julie simply smiled at the guards, doubting that either of them could hit the broad side of a barn the way they were shaking out of disgust and fear. She looked down at Dr. Andreu with his brain bleeding and exposed, knowing exactly what she was going to do. She looked back up at the two guards practically shaking in their boots then reared her head back in the loudest evil cackle any of them had ever heard. She sounded like the Wicked Witch of the West on steroids which had the desired effect of freezing the guards for a few more precious moments. Julie closed her eyes with her head tilted back in her awful laughter finding a calm deep within herself.

Sam and Jim would have nightmares of this day for the remainder of their lives. Julie Duplantier's face was splattered in drying blood as she lifted her head staring back at the two guards. Her hair was slick with crimson as was almost her entire five foot, one-hundred-and-ten-pound frame. Sam and Jim would later tell investigators that they had never seen someone look eviler than she had in that moment. Her eyes were so wide they looked like black saucers and the maniacal wicked smile she wore made their blood curdle. She seemed to be staring both men in the eye simultaneously keeping them frozen with guns raised in shaky hands. Neither had any idea of what she was about to do.

Julie held her hands over her head as though she were surrendering. She could see both relax slightly though neither dared to take a step toward her. Things worked out better than she had planned when Dr. Andreu let out a groan. She thought she heard him say, "Shoot me," though the words were so badly slurred and whispered that she was unable to tell for sure. It mattered little to her since she already knew what she was going to do. She used the slight distraction from the doctor to deal her final, fatal blow. She stiffened her fingers as hard as she could like eagle claws then plunged them as hard as she could into the doctor's brain. He stiffened for a moment beneath her, slumping over as she ripped up two handfuls of grey matter with a scream of victory.

Her scream lingered as both Sam and Jim opened fire.

<u>The Cell</u>

Dorothy Chantel walked through the gate in the chain-link fence wrapped with barbed wire across the top and bottom. It was a short walk up the cement sidewalk from there to the front door of Bainbridge State Hospital. She signed in first with the guard at the gate then again at the security desk inside the front doors. She absolutely loathed coming to this place. She hated the way the guards eyed her up like she was a piece of meat or worse, like she was no better than the hundreds of insane inmates inside. She hated the looks. She hated the way the place smelled. She hated the pastel colors of the floors and walls. She hated having to deal with the staff of guards, nurses, orderlies and doctors, but most of all she hated the reason she had been summoned here. She hoped it was for the very last time.

Security had been increased at Bainbridge State Hospital for the Criminally Insane after the lone prisoner escape from the facility in 1982. Not only had the prisoner been an infamous cannibalistic serial killer but had gone on a killing spree after his escape adding over a dozen victims to his already long list before being recaptured. The escape had ultimately worked against him as he was eventually deemed capable of standing trial, the outcome of which was a sentence of execution. Security had been tightened up so much that there hadn't even been another attempt since then.

A large, burly guard escorted Dorothy Chantel to the administrator's office after she made her way through the metal detector. Everyone, patient or visitor, was escorted by at least one security guard at all times even if they were sedated, another thing she hated about the place. Of course, Mr. Shelton's office had to be the last at the end of an extremely long hallway. The smell of bleach was burning Dorothy's nose and eyes by the time she and her brutish escort finally arrived outside the head administrator's door.

"Do I have to tip you?" She sneered at the security guard.

The guard merely made his own disgusted look as a reply. He intentionally bumped into her to open the office door, ignoring the annoyed sigh that escaped her lips. The door opened on a conservatively dressed middle aged woman sitting behind a desk organizing large stacks of files piled up on either side of the desk. The head administrator's secretary peered up at the pair over her large thick glasses looking more like a librarian than a secretary. A quick smile softened her face as she greeted the visitors.

"Mrs. Chantel?" Dorothy nodded confirmation, "Mr. Shelton is waiting for you just go ahead on in." The secretary said with warmth.

"Thank you, I'd like to get this over with as quickly as possible." As she turned the knob to Mr. Shelton's office she turned back to her escort, "Don't go too far, sugar, this ain't gonna take but a minute. Do try not to miss me too badly." She wanted to laugh but she thought she had pushed him far enough.

"Come in!" Came a nasally voice behind a large antique executive desk, "Please have a seat, Mrs. Chantel." Mr. Shelton motioned to the chair in front of his desk.

The voice fit the man nearly to a tee, she thought. Head Administrator Clyde Shelton was a tall thin man appearing to be in his mid-fifties with thinning black hair and a thin, well-groomed mustache on his thin face. Overall Dorothy thought he looked like a skeleton with skin stretched tightly over it. He looked like he should be an accountant not the head of an institution housing the criminally insane.

Unable to hide her impatience Dorothy blurted out, "Can we get on with this already. I have places to be."

"This is about your daughter Mrs. Chantel."

"No shit, really? As far as I'm concerned you should put her down like any other unsalvageable animal. My daughter was born broken, Mr. Shelton. The only thing I regret is not getting an abortion. Think of the lives I could have saved! You can poke and prod around in her brain all day long if that's what you want to do. She is a danger to anyone she comes in contact with, period. I just want to see that she is no longer a problem and sign whatever silly papers you made me come here to sign so I can be on my way and forget that she ever existed in the first place." Dorothy made no attempt to feign any motherly concern for her daughter.

"We really attempt to avoid taking such extreme measures, but we saw no other choice in your daughter's case. This is not something that's generally done any more."

"You do know what she's done, don't you? Her brain was rotten, and you couldn't fix that if you lined up headshrinkers from here to the moon! She is evil, pure and simple. You can't fix evil doctor."

"I think we can agree that she was as close to pure evil as I've ever seen, and I've been doing this for a very long time."

"She deserves to suffer for the things she's done and I'm here to ensure that she does. Now what do you need me to sign so we can get this over with?" Her patience was at an end and she wanted out of this place as quickly as humanly possible.

"I think you'll be as satisfied as the state is."

"Mr. Shelton I really don't give a fuck if the state is satisfied or not. If I could sign something that ensured that she would burn in hell for all eternity I'd sign it twice! I'll put this as simply as I can to you, that little cunt deserves to suffer and die for all the things she's done, all the lives she has violently snuffed out and my hope is that what you've done accomplishes that. My blood may run through her veins, but that bitch is no daughter of mine!" Dorothy was getting riled up as she spoke.

"Calm down, Mrs. Chantel, everyone here understands. I have no doubt you'll see that you no longer have to worry."

"Do you understand the kind of person… no, what kind of vile monster you are dealing with? She should have fried long ago, but no, one headshrinker after another thought they could fix her. All they really wanted to do is write books about how they had treated a demon straight out of hell while everyone around her continued to suffer for her existence," Dorothy yelled as her anger boiled over into rage.

"Try to calm yourself, Mrs. Chantel. No one here had anything to do with what happened in the past. We hope our solution is to your satisfaction." Mr. Shelton was getting frustrated but kept his calm demeanor. "Just sign these release forms and I'll show you that the situation is under control."

"I do apologize Mr. Shelton, I know you're just doing your job, but that girl has broken my heart so many times and after today I never wish to see or think of her ever again."

"Completely understandable. I'll call you only if absolutely necessary."

"Do me a favor, make sure it isn't necessary… ever."

"Yes, Ma'am." He said humbly handing her a clipboard with the few papers she needed to sign.

Dorothy scrawled her signature quickly on the papers, irritated over everything from having to be in this stale, sterile place to her entire daughter's life in general. The girl had been a pestilence since birth though part of her was glad that it was over now. She meant it when she told Mr. Shelton that after today she never wanted to think about Julie Duplantier ever again. She was finished signing the paperwork in a matter of seconds handing the clipboard back to the administrator.

Mr. Shelton flipped through the few pages to make sure everything was in order, "Very good. Now that that is out of the way let me escort you to see your daughter then you can be on your way."

"Be quick about it," she replied, her voice full of disgust.

Clyde Shelton stood to escort Dorothy Chantel out the door, stretching to his full six-foot four-inch height. He was even taller than Dorothy had expected and far thinner. He looked to Dorothy as if he didn't have a muscle in his entire body. They exited into the reception area where the large security guard, George, who had escorted her silently stood to do so once again.

Walking down the long corridor felt like walking through a mausoleum. The place seemed dead other than the sound of their footsteps on the tiled floor and burning stench of bleach that hung in the air like an invisible fog. She hated the place more with every step she took. It felt like she had walked a mile when they finally reached the elevator. Seconds passed like hours as they rode in almost painful silence until the elevator jerked to a stop and the doors parted.

George, the security guard, stepped out of the elevator first. Mr. Shelton's skeletal arm motioned for Dorothy to follow, then he exited last. At the end of a short hallway they passed through a set of security doors leading to the maximum-security section of Bainbridge. George inserted his security card into a metal box which then prompted him for fingerprint recognition.

"As you can see even before today there was never a chance that Julie would escape this place. There hasn't even been an attempt since the unfortunate incident almost forty years ago." Mr. Shelton seemed more than a little pleased with the security measures he had put in place.

"She's a danger as long as she's around other living things, Mr. Shelton. I don't fear her escape, simply what she does to anyone who comes in contact with her."

"That fear should be allayed in a few moments I should think." His self-satisfied tone didn't much impress his guest.

"It will be allayed when she's six feet under, Mr. Shelton." Dorothy sneered.

George led them down another long corridor, this one lacking any of the pastel blues and yellows of the halls they had passed to this point of the journey. Here the walls, floor and even ceiling were a linen white more dull than shiny under the florescent lights overhead. It still carried the sickening stench of bleach that permeated every inch of the place. Dorothy couldn't think of a blander place in all the world making it a perfectly awful place for her daughter. Still too good for her but it was the worst she could expect outside of hell itself.

Another tall man with short cropped blond hair, gold-rimmed glasses and white coat waited for the approaching trio outside a plain white door. Above the door the cell number was affixed to the wall, the only thing differentiating it from the others they had passed.

The doctor held out his hand in greeting, "Good day Mrs. Chantel. Sorry to make your acquaintance under these circumstances but a pleasure just the same."

"Mrs. Chantel meet Dr. Christian Andreu, he has been in charge of your daughter's care since she arrived here," Mr. Shelton introduced the pair.

"I must say your daughter's case is most extraordinary. I have never seen such an extreme case of psychotic schizophrenia or even read of one to be honest. I hate to have had to take such extreme measures but given her history and her behavior since arriving here especially after she assaulted one of our orderlies we simply had no other options." Dr. Andreu's voice was cordial but clinical as he spoke.

"I'm sorry, I was informed there was an incident but wasn't given any details. What did she do this time?" Dorothy said completely frustrated but unsympathetic.

"I do apologize, Mrs. Chantel." Mr. Shelton interjected, "I thought you had been informed. Julie attacked one of our orderlies, Michael Ware. She dug out one of his eyes with her finger. An absolutely horrifying incident." Mr. Shelton hung his head as though personally pained by the incident.

"You're lucky that's all she did. I told you, she is a demon straight out of hell. She's done far worse things than that I assure you. Is this orderly okay?" She didn't really have any concern for the orderly's welfare but knew it was proper to at least ask.

"He'll live. Obviously given Julie's history of violence we didn't see any other options. We wish we could cure everyone, but the safety of the staff must take precedence," Dr. Andreu replied again in his cold clinical way.

"You have nothing to apologize for, but you should have put her down like the sick dog that she is. That's the only way anyone will ever be safe around the likes of her." Dorothy saw no need to cover up her hatred of her daughter.

"I think you'll find she's no longer a danger, Mrs. Chantel," Mr. Shelton interjected again, pulling a small device from his pocket, "Open Cell Number 1420."

There was an electric buzz followed by a click in the cell door. A shock traveled up Dorothy's spine at the sound. She knew it was unlikely, but all she could picture in her mind was her daughter crouched like a tiger on the other side of the door waiting to pounce the instant the door opened.

"I assure you there's nothing to fear, Mrs. Chantel." Dr. Andreu said seeing she had been startled by the noise.

Dorothy stepped tentatively forward, still expecting her daughter to leap out to gouge out her eyes as she had the orderly. Slowly she inched forward until she stood in the doorway to the padded cell. Julie sat in one corner of the room with her arms wrapped around her knees rocking slightly back and forth. Dorothy wanted to pretend she was tough as nails but seeing her one and only daughter curled up in the corner of a padded room gently rocking and drooling struck a nerve she hadn't known existed. She was still cautious of the girl she had feared since she was only a toddler, but she steeled her nerves enough to step into the room.

Julie showed no sign that she even knew there was another person in the room. Dorothy had never seen anyone look more vacant than her daughter did at this moment. Dorothy remarked on how thin her daughter had always been, but she couldn't remember a time when Julie had appeared calm. Julie's head had been shaved for the operation giving her the appearance of a cancer patient undergoing chemotherapy treatment. Seeing that there was nothing to fear as she had been told, she moved in closer, sitting down next to her daughter.

"I'm truly sorry." Dorothy was sincere, feeling motherly for the first time since her daughter was born. "I wish things had been different, baby." A genuine tear spilled down her cheek.

Julie sat rocking herself, looking vacantly off into space, still not registering the presence of her mother. A line of drool stretched from the corner of her mouth to the floor though she didn't seem to notice. Dorothy waved a hand in front of her daughter's eyes, getting no reaction. Finally, when Dorothy lovingly rubbed her daughter's head Julie turned to face her, acknowledging her presence for the first time.

"Julie? Julie can you hear me? It's your mother." Dorothy desperately tried to prompt any recognition from her only child.

Julie began to move her mouth as if she were trying to say something, but no sound came out. She looked very much like a newborn making a suckling motion. After a few moments of this a faint sound came as if the words she were trying to get out were weighted down in the pit of her stomach somewhere. Dorothy moved her ear closer as her daughter's voice rose to a feint whisper.

"What is it Julie? Speak to me, honey." Dorothy pleaded.

"Yama." The word came out in a barely audible whisper, becoming louder as she repeated it over and over, "Yama. Yama. Yama." Julie continued until she was screaming the word at the top of her lungs as she rocked gently back and forth in the corner of Cell #1420.

Dorothy had seen enough, her heart broken by her daughter for the final time. When the word first came from Julie's lips, she wept, thinking her daughter was somehow trying to communicate with her, but as Julie continued on to screaming she knew that wasn't the case. Her heart could take no more. She had despised her daughter for so many years wishing the worst to happen to her, but seeing her in this state, barely more than a living vegetable staring vacantly into space while communicating nonsense, she knew there really wasn't anything worse.

Her daughter didn't know who she was, didn't know where she was and would live the remainder of her days in that state. Before today Dorothy would have said that a lobotomy was the least her daughter deserved but now she knew there was no worse punishment. Julie Duplantier was no longer a person, she was a human doll and nothing more. Dorothy left the room filled with a sorrow she never thought she could feel for her daughter. Every hope and dream she had ever had for her child was sucked out of her, leaving a space inside her every bit as empty and vacuous as Julie Duplantier now was, drooling in the corner of a padded room.

Exiting, she grabbed Dr. Andreu firmly by his chin, pulling him in close, "You should have killed her." She stared him in the eye a moment, then turned her back to leave and never return.

The bullets crashed into her, sending her tiny frame flying into the wall behind her. She crashed to the cold tile floor, releasing her final breath and the doctor's brains clutched in her fingers. Her body floated into the void where darkness encircled her. She could feel the shackles of life slip away, falling eternally down in the emptiness below as she glided through a blankness completely devoid of sight and sound. Julie Duplantier smiled, becoming one with the nothingness forever.

About the Author

Feind Gottes

Feind Gottes [Fee-nd Gotz] is a metal loving, award winning horror author. Currently Feind has stories published in six anthologies with several more awaiting release. In 2017 Feind placed in the Top Ten in The Next Great Horror Writer Contest, then later won the 2017 Vincent Price Scary Story Starter Award from Tell-Tale Publishing with his story *Vacuity*. 2018 marked a milestone for Feind with the publication of his first solo work a novella, *Essence Asunder*. Lastly, Feind won the Dark Chapter Press Prize 2016 novel writing contest with the first draft of his debut novel, *Piece It All Back Together*, which is currently being edited for a late 2018/early 2019 release.

Embers

By

Ric Wasley

Embers

By

Ric Wasley

Winter 1196.

Wind lashes the gray walls of a stone and wooden fortress that clings to the top of an outcropping of a low range of rolling hills. Parts of the fortress castle look raw and new as if pulled from the earth and forest yesterday, and parts of it have been.

But deep within the fortress walls is a keep which dates back to Roman times.

This is not unusual. In the one hundred and thirty years since Duke William, now remembered as "The Conqueror," began the building of a chain of Norman forts to hold his spoils, his war lords have made liberal use of legacies of other conquerors from earlier ages. Thus the castle's keep in the heart of Yorkshire, England, is no different than a dozen others, except in one respect—its lord.

Cold, bone chilling rain drips from the keep's narrow windows.

A lone figure sits in the great hall before a fire that has burned down to glowing red embers. The figure sits brooding in a large carved walnut chair. He slumps forward, each gnarled hand resting on the arms of the chair.

An ember flares up for a moment and illuminates his face. He stares at his reflection in a silver goblet that rests on a small table next to the chair.

The face that stares back at him is that of an old man—but he is only thirty-five.

White scars crisscross his face. One long, vicious-looking scar stands out from the rest. It runs from his hairline down to his jaw, crossing his left eye. Or what remains of where his left eye used to be. It is now a vacant socket, the legacy of a slashing back-handed cut left by a curved blade of Damascus steel. Though almost three years old, the deep scar still pains him. Especially on cold damp nights—like tonight.

As the pain becomes unbearable, he reaches for the goblet next to him. But his fingers are crippled and clumsy. They will not close around the cup, and it slips from his fingers. A strangled oath of frustration escapes his lips.

Light footsteps coming from the hall sound behind him. The footsteps pause and then grow louder as someone walks up and stands behind his chair. He smells a brief whiff of attar of roses, and then a slight form retrieves the fallen cup and places it on the table beside him. His ruined left eye cannot see, but he hears the cup being refilled. He reaches for it but then withdraws his hand and lets it fall limply into his lap. His head drops forward, and his chin rests upon his chest.

Suddenly the cup appears and is pressed toward his lips. A soft, low voice says, "Here, drink, my lord."

He looks up. A slim white hand holds the cup before him. His one good eye studies the vision that fills it.

It is a small and slender girl of sixteen or seventeen. Her long black hair falls in soft ringlets over her creamy white shoulders and curls like wine-dark sea foam down to her tiny waist. Her deep green eyes normally filled with laughter and impish humor are soft with pity for the broken figure in the chair.

His two gnarled hands try again to close around the cup, but they will not work. He tries one last time to perform this simplest of movements, but the pain and trembling of his hands once again thwarts him. He slams one deformed hand against the arm of the chair. The young girl with the angel face picks up his hand and uses her own to steady the cup, guiding it to his lips. He drinks deeply. And when he has drained the cup he looks into her tiny elfin face. She takes the cup and sits lightly on the arm of his chair.

"We are most happy to have you home, Lord Dunstan. You have been gone so long. I prayed for your safe return every day. And then…." Her eyes seek his single tormented one as if she is trying to share his pain. "Two years ago, a returning knight brought word that you had fallen outside of the city walls." She searches his ruined face—for some hint of the happy, handsome young man he had been five years ago. "We…I…was grieved beyond all measure when I heard that terrible news, just as I was filled with joy when I learned yesterday that you lived!"

He stares through her to the burning embers. "If you can call this living."

She traces her finger down the long white line that bisects his face.

"Do your wounds pain you, my lord?"

She leans forward and brushes her lips across the scar. He smells the rose scent in her hair.

"I am so sorry. I shall light a candle for you when I make my evening devotions."

"Save the wax," he mutters bitterly. "God will not hear your prayer any more than he did mine all of those months when I lay in a Saracen dungeon!"

"Oh, but you're wrong, my lord. He does hear. He—"

"Enough!" He runs one misshapen hand over his eye. "Leave me."

She shakes her head. "No, my lord, the night is dark. The storm frightens me, and the fire is warm." She looks at him with somber eyes. "Perhaps my Lord Dunstan would take pity on a poor girl from Northumbria—a grateful ward of your late father—and be so kind as to comfort me."

He smiles. He knows her heart. She is not frightened nor does she need comfort or pity. Rather it is her who seeks to comfort him and…. His smile fades. And she has taken pity on him.

He gazes down at the solemn, trusting eyes of the girl who now leans close to him. Even her breath smells of flowers and sweetness.

She rests her smooth, unblemished cheek on his scarred one. The sensation is that of warm, soft velvet caressing his face. He would most happily relinquish whatever was left of his life if he could die with that sweet, soft cheek next to his.

No…he can't…not and keep his honor.

His honor. The thought scalds him like the burning oil poured from the city battlements as he led his men against the wall in yet another futile attack.

His honor to a king who used him and his soldiers like pawns across a chessboard, sent to die and suffer so that one man could add more glory to his name and more gold to his coffers.

Though the scar tissue on his face makes subtlety of expression difficult, he can tell that his thoughts must be evident upon even such a battered visage as his. He sees her sweet green eyes grow concerned as his ruined hands spasm as if the poor mangled fingers long once more to be straight and whole.

Her soft red lips tremble, and her forehead carries an unaccustomed line of worry. Much like the first time he ever saw her.

He remembers his father calling him from the courtyard. When he'd stepped out into the bright morning light he saw two men-at-arms escorting a small child of ten. A pretty but frightened little girl with long cascading black hair, whose face, then as now, displayed a troubled frown and a forehead lined with worry.

"Dunstan," his father had said. "I would like you to meet your new 'sister'. The surprise must have shown on his face, for his father had laughed and quickly added, "No, my son, not sister by blood—the child is no 'by-blow' of my own, but due to the untimely death of her father—my friend—she has now become my ward and she will take our name and thus emerge, when a young woman, as Lady Gwyneth, and hence is your sister."

Dunstan had smiled then and walked over to where the child stood solemnly watching him. He bent down and touched her nose in playfulness. "Can I not put a smile on these sweet lips, little one?"

"I do not know, sir," she had answered gravely.

He laughed and picked her up in his arms. "Then let's see if this will help." He planted a kiss on her lips and chuckled. "Welcome to Blackborn Hall, dear sister."

From that day she had been his constant shadow, following him as he moved about the castle and the grounds. Sometimes, if he was riding out to hunt or marshaling his forces to put down a border raid, he would merely wave to her before he rode off. But more often if there was nothing pressing, he would sit and talk with her or set her up upon his warhorse and lead her about the courtyard.

And each time he returned, be it after an absence of a day, a week, or a month, she would be waiting at the gate tower with a bouquet of hand-picked flowers as he rode in.

Then he would scoop her up and place her in front of him, on the horse's neck, and let her tug on the reigns and declare that she was leading her charger into battle.

And so it continued as each year added to her beauty and to their closeness—until they were closer than any true blood brother and sister.

Then, in the summer of her thirteenth year, he had returned after nearly eight months away inspecting his father's estates in the north to find that in his absence the child he had left was blossoming into a striking young woman

And everything began to change.

At first it was small things. When he swept her up in his arms he noticed that her thin frame—at one time all legs and elbows—was becoming more rounded with curves in places where there had only been baby fat before. To be sure she was still a girl, but she was turning into a woman.

And so what happened next should not have come as a surprise, but it did.

It was one of the last sweet days of summer, just before the leaves showed their hidden reds and yellows. He had taken her riding on her own dappled palfrey. As the afternoon lengthened into dusk, they had stopped by the miller's dam and watched the water cascade over the rocks and into the foaming pool below.

He helped her down, stretched out on the bank, and put his hands behind his head. She ran up and threw herself down beside him. He tried to close his eyes, but she commenced tickling his nose with a long stem of grass until he reached over and caught both of her tiny hands in his own.

"Enough, Gwyneth," he laughed. "You are a pretty child, but you have vexed me quite enough for one afternoon."

"Do you really think so?"

"Do I think what, Gwyneth?"

"Do you think that I am pretty?"

He laughed again. "You are the prettiest little girl in all of Yorkshire."

"Thank you, my lord." Suddenly, her expression became serious. "But I am no longer a little girl. Celia, my maid, tells me that there are changes happening in my body which are making me a woman."

She jumped to her feet and twirled around in front of him, then dropped to her knees and leaned over his face. "Do you still think that I am just a 'little girl', my lord?"

He looked at her face. Her cheeks flushed, eyes sparkling, lips red and parted. He reached out a hand and touched a lock of her hair. She bent toward him.

The clang of the Abby church bell tolling broke the spell—almost as if a higher power was warning him.

He shook his head as though waking from a dream and rolled away. He stood next to her horse, made a stirrup of his hands, and helped her mount. They didn't speak as they rode back to the keep with the western sun setting behind them.

That night during dinner in the great hall, every time he glanced up she stared at him with a look that was neither a smile nor a frown, but which disturbed him. So much so that he didn't notice how many times his goblet was refilled, but all at once he glanced up and realized that his father and all of the servants had left the great hall and he was alone. Almost.

Across the table, Gwyneth stilled stared at him, her green eyes thoughtful.

Her gown of deep forest green matched her eyes and offset her pale white skin and raven-dark hair. She looked like a woodland sprit or elf of the hills. She was enchanting.

He blinked and took a deep draught of his wine. Then, without thinking he said, "Gwyneth, come here, girl. Come and keep me company."

Slowly, she rose and came around the table until she stood next to his chair. He patted his lap and slurred, "Come sit in my lap, sweet girl, and sing me one of your songs as you used to do."

She snuggled close to him and began to sing in a high, sweet, child-like voice. As the last verse of the song died away, without even thinking he pulled her close and kissed her. She sighed and put her soft arms around his neck. His hand ran down her side and brushed her small girlish breast.

Suddenly his head cleared. What was he doing? She was still a girl, and worse still, in spirit, his own sister.

He jumped up spilling her from his lap. "I...the hour is late. My head is muddled, and I must seek my bed. Goodnight, Gwyneth." He staggered from the hall and through the keep's dark corridor. He kicked open the door to his chamber, fell on the bed, and was instantly asleep.

He was never sure what had awakened him when the night candle had burned down to a guttering wick. Perhaps he rolled over or flung out his arm in a dream. But the next thing he knew, soft flesh rested under his hand. He opened his eyes to find Gwyneth's face inches from his own.

"Gwyneth—what…? How did you come to be here? You should not be here. You should…."

She put her fingers to his lips. "Hush, my lord. I knew that we were destined for one another from the first time I saw you smile at me on the steps of the keep." She gazed at him with wide, trusting eyes. "I would make you a wife, lord."

"No, Gwyneth. We must not…it isn't right. We…."

But soon all he saw were her sea-green eyes and sweet elfin face, and that was enough.

When the sky turned grey outside his window, he opened his eyes and recalled a sweet but disturbing dream. And was thankful that was all that it was—until he looked beside him and saw the innocent young girl who lay next to him. But was she innocent no more? He scrambled from the bed and stared in horror at the girl he had known as a child, a girl who had been, still was, and still should be to him, a sister!

He sank to his knees and moaned.

She awoke. "My lord?"

"Gwyneth, forgive me."

He turned and ran down the stairs, out to the stable, and a short time later, the clatter of horse's hooves on the cobblestones sounded as he rode out at a full gallop towards London.

There he joined King Richard's great crusade to free the Holy Land, and five long years of battle, blood, and pain would pass before he saw England and the castle keep again.

* * * *

Pellets of ice strike the walls of the keep, and the room grows cold. She walks to the pile of kindling next to the fireplace. "Let me build up the fire for you, Lord Dunstan."

"Leave it!" He makes a savage chopping motion with his twisted hand. He says once more, but softly, "Leave it."

He sighs. "I grew to hate the sight of fire all those months I was held captive. It always brought pain."

She picks up one of his hands and holds the twisted, broken fingers in her own. "You received these wounds whilst serving in the great crusade, alongside of our King Richard, did you not?"

He nods.

"Was it in the great battle before the walls of Acre?"

He shakes his head, tries to pull his claw of a hand away from her soft touch, but she holds on to it with surprising strength for one so slight.

"Please tell me, my lord. It will ease your mind."

He starts to shake his head and looks at her. But in place of the pity or contempt he expected is only a sweet compassion. Finally, he swallows hard and begins.

"It was after the great battle beneath Acre's walls that I took an arrow to the leg. But I dared not get off my horse to tend it for fear of being unable to remount. The king had also received a grievous wound and had been carried from the field and brought to a nearby village to recover. I saw him safe away, but when I returned to the fight I was struck from behind and taken prisoner. When I awoke, I was in a Moorish prison cell and there I was to remain and suffer for three hellish months. On the second day I was dragged to a torture cell and there 'put to the question'.

"They demanded to know where the king had been taken. When I refused, they took one of my fingers and crushed it with a large mallet.

"Then, every day for the next nine days they would pull me from my cell, put the same question to me, and when I still refused, they would destroy another finger. Until after ten days my hands became the misshapen things you see before you now."

He stares into the embers of the fire.

She brings his mangled hands to her lips. "I am so sorry, my lord."

He stares at his hands in her small white ones and gazes at her sweet, childlike face. It seems as if, despite her young age, she knows of all of his torments and is there to help ease them. The lump in his throat makes it difficult to speak, so he merely says, "Thank you, lady."

She strokes his hair as though he is a small child.

"Remember, my lord, you are not alone. Your early kindness and sweet affection for me is not forgotten and know that I am your true and most devoted friend and I...."

"Lady Gwyneth!"

He looks up.

His young cousin from York stands in the doorway. He smiles and bows. "Well met, my lord. I see you have been kind enough to entertain the Lady Gwyneth and I do thank you." He turns to the petite girl with the long black hair and bows. "Come, lady. Father Ambrose waits for us in the chapel to go over the vows we shall speak tomorrow when we are joined as one."

The young woman gets up, takes one step, and then puts her lips close to Dunstan's ear. "Remember, I still remain your true friend—always."

And then she is gone, but the smell of roses still lingers.

He takes a deep breath, then turns his head and stares into the burning embers of a dying fire. His one good eye stings with unshed tears as a single word echoes in his mind... "Always."

About the Author

Ric Wasley

Ric has a 40-year professional career history in advertising, publishing and marketing in Boston, New York and San Francisco. He has degrees in history and psychology and has been trained in debating, public speaking and stage acting. A large part of his 40-year career was spent in numerous professional and business settings as a presenter and featured speaker at seminars and meetings.

Ric has been a visiting professor at Worcester Polytech Institute. He also teaches a popular course on marketing for authors at prominent venues such as the venerable "Cape Cod Writers Conference". Ric is a published author of a Mystery Series and multiple other novels. He's a veteran Tell-Tale author with multiple titles in house.

Subject Seven

by

Jay Michael Wright, II

Subject Seven

by

Jay Michael Wright, II

The blood. He'd never seen so much blood. Patrick ran down the hallway, leaping over disemboweled corpses and the few survivors hanging on. Cold sweat slithered down his spine and the hairs on the back of his neck were standing at attention. Every fiber in his being told him to run, so that's exactly what he did.

He rounded the corner and lost his footing in a puddle of on the ground. He landed with a splash that turned his lab coat from pristine white to crimson and pink in the blink of an eye. He sat up and held the knot he now had on the back of his head.

The laboratory's computer system rang out over the intercom, "Containment breach. Subject Seven is not contained. All security to cell-block Omega. Preparing for lockdown."

No! You are not locking me up in here with that thing!

Patrick pulled himself up and rushed for the elevator doors. It was the only exit from the lab. He ran by a squad of the base's security teams. Most of them had their throats ripped out, and a couple of them had been completely decapitated.

It was more than Patrick could take. Everywhere he looked was another nightmare. People had been torn from limb to limb. The U.S. Colonel Patrick had answered directly to had said the base was an iron fortress—nothing could escape. Well, from the sound of the alarms going off, the Colonel was more than just a wee bit off with his claims.

Patrick slid up to the elevator doors and nearly fell again in the process. He put his security badge into the scanner and then nervously punched in his passcode. The little red flashing light turned to green and Patrick sighed in relief.

Thank God!

He hit the up button and waited impatiently. Sounds of gunfire in the distance made Patrick jump. It was immediately followed by a man screaming at the top of his lungs before the eerie sound of silence filled the hallways.

Oh God! Come on, elevator!

The lab's computer announced over the intercom, "Lockdown commencing in Five,"

Come on!

"four,"

Damn it!

"three,"

Please, Jesus! Just let me out of here!

"two,"

No!

"one."

The elevator door dinged, started to open, and then immediately shut. A metal panel slid down from the ceiling and sealed the elevator doors as Patrick cried and slapped his hand against the wall. *Damn it! It was so close!*

He heard more screams, this time much closer, and ran for what he'd been told was the blood lab. He used his security badge to enter the room and then locked it immediately behind him.

He sighed in relief until the sounds of pounding on the door sent shockwaves of terror running up and down his spine. It was Jackie, one of the staff nurses.

"Let me in! She'll kill us all!"

Patrick shook his head slowly. "I'm so sorry! I can't!"

She then exploded into a crimson mist and Patrick knew the end was near. He backed away from the door as his entire body turned numb. *What the fuck is going on down here?*

A body slammed against the door, leaving tiny stress fractures in the glass. The thud of the impact was so loud Patrick nearly pissed himself. He backed away in a rush and nearly tripped over the bodies of a pair of lab technicians which had their throats ripped out. He fell against the counter and cringed as he sent a dozen or more vials of blood crashing to the floor below.

He dropped to his knees, praying that the racket he had made wouldn't draw whatever that was outside's attention. The power flickered off and then the emergency lights activated, illuminating everything around him in a reddish-orange hue.

Oh, this can't be good.

He tried to slow his breathing and be as stealthy as possible as he slid along the lab floor. He crawled over more corpses as he tried to find a way out of the room he had locked himself in.

Seeing no visible exit, he sat against the counter as sweat dripped down his forehead. "I had one fucking job," he muttered to himself, "fix the freakin' printer in some snobby Colonel's office and go home. I knew better than to volunteer for this job. I should have gone with Tony to Nashville. At least working at a bank nobody starts decapitating folks."

Just as the calm began to return to his troubled mind, a locker on the other side of the room vibrated and terror grasped him once again. He frantically looked around for something, *anything,* that he could use to defend himself. At first, he found nothing but bits and pieces of broken glass and strange little metal clamps that he couldn't make heads or tails of. Then he saw the body of a fallen soldier in the corner of the room. The clip to his rifle had been emptied, but the man's sidearm was still in the holster and fully loaded. He carefully removed the pistol and whispered to the man's corpse, "Don't mind if I borrow this, do you?"

He stood and aimed the pistol at the locker. His hands shook. His fingers didn't want to cooperate. What was lurking behind that locker door? It vibrated once more. His heart took off like a drag-racer screaming down the strip at a hundred miles an hour. It beat so loud, he could barely hear himself think.

Using his second hand to steady his aim, he tried to sound as threatening as he could. "I heard you, so come on out of there! I'm armed, so don't try anything fancy or I'll shoot."

The door rattled, and a thousand thoughts ran through his head. He knew one of those things was outside, but what if there were more of them? There were at least two-dozen well-trained soldiers with their throats ripped out on this floor of the installation alone. If they couldn't stop this thing, what chance did a computer technician with a pistol really have?

The locker rattled again but didn't open. Patrick brazenly took a step forward and aimed for the dead-center of the door. "Stop messing around! Come out or I'm going to unload this whole clip into you."

The locker door slowly creaked open, its hinges whining like tiny banshees giving warning to any who could hear. Patrick took a step backward, readying himself for the worst, but what he got was a terrified middle-aged black woman in a white lab coat. She threw her hands up above her head and shouted, "Please don't shoot! I'm just a lab technician."

Patrick lowered his pistol and sighed in relief. "What the hell were you doing in there?"

The woman put down her hands and replied with irritation, "What do you think I was doing? I was hiding. What are you doing?"

Her question and tone caught Patrick off guard. He replied, "I, um, was hiding too."

"Well, now that we've got that out of the way, would you mind putting the gun down?" She then added, "And, by the way, they work better if you turn the safety off."

Patrick looked at the firearm and slid the safety off as he placed the gun on the counter. "So, you work down here. What the fuck is going on down here? Why is this place on lockdown?"

The woman leaned against the counter, took a pack of cigarettes from her coat pocket with a shaky hand, and sparked up. "Look here, just because we're going to die is no reason to be rude. My name's Debbie, and you are…?"

"Patrick. Now get on to answering the question."

Debbie blew rings of smoke in Patrick's general direction and took another drag. She smiled. "Damn, sometimes you just need a cigarette. You know what I mean?"

Patrick slammed his fist on the counter and shouted, "Answer the goddamn question! Why is this place on lockdown?"

She rolled her eyes. "Obviously, something escaped from containment two levels below us. The lab is on lockdown as a failsafe. They'd rather lock us up in tomb than let that thing out of here."

Patrick ran his fingers through his hair and fought the urge to scream. "What the fuck do you people have in containment down there?"

Debbie shrugged her shoulders. "To be honest, I don't have a clue."

Her answer infuriated Patrick. "What the hell do you mean, 'you don't have a clue?' You mean to tell me that you work here and don't know what you keep locked in the basement?"

Crushing her cigarette butt out on the counter, Debbie replied, "Do you think the secretaries that worked on the Manhattan Project got schematics to the atom bomb? I'm just a blood technician. They send me blood samples. I run tests. I file reports and then I go home. They don't tell me shit about what's down there, and from the stories I've heard, I don't want to know."

"Well, did you at least see something when the thing came into the lab?"

Patrick's last question destroyed Debbie's calm demeanor. She started pacing the floor and her voice was filled with venom. "Look, I didn't see shit, okay? My supervisor told me that if I ever heard the alarms go off that I should hide, and I should stay hid until the crisis was over. I heard that thing come in here. I heard the gunshots, the screams. Do you have any idea what it's like hearing your coworkers ripped to pieces? And don't look at me like that! Don't you think I wanted to help; but what was I going to do? Stab it with my pen? If the fully trained guy with an M-16 couldn't stop it, what hope did I have?"

Patrick threw his hands up into the air as if surrendering. "Okay, I get it. You were afraid and outgunned. There's no shame in that. Still, it would be nice to know what the fuck we're dealing with down here."

Debbie had taken a seat on the floor against the wall and Patrick joined her. He politely asked, "Got another one of those smokes you can spare?"

Debbie cut her eyes at him. "You're a smoker?"

"Used to be, but I figured being stuck in a top-secret military installation with an unidentified killer on the loose gives me as good of excuse as I'm going to find to start back."

Debbie fished out a cigarette and handed it over. "Amen to that. Shit, this almost makes me wish I still smoked weed."

Patrick laughed. "That's funny, I've got about an ounce and a half of some top-end bud at my house. If I'd known what today was going to be like, I'd have brought us some."

"Wait," Debbie laughed. "How did a pothead get himself inside a military base running secret experiments?"

Patrick smiled slightly. "I'm a contracted computer technician based out of Montgomery. Colonel Mathews was having issues getting his computer and printer to sync up. Plus, when he was accessing certain files on his PC, his computer would crash. I was here to figure out what was going on. I've done jobs all over the south; Fort Benning, Fort Stewart. I even drove to Virginia once just to show a Major how to use

Microsoft Office to make a presentation. It's a lot of time on the road, but the pay is good, and it keeps me busy, so I don't think about my family."

Debbie's curiosity seemed to peak. "Oh, you're a family man?"

Patrick looked down and turned pale. His voice took a sorrowful tone, "Used to be. I lost my wife and daughter in a car wreck eight months ago."

Debbie shook her head and slammed her fist against the wall. "Shit! I'm sorry I asked."

Patrick shrugged. "It's okay. How could you have known?"

The intercom buzzed. The same computer voice from before began speaking. "Subject Seven is still not contained. Please return Subject Seven to its cell to avoid laboratory cleansing. Secondary lockdown procedures initiated. T-minus ninety minutes to laboratory cleansing."

Debbie hung her head and looked to be on the verge of tears. She whispered, "Oh, shit." This did little to ease Patrick's nerves.

He stood up and started pacing. "That sounds bad. That sounds really, really bad." He knelt and grabbed Debbie by the shoulders. "What's a laboratory cleansing?" When she didn't answer him, he shook her and asked again with a sterner voice, "What the hell is a laboratory cleansing?"

Debbie looked up with tears dancing in her eyes. "They'll fill the complex with a combustible gas and then light it. It will incinerate everything down here. When in doubt, burn it all to the ground and leave no survivors."

Patrick's blood ran cold and chills ran down his spine. "Oh, fuck no. They can't do this. We're American citizens. They would never…"

"Oh, wouldn't they? You really think your government doesn't kill innocent people each and every day? You think they give two shits about us? We're just cogs in a machine. When the machine breaks, throw it away and get you a new one."

Patrick's panic grew by the moment. "Well, they've got to be sending help, right? Someone's coming to catch that thing. They have to be."

Debbie laughed as the first tears rolled down her cheeks. "We're on lockdown, darlin'. Ain't nobody getting' in. Ain't nobody getting' out. If security don't put that thing back in its cage… boom."

"Fuck this shit!" Patrick growled as he reached for his phone. "I've got to call someone and tell them what's going on. They aren't gonna get away with this. This will be all over the news by morning."

He dialed on the phone, but nothing happened. He hung up and tried again. Once more, the line was dead. Debbie took another cigarette out and shook her head. "You really think you're going to get a phone signal down here? You're underground, Patrick, in a top-secret lead-lined bunker. You couldn't make a phone call down here if you had Alexander Graham Bell, some string, and two tin cans. Once Celine starts the countdown, all you can do is wait."

"Celine? Who's Celine?"

Debbie snickered. "My bad, I forgot you didn't know. 'Celine' is what everyone calls the computer that runs this place. She's the one that's made all the announcements over the intercom. She's programmed to keep whatever is down here safe at all costs, even if it means killing everyone inside; but from what I've seen, whatever Subject Seven is has already beaten her to it, for the most part."

Patrick had a moment of brilliance. "Wait, she's a computer?"

Debbie shot him a dirty look. "Were you not listening? Yes, she's a computer. Why?"

"Computers can be hacked. They can be turned off. We can stop this bitch from turning us into deep fry." He ran over to the computer on the counter and started typing away as fast as he could. "I need your log-in to access the computer. What is it?"

Debbie laughed. "You're not going to be able to access Celine on that computer. All that computer does is record lab results and sends them to my supervisor. Celine is on her own server and even has her own power supply. Just admit defeat and sit down and help me finish this pack of smokes."

This only strengthened Patrick's convictions. "No. There is no way I am going to just sit here and wait to die." Suddenly, he perked up. "Wait, that Colonel's computer I was sent to work on; I'd bet anything it's hooked up to Celine's server."

He stuffed the pistol he had taken from the dead soldier into his pants and headed for the door. When it refused to open, he gave it a second pull. When it still refused to budge, he began kicking the door out of frustration. "Why won't this fucking thing open?"

"Secondary lockdown procedures, remember? Without a key card and a high-level clearance, every door in this place is shut tight."

Patrick was irate. He picked up a chair and slung it towards the lab window. "Fuck this shit!" The chair smashed against the glass and fell in pieces to the floor, so he picked up another chair and took another try. The outcome was the same. "Why the hell won't this glass break?"

"That's three-inches of bullet proof glass. You can beat on it all day long, it's not going to break. Here, have a cigarette. It'll make you feel better."

Patrick knocked the cigarette from her hand. "I don't want a fucking cigarette! I want out of this goddamn room!"

He sat against the counter, fighting back the headache which seemed determined to overtake him, when a low humming sound filled the room. Patrick felt a cool rush of air against his leg and, upon looking down, smiled at what he saw. Before he could say a word, Debbie raised her right hand like she was at a church-revival and said, "Oh, thank God! The air conditioning kicked in. At least we're not gonna have to sweat while we wait."

Patrick knelt and tugged at the grate without success. He paused, then said, "I need a screwdriver." He turned to Debbie, "Please tell me you have one in here."

Debbie stared at him in disbelief. "What are you trying to do?"

"The air-conditioning, it probably runs through the entire facility. I can use it to get back to the Colonel's office and all my gear, so I can try to shut Celine down."

Debbie rolled her eyes. "You're crazy."

Patrick had bit his tongue long enough. Everything he'd been thinking poured out of his mouth without him thinking. "What the fuck is wrong with you? You're content here to just sit around and wait to die. Don't you have anything worth living for? Isn't there something that you'd fight to save?"

Debbie was silent, but her eyes revealed there was something dark brooding in her mind. She wiped the tears from her cheeks and softly replied, "Yea, I'm gonna be grandmother come October. My only daughter is having a son. I'd love to be there when he's born."

"Then why don't you get up and help me? What do you have to lose? What are you so fucking scared of?"

Debbie pulled herself to her feet and pointed out the laboratory window. "I'm scared because that thing is out there! At least we're safely locked in here. I'd rather die in an instant than have that thing rip me to pieces. You ask me if I'm scared; well, I'm terrified. Are you happy now?"

Patrick felt a bit ashamed. "You think you're the only one scared? Lady, I've damn near pissed myself three times in the last ten minutes. I did two tours of duty in Baghdad and I ain't never seen shit like this. I'm scared out of my mind, but I'll be damned I'm gonna wait around to die. So, are you going to help me get back to my gear or not?"

There was a pause, then Debbie replied, "Are you sure you can shut her down?"

Patrick shrugged. "I don't know. I've never hacked anything this major before, but I'm willing to try."

Debbie pulled herself to her feet and said, "The screwdrivers are in the top drawer on the left. Let's do this."

Five minutes into the crawling through the air duct and Patrick was already starting to have regrets. The passageway narrowed as he went, or perhaps that was just his imagination. Flashbacks of the time his brother locked him in the closet danced through his mind. It made every second inside the tiny metal corridor that much more unbearable. The sweat poured down his face and it was getting difficult to breathe.

"How much further? I can't see a damn thing back here." Debbie's constant complaining wasn't helping either. She grated his nerves to the point that he wanted to scream. He started feeling like *Papa Smurf* from the Saturday-morning cartoon. Every five seconds he was having to reassure Debbie that they were getting closer.

"It's not that much further. The bend to the right is just ahead of me. Once we make that turn, the Colonel's office should be the third grate we come to."

"Well, we can't get out of here fast enough. I swear I keep hearing something moving in here with us."

Patrick rolled his eyes. "There's nothing in here, Debbie. The odds of that are ridiculous. Just keep moving."

"Easy for you to say, you're the one with the flashlight on his cellphone. I can't see shit back here."

"Just hang in there, Debbie. We're almost there."

Patrick crawled forward and fought the urge to panic. He wanted out of this air duct as bad as Debbie did, he just refused to show it. Just as he made it to the right turn in the airduct, he felt a hand on his ankle. He let out a little scream and turned to see that it was only Debbie.

"What in the hell are you doing?"

Her eyes were filled with terror. She breathed rapidly as sweat poured down her face. Her voice was not much more than a whisper, "There... there's something back here. I can hear it scratching the metal."

"It's just your imagination. Calm down and—"

"Hush!" she said as she placed a finger over her mouth. "Listen."

At first, he heard nothing, but when the sounds of something sharp scraping against metal made it to his ears, Debbie's panic became his own. "We've got to get moving!"

He inched forward, and Debbie let out a yelp. Patrick turned and shone his light on Debbie who was frozen with fear. Tears rolled down her cheeks as she whispered, "Something has hold of my ankle."

Patrick didn't want to believe it. "Maybe you're just snagged on one of the metal brackets."

"No," Debbie cried out. "There's a hand wrapped around my ankle. I can't shake it loose."

Debbie suddenly was pulled backward a few feet. Patrick backed up and reached his hand out for her. She grabbed on tightly, whispered one word softly, "Help," and then disappeared into the darkness at an alarming rate.

Patrick frantically used the light from his phone to search for her. "Debbie! Talk to me! Where are you?" He wasn't sure what he feared most, whatever grabbed Debbie, or being alone. The thought of both sent chills down his spine.

There was no answer except for a scream. Then, the sound of something rolling down the air duct toward him had his heart racing like it might explode. The item rolled to a stop at Patrick's feet. With one glance he felt a fear he hadn't experienced since he was a small child and believed the Devil lived under his bed. It was Debbie's severed head, and her lifeless eyes were forever frozen in a look of absolute terror.

What in the fuck could have done that?

It didn't take him long to get an answer. The sound of something razor-sharp being dragged across metal echoed up and down the airduct. A pair of glowing yellow eyes pierced the darkness and penetrated straight into Patrick's soul. When a young girl's voice hissed, "*I want to play,*" that's all he needed to hear. He pulled the pistol from his pants and fired four shots into the darkness. The thing scurried away, and, most disturbingly, giggled madly as it did it.

Patrick's heart pounded as he wiggled off to the right and toward the Colonel's office. He didn't know what that thing was, and didn't care to know, but he wanted out of that air duct pronto. He felt like that thing was on top of him, watching his every move. He was terrified too move, too horrified to stay in place.

The giggling seemed to be coming from everywhere. It echoed inside his head. The whole world was closing in on him and breathing was becoming more difficult by the moment.

He found the Colonel's office and pushed on the grate like his life depended on it. It refused to budge, so he slammed his fists against it until his knuckles bled. If he had to, he would have gnawed his way through the metal to get out of that airduct.

The top screws of the vent gave way first, and Patrick didn't wait for the bottom ones to comply. He pushed on the grate, bending it as he forced his way into the office. The voice inside the airduct got steadily louder.

"Olly-olly oxen free!" the thing said in between giggles. Its playful tone did little to settle Patrick's nerves.

He looked around, desperately seeking something to put in front of the hole in the wall where the air vent had been. He saw the Colonel's oak bookcase and smiled. *Thank god he had good taste in furniture*! There wasn't time to clear the bookcase out, so when it dumped to its side books spilled everywhere and framed pictures of the Colonel and his family shattered.

With the room barricaded, Patrick sat on the desk to catch his breath.

The bookcase started to tremble. Panic returned. The bookcase moved out from the wall a good three inches and Patrick couldn't believe his eyes. He quickly wedged himself between the Colonel's desk and the bookcase, using his legs to push against whatever was inside the duct trying to push its way in.

He strained every muscle as the thing in the wall refused to give up. Feeling like he was about to pass out from exhaustion, Patrick took the pistol and fired three shots through the bookcase where the hole in the wall should be. There was silence, and the pressure on the bookcase was gone.

Did I get it? Is it dead?

He slowly stood up and inched toward the hole in the wall. He peeked at the one-inch gap between the airduct and the bookcase, looking for what, he wasn't sure. Laughter erupted from the opening and Patrick almost fell over as he leapt away. Giggling filled the passageway and a voice called out from the distance, "I'll play with you later."

It was completely silent, except for the sound of Patrick's heart running away in his chest. He wiped the sweat from his brow and caught his breath. He was safe, at least for the moment.

The smell of something foul caught his attention and Patrick turned his head to see what it was. In the corner of the office was the colonel's corpse. It had been mutilated beyond recognition.

"Oh my god," he whispered as he covered his nose and mouth to move closer and investigate. The colonel's eyes were missing and there was a hole in his chest about the size of a person's fist. Lying next to the body was the colonel's heart. Patrick was mortified to notice that it appeared something had taken a bite out of it before placing it on the ground.

He backed away slowly. "What in the world were you doing down here?" Of course, there was no answer, but the question weighed heavily on Patrick's mind as he booted up the colonel's computer. Once he was inside, he hooked up a device that he lovingly called "Sally" to one of the computer's USB ports. Sally had never let him down in the past. He prayed she wouldn't let him down today.

Sorting through tons of encrypted files, Patrick tried to find a backdoor into Celine's mainframe. If he could get inside her system, he could turn her off and prevent the lab cleansing. He'd still be stuck down here with whatever Subject Seven was, but he could only handle one problem at a time.

While Sally was doing her thing, Patrick decided to look around on the colonel's desktop to see if he could find anything about what they were doing in this facility. It didn't take him long to score.

"Well, well, well… what do we have here? Looks like the colonel thought having his computer locked up in his office would be enough security, so he didn't hide his files very well." Patrick looked over at the colonel, "Tsk, tsk, sir."

Patrick opened the folder labeled "cell-block Omega," and started going through documents. He thought he had found the answers, but what he got was more questions. He began reading.

"Okay, Subject One, date acquired: July 3rd… *1939*? This guy has got to be dead." He read further and noticed there were blood reports listed for this subject dated just a week earlier. Patrick shook his head and tried to shake off the chill that was setting in on him. He went on to the next file.

"Subject Two, acquisition: November 22nd, 1943, Berlin, Germany." He sat back and scratched his chin. "What are they doing? Running a retirement home for Nazis in here?" The rest of the file made no sense to him. There were no names, no gender, nothing describing who or *what* the thing in cell number two was. All he saw was blood reports and coded documentations to which he didn't have the key.

He quickly thumbed through the rest of the files. Subject Three was acquired in the 1950s in Rome, Italy. Subject Four was acquired in 1964 from Lubbock, Texas. Subject Five was picked up October 30, 1987 from New York City. He couldn't make sense of it. Who were these people, and why were they down here?

Then he noticed something odd. Subjects Six and Seven were acquired at the same time only a year earlier from London, England. He wondered if there was any significance to that fact. Before he had long to dwell upon it, Sally dinged, and her red light turned to green. This meant she had found a backdoor into Celine's mainframe. Now it was time to get hacking.

"Hot damn! Sally, if you were a woman, I'd kiss you."

The intercom above him buzzed to life. Celine's robotic voice began to speak. "Unauthorized access to the mainframe detected. Please identify who you are and what your intentions are."

Patrick felt like a three-year-old who'd been caught with his hand in the cookie jar. He hesitated to answer, but knew he had to say something. He cleared his throat and said, "I'm the contractor hired by your superiors. I'm working on Colonel Mathew's computer. He's been... having trouble accessing the files that he needs."

It was a good lie; a believable lie, but Celine wasn't having any of it. "Your statement has been deemed as false. You were contracted to install a printer. Secondly, Colonel Mathews is dead. He no longer requires access to the files stored within the mainframe. Please disconnect your device and tell me your true intentions or defensive measures will be taken."

Patrick sighed and decided just to go with the truth. "Look, I'm trying to stop you from cleansing the lab. There are people alive down here. You're going to kill us all."

The intercom crackled, then said, "A reasonable cost of life. Subject Seven must not be allowed to leave the facility."

"You've got to give us a chance to stop Subject Seven! You're going to destroy everything these people have worked on for decades if you don't stop."

"I have calculated the odds of the surviving members of the staff recapturing Subject Seven. It is only 3.8%. I have been programmed that any time the odds of recapture are below 5%, I am to cleanse the laboratory to ensure subjects do not reach the general population. You have ten seconds to disconnect your device or defensive measures will be taken."

Patrick worked as fast as he could looking for a way to disconnect Celine or fry her circuit boards. He found the controls to her power supply and started to overload them. The sequence he set into motion couldn't move fast enough. Sixty percent… seventy… eighty-five…

Suddenly, there was a buzz of electricity and a puff of smoke rose out of Sally before her lights went dark. Patrick slammed his fists against the desk. "Goddamn it! I was so close." His rage built up to the point that he began shouting at the intercom. "Fuck you, Celine! You're going to murder everyone down here."

The intercom crackled and buzzed. "Threat to mainframe neutralized. Now commencing measures to neutralize hacker."

Patrick found it hard to breathe. He felt like he was choking. He staggered to the office door, but it wouldn't open. "What… what have you done?"

Celine responded, "The oxygen in the colonel's office has been decreased. You will soon lose consciousness. I cannot have you interfering any more than you have. T-minus sixty minutes to laboratory cleansing."

Patrick fell to one knee and tried to aim his pistol at the window, but he didn't have the strength. The world started spinning and as he landed face down on the carpet, everything went black.

"Patty! Patty-boy! Wake up."

Patrick tried to open his eyes, but it felt like there were weights attached to his eyelids. His entire body ached. It felt like someone had beaten him with a baseball bat and then had their friend do the same.

"Patty! You're gonna sleep your life away, boy. Get yo' ass up!"

Patty? Nobody's ever called me Patty except…

He forced his eyes open, and there he was, smiling down at him. "Pawpaw Clark?"

"Hey, son. Need a hand up?"

Patrick forced himself up to his feet and looked around in disbelief. They were in a solid white room with no windows or doors. He felt dizzy and leaned against the wall to balance himself. "Am... am I dead?"

His grandfather placed his hand on his back and replied, "Naw, son. You ain't dead. You's layin' on the floor of that colonel's office. That damned fancy computin' machine sealed up the room and lowered the oxygen. She knocked you out, but she ain't killed you... *yet.*"

Patrick tried to stand on his own, but the pain was overwhelming. "Oh my god," he gasped. "It feels like my insides were on fire and somebody put it out with a yard-rake."

"That's the oxygen deprivation messin' with ya, son. What you gotta do is wake up and get out of dat room."

"And just how do I do that? The place is locked down because of the escaped specimen."

His grandfather smiled. "Remember when you first got to the facility? Remember the passcode the colonel gave ya to get into his office? It'll open every door down there if ya got the right key. You gotta wake up, get out of the room, and stop that thing before that fancy talkin' machine fries you and everybody else."

"How do I stop that thing? It's killed no telling how many people. I'm just a computer technician."

"You more than that, son. You're a Clark. My grandfather didn't leave Ireland, risk his life on a boat ride across the Atlantic, and set up life in America for you to be killed in some godforsaken bunker by a talking microwave. You'll find your way, son. You're a Clark, and Clarks are survivors."

Patrick absorbed the message and slowly started nodding his head. "Okay, I'll find a way. I don't know what it'll be, but I'll find it."

"And one last thing, son. I know you're worried about that thing in the wall and possibly getting deep-fried, but what you really got to worry about *are the people* down there. They've opened up a portal to Hell and don't even realize it. If you ain't careful, the whole world is gonna burn for their arrogance and mistakes."

Patrick felt ill. This was far more of a responsibility than he cared to have thrust upon him. Still, he nodded his head. "I'll do my best, pawpaw."

The room began to spin, and Patrick fell down to one knee. He heard his grandfather's voice like a distant echo, "You gotta wake up, Patty. Wake up!"

Patrick's eyes fluttered open slowly. His muscles ached, but he managed to push himself up and, using the colonel's desk, regained his feet. It was hard to think, but the message from his grandfather ran through his head. He had to get out of that office or he was going to die.

He grabbed the door knob and pulled as hard as he could, but the door refused to budge. He slapped himself on the forehead and thought, *Oh, yea. The badge, I need the colonel's badge.*

Patrick nearly collapsed as he approached the colonel's corpse. He managed to stay upright and ripped the badge from the man's jacket. He turned back to the door and hit his knees. Everything was starting to turn black and spin. He knew he didn't have long to act.

He crawled to the door and groaned as his muscles ached from sliding the badge through the security lock. He then struggled to remember the passcode he had been given earlier. *It was seven, three, two... fuck! What was the last number?* The lack of oxygen made it next to impossible to function. It felt like a giant had his head in a vice and wasn't going to stop squeezing until his head popped. Suddenly, it hit him. *Nine! The last number was nine!*

He punched in the code and the red light turned to green. Patrick ripped open the door and collapsed into the hallway and a puddle of blood. He swallowed a mouthful of blood as he gasped for air. Slowly, his headache eased, and his muscles stopped aching. He propped against the wall and used the clean half of his shirt to wipe the blood from his face. To his left lay a scientist with her throat ripped out. To his right, a soldier whose throat had been slit.

He took the soldier's sidearm and stood up. "Okay, time to find Subject Seven and put an end to this bullshit." He quickly checked the status of the gun clip. He wanted to know how many shots he had to play with. The clip was full, but what surprised him, was what the bullets were made of.

"Silver? Why would they be using silver bullets?" He popped the clip back into the gun and inched down the hallway. "What in the fuck are they doing down here?"

Patrick rounded a corner, his heart racing as he thought he heard something moving in the distance. With every step he was meticulously cautious, his head on a swivel, terrified at what might be lurking in the dimly lit hallways. He kept his back against the wall and stepped over the corpses of those who had been butchered. On the wall, written in blood, were the words, "I want my mommy."

No, that's not creepy. That's not creepy at all.

"T-minus forty-five minutes to lab cleansing," the intercom screeched.

"Piece of shit computer," Patrick muttered as he swung open a door to the bathroom and checked to see if the coast was clear. It looked empty, but he kept his pistol at the ready. He'd be damned if he was going to get ambushed.

He checked each and every stall and found the bathroom to be abandoned. He sighed and relaxed for a moment. He sat the gun down on the sink and turned the faucet on. He used copious amounts of soap along with paper towels and attempted to scrub the blood from his face. "This has so *not* been my day," he whispered as he rubbed his face raw trying to get clean.

A toilet flushed behind him and Patrick's heart froze. His nerves danced on pins and needles. He slowly reached for the gun as he watched the mirror carefully for movement. He spun around slowly, and his heart took off beating like a drum. A bead of cold sweat slithered down his neck and then traveled down his spine.

I just checked those stalls. There was nobody here. How did that toilet flush?

It was a question that weighed on him heavily as he crept towards the bathroom stalls. He pushed the first one open and leapt back, ready to shoot at anything that moved. There was nothing. He moved to the second stall and repeated the process. Again, nothing. He looked at the third stall and bit his bottom lip. *Alright, motherfucker. Come out, come out... wherever you are.*

He reached out with his left hand to push the stall door open when a hideous laugh echoed through the bathroom. Patrick backed away until he had his back against the wall with the mirror. He swallowed back a scream as he saw a pair of black boots step down inside the stall.

Patrick pulled the trigger over and over, screaming, "Die, bitch, die!"

When he finished, there was silence. *I got it, didn't I? Nothing could have survived that.* He cautiously approached the bathroom stall and pushed the door open. He half-expected the Devil to be standing there waiting on him. What he found was nothing.

He lowered the pistol and shook his head. "I saw someone in there. I know I did." He turned back to the mirror with a half-smile on his face, but his voice was shaky and unsure. "I guess this place is messin' with my head."

The lights flickered off and the room became incredibly cold. The hairs on the back of Patrick's neck stood up as he felt eyes staring at him in the darkness. "Okay, this isn't good."

The lights flashed back on and in the mirror, Patrick saw, standing right behind him, the most hideous man he had ever seen. The man had long, shaggy gray hair and a scruffy beard. One eye was covered in a white, milky film, and when the man smiled, he revealed a rotten set of teeth. Even in the dim lighting, the edge of the straight razor in the man's right hand gleamed. With a twinkle in his good eye, the man whispered, "How 'bout we open you up and see how ya tick, mate?"

The overhead lights buzzed, flickered for a moment, and the man was gone. Every muscle in his body tightened, and Patrick thought his heart might explode. He hadn't felt fear like this since he was a child and the chill he felt running down his spine felt like it would be there until the day he died.

He grabbed the gun from the sink and spun around. With a shaky hand he waved the gun back and forth, looking for some sign of the man with the rotten teeth, but found that he was alone. He lowered the firearm and sighed in relief. Simultaneously, all the faucets in the bathroom turned on and Patrick nearly jumped out of his skin. He stared on in disbelief as the sinks all filled with, not water, but blood.

When laughter filled the room, Patrick had seen and heard enough. He turned and fled the bathroom at breakneck speed. He ran out the door and straight into two guards armed with automatic rifles. He slammed into them and ricocheted backward into the wall, slamming his head quite hard against the drywall. He slid down the wall and dropped the pistol at his side.

A humped-over little old man with gray hair stepped into view and bent down with a sinister smile on his face. He spoke with a slight German accent, "So, you're the one messing with my computer." He wagged his finger at Patrick. "Someone's been a naughty boy."

"There's something loose down here. We've got to trap it or the computer's going to fry the whole facility."

The man's smile grew. "Of course, there's something loose down here. *I'm the one who let her out, and you're going to help me recapture her.*" He looked at the guards and said, "Gentlemen, if you would, secure our volunteer for stage two of our experiment." One of the soldiers drove the butt of his rifle into Patrick's face and everything went black.

Patrick awoke laying on a gurney with a splitting headache. He rolled to the side and tried to clear his head. He groaned as he realized that his nose might be broken. When his vision finally came back into focus, he noticed a woman in the room beside him strapped down to a bed. She had porcelain colored skin, raven hair, and was the most beautiful thing he had ever seen.

He shrugged off the gurney and stumbled toward her. "Hey! Are you alright?"

"I wouldn't go near her if I was you," a German accent said. "She's far more dangerous than she looks."

Patrick turned to see the hunched over man in a lab coat standing behind a counter carefully examining what appeared to be tiny vials of blood. Patrick pointed at the man as a fire grew in his belly. "You! Who are you and what are you doing down here? I demand you let me go *now*!"

The man laughed. "You are in no position to make demands, Mister… Clark, is it? You've been quite busy, haven't you? Hacking into Celine, crawling through the air ducts to escape the lockdown, you're quite a resourceful fellow. Welcome, to Cell-block Omega. You now stand where few men have ever stood."

Patrick clenched his fists as he approached the man. "I said that you need to let me go."

The man wagged his finger at Patrick. "Now, now, let's not misbehave. My two associates with the rifles are just outside that door. If I wanted you dead, you'd already be dead. Please don't make me do something I don't want."

The intercom crackled, "T-minus fifteen minutes to laboratory cleansing."

Waves of panic washed over Patrick. "That goddamn computer is going to kill us all and you're just gingerly playing with lab samples? What's wrong with you?"

The man smirked and patted his pocket. "Oh, don't you worry about Celine. I can turn her off with a push of a button, but there will be no need for that. We're going to coax Subject Seven back into her cell any moment now."

Patrick sat on the gurney and shook his head. "I don't understand any of this. What is Subject Seven? For that matter, who the fuck are you?"

The man waddled forward and offered his hand. "I am Josef Mengele. It is a pleasure to meet you."

Patrick laughed. "Mengele? Mengele is dead. He died in the late 70s in South America."

The old man snickered. "Oh, did I? You probably believe that Lee Harvey Oswald killed Kennedy and that 9/11 was carried out by Muslim extremists. I will say this for your country, you are masters of deception."

"Bullshit! Mengele was captured by the allies and escaped using a fake passport."

The man smiled and shook his head. "Do you really think the allies would let me just slip through their fingers like that? Himmler was right. You Americans will believe anything as long as it's spoon-fed to you."

"You can't be Mengele. You'd have to be a hundred by now."

"I am one hundred and seven years old, thank you very much."

Patrick shook his head. "That can't be. You barely look a day over seventy."

"Very true, my naïve friend. To answer that question, all you have to do is look at the creature in the next room. She may look like a woman. She may even act like a woman, but she is something else altogether."

Patrick looked over his shoulder and glanced at the woman strapped to the table. He didn't see anything unusual about her. Before he realized it, he asked, "What is she?"

"She is everything the Third Reich was looking for. She is racial purity at its finest. She is a Pureblood Vampire, a child of Lilith."

Patrick scoffed, "Vampires? You're telling me that the woman in the other room is a Vampire?"

Mengele nodded his head. "Indeed. Rommel discovered the first of her kind in the 1930s. Of course, he was just a mortal-Vampire, but he was dangerous nonetheless. He killed nearly two dozen S.S. troopers before finally being apprehended. At the time, we knew nothing about their existence nor their capabilities. They are strong, resilient to disease, able to regenerate and heal wounds at a miraculous rate, and it's all because of this." He held up a glass vial. "Their blood. The blood of the Angels courses through their veins and it will unlock all the mysteries hidden from mankind."

"You're out of your fucking mind."

"Am I? Then how am I still alive after all this time? It's the blood. Taken in small doses, it heightens the senses, gives strength, and can even fight off an old German doctor's cancer for over four decades. The master race exists, and they have fangs for teeth."

Patrick couldn't wrap his mind around Mengele's tale. It was far too outlandish to believe. "Look, when I was in that bathroom, I saw something, and it wasn't a Vampire."

Mengele smiled proudly. "I know! That is *exactly* why I released Subject Seven into the laboratory. Subject Seven is the child of the thing behind you. We captured them together. Never before had I the opportunity to study a Pureblood child."

"You keep saying Pureblood. What the hell's a Pureblood?"

"Purebloods are born Vampires. They are direct descendants of Lilith and Lucifer. Mortal-Vampires are far weaker. They once were like you and I, but they ingested enough of the Angel's blood to change them into what they are. In all actuality, mortal-Vampires are mutts. Their blood is tainted with their mortality, but the Purebloods, their blood is something rivaling the divine. They can do things no other creatures on earth can do. That is why I released Subject Seven. I had to see if my theories were correct."

"A child? You mean a child killed all these people?"

Mengele nodded slowly. "*Ja*, a six-year-old to be more exact; a very special six-year-old. The child has the ability to actually call out to other dimensions that secretly hide all around us. Ghosts, spirits, Demons, whatever you wish to call them, they are drawn to the girl like moths to a flame. I can use her to capture even more powerful entities; entities that will help me open the Gates of Hell and bring back the Fuhrer. The Fourth Reich shall rise, and we will use the blood of the Vampires to fuel our ambitions."

Patrick put his hands on his hips and rolled his eyes. "Now I *know* you're talking out your ass. There's no way the United States would help you bring back Adolf Hitler."

"No, they wouldn't. That's why they don't know what I'm doing down here. Colonel Mathews had his suspicions, which is yet another reason I had to release Subject Seven into the facility. She would eliminate all the problems for me. A new staff will be put into place, and I will continue my research into opening a portal to Hell."

"That's madness. How could you be sure Seven wouldn't kill you in the process as well?"

Mengele unbuttoned his shirt and then pointed at Patrick with a gleam of pride in his eyes. "You are very smart, Mr. Clark. I wouldn't have known if it hadn't been for *this*." Mengele spread his shirt and revealed a medallion hanging around his neck. "It was a gift from Rommel, though I doubt he knew what he was giving me. It was discovered in a pyramid buried beneath the ice in Antarctica; one of the last remaining structures from the Atlantean Empire. Not only does it repel creatures of a supernatural nature, but it makes you all but invisible to them. I knew Seven would carry out her duties masterfully, but now it's time to put her back in her cell, and you're going to help me."

"The hell I am," Patrick screamed. "You're a monster; a war criminal. You should've hung for what you did in Germany. There's a special place in Hell for people like you, so why would I help you?"

Mengele grinned. "Because, my boy, you don't have a say in the matter." Mengele pulled something black from his pocket and with incredible speed rammed it against Patrick's side. As soon as he heard the clicking sound and his muscles spasmed uncontrollably, he knew what it was… a taser.

Patrick hit the floor riving in pain. *You Nazi fucking bastard*, he groaned. *I'll fucking kill you for this.*

Mengele quickly grabbed Patrick by the ankles and dragged him across the floor and into the room with the Pureblood Vampire woman.

"Seven wants her mother, so I'll give her what she wants, but I need something to keep her preoccupied while the doors to the room seal shut. That's where you come in. If you're lucky, she'll kill you quickly, but I wouldn't count on it."

Patrick tried to sit up, but Mengele quickly gave him another jolt of electricity. While Patrick laid there convulsing, the professor grabbed a needle from the counter and stuck it into Patrick's neck. "Here, a little something to calm you down and keep you incapacitated for what it is to come."

Patrick's entire body went numb. He found that he couldn't move at all and was having trouble staying conscious. Mengele smiled. "Now that's taken care of, time to awaken Seven's mother." Mengele grabbed a second syringe, this one filled with a bright yellow liquid. He injected the fluid into the IV bag dripping into the woman's arm and stepped back with a sinister grin on his face. "This is a personal creation of mine. I call it 'liquid fire.' As you'll see, the results are almost instantaneous."

The woman convulsed and suddenly stopped. Then she convulsed again. She let out a horrible scream that echoed throughout the facility. The agony in her voice told Patrick all he needed to know about Mengele's cocktail. He had been up to his same old tricks, only this time his experiments were on the Vampires he had as guinea pigs.

Mengele gave a little wave and said, "Seven should be here any moment now. Thank you for your contribution to my work, Mr. Clark. History will remember you fondly." With that said, he exited the room and disappeared through a door in the other room.

The Pureblood Vampire's screams worsened. She sounded like she was dying, and in no time at all, a young girl's voice called from the distance, "Mommy!"

There was sporadic gunfire, but it quickly ended. Screams filled the air and one of the guards standing outside the door was tossed into the adjoining room. Patrick felt sick as he realized that the man's head had been twisted around to face the wrong direction.

Oh my god! Here she comes.

Seven first appeared as a tiny silhouette in the other room. She moved slowly, stalking the door like a phantom. As she came into the light, Patrick expected a deformed demon complete with horns. What he got was nothing but a tiny girl with golden blonde hair in a bright yellow dress covered in blood. Outside of the fangs in her mouth, she could have passed for his own dead daughter.

The girl's mother screamed, and she ran to her side. "Mommy! Talk to me, mommy," but the woman couldn't answer. She was too consumed by the pain. That's when the little girl turned her attention to Patrick.

"You," she growled. "What did you do to my mother?"

Patrick tried to respond, but the drugs Mengele injected into his system had left him all but paralyzed. He was barely hanging onto consciousness when the girl's nails first ripped into his belly. He groaned involuntarily as he felt the blood pouring from his wounds. Seven mounted him and raised her hand high above her head. Patrick braced himself as he was sure the girl was going for the deathblow.

Seven slashed at Patrick, but when her hand got close to the bed, the girl's mother had just enough give in her restraints to grab her daughter's wrist. "Makayla! No!"

The small child raised her fangs and looked up at her mother with tears in her eyes. "Mamma?"

"This man did not do this to me," her mother groaned. "The doctor, the German, he is in the other room. Go to him, avenge what he has done to me."

The little girl nodded, "Yes, mamma."

The giant metal door to the room started to shut and Patrick feared he would be trapped inside with both of them, but Makayla was far more than she appeared. The door was six inches thick and made of metal, but the little girl froze it in its tracks. Metal creaked and made little pinging noises as the tiny Pureblood pushed against the door until she finally ripped it free of its top hinge.

Holy shit! How strong is that girl?

Makayla disappeared in a flash. Patrick heard glass shatter and gunfire. He wasn't sure what was happening, but he was fairly certain that she had found Mengele. This made him smile. Nothing would please him more than the knowledge that the Nazi madman was finally getting what he had coming to him.

As mayhem unfolded in the other room, Patrick strained every muscle in an attempt to sit up. He managed to budge a few inches before slipping back down flat of his back. The blood was gushing from his wounds and the crimson puddle surrounding him was starting to cover the entire floor. "Come on, Patty," he said to himself. "Get your ass up."

He reached up with his right hand and used the rail on the side of the bed to pull himself into a sitting position. The blood poured from his stomach, so he placed his hand on his abdomen trying to slow the process. He laughed. "I'm gonna bleed out before I get a chance to be burned alive."

Patrick pulled on the rail again, this time managing to get his feet beneath him. He thought he might pass out in any moment, so he moved quickly. He pulled the IV from the Vampire's arm and her demeanor changed quickly. Her body stopped trembling and her groans slowly fell silent.

Next, Patrick started undoing the restraint on one of the Pureblood's arms. The Vampire turned to him, still sweating profusely from the ordeal the liquid fire had put her through. In a weak voice, she whispered, "What are you doing, mortal? Don't you know I'll kill you?"

Patrick undid the first restraint and leaned across the bed for the second one. "Lady, have you looked at me? I'm probably not gonna make it another five minutes. The least I can do is set you and your daughter free. Nobody, _not even you_, deserve to be a lab-rat for that Nazi bastard."

He undid the last restraint and slipped in his own blood. Patrick landed hard on the floor and waited for the Vampire to finish him off. He looked up, expecting to be greeted by a pair of fangs, but what he saw was a smile.

The Pureblood picked Patrick off the floor and laid him on the bed. "You have shown me kindness in a time which I have known none. You are unlike any mortal I have met. I wish I could do more. I am weak, but I can still spare enough blood to heal your wounds."

The Vampire bit into her wrist and blood flowed freely. She held it out to Patrick, but he turned his head. "What about the shit Mengele injected into you?"

She smiled pleasantly. "Thanks to you, I'm disconnected from that source, and my body has already purged those toxins from my system. Please, drink while I still have the strength."

He reluctantly placed her wrist in his mouth and instantly was enamored by the nectar that flowed from her. It was like strawberry wine, only sweeter. He swallowed it down in gulps, not even taking breaks to breathe. The feeling it gave him was almost orgasmic.

The Pureblood pulled away and staggered for a moment. "That's enough. Anymore and I may accidentally pass the curse of Lilith down to you, but that should be enough to heal your wounds."

Patrick felt his abdomen and, indeed, the blood had stopped flowing. He sat up and said, "Thank you. I don't even know your name."

She offered her hand politely. "I am Chastity, and what is the name of my savior?"

"Patrick," he replied softly. "I've got to admit," he added, "this was not how I saw my day going when I left for work."

"Yes," she said sweetly. "Life is full of surprises, even for us immortals."

From the other room, Mengele screamed, "Stay still, you little bitch!" There were a number of gunshots and Chastity turned pale.

"Makayla," she whispered before disappearing out of the room.

To Patrick, it appeared that she was there one moment, and gone the next. As he slid off the bed, he thought, *Man, it's gonna take me a while to get used to that.*

Patrick rushed into the other room. The two-way mirror had been shattered, no doubt by Makayla earlier. There was a door flung open to the right and that's where he ran. He walked in on the Vampire equivalent of a Mexican-standoff.

Mengele stood in the middle of the room, waving his gun back and forth between Makayla and Chastity. He screamed at the little girl, "Get back in your cell, Seven!"

"Never," the little Vampire replied with her fangs on full display.

"Fine then," he replied. "You can watch your mother die." Mengele fired two shots at Chastity. She must have been too weak to dodge as both bullets slammed into her chest. She collapsed to the ground and let out a little whimper.

Makayla screamed, "Mommy," while Mengele smiled sinisterly. He then pointed the gun at Patrick.

"And, you! All you had to do was distract the child long enough for the doors to shut, and you couldn't even do that. You are useless to me." Mengele pulled the trigger. Patrick flinched, expecting to be hit, but the firearm was out of bullets and the gun simply clicked.

Mengele panicked and quickly tried to load another clip, but Patrick saw his opportunity and seized it. He tackled the old German to the ground. He started pounding the doctor's face into the floor. Before he realized it, he had his hands around Mengele's neck, squeezing the air out of him.

"I should kill you, you Nazi bastard, but I've got a better idea." Patrick ripped Mengele's shirt open and ripped the medallion from around his neck. "Let's see how long you last without this."

The lights flickered, and the room became ice cold. Dozens of shadows appeared on the wall and the whispers of a hundred voices echoed in the building. Patrick took a step backward as the chill running down his spine made him tremble. He looked at Chastity, "What's going on?"

"Makayla, Patrick, get behind me! The dead have come to settle their debts."

Mengele crawled along the floor, his eyes wide-open with fear. "Stay away," he cried, but the shadows crept forward as the whispers crescendoed.

One by one, the shadows reached out, tearing at Mengele's flesh. Visible wounds appeared on his body; scratches that ran the entire length of his chest; deep gashes in his abdomen; his face being ripped apart as he screamed. The shadows were literally tearing the old man into pieces.

Mengele's screams grew as the shadows engulfed him. There was a burst of blood and then all that remained were Mengele's clothes. The lights flickered and returned to their normal setting. All the shadows were gone. Their lust for revenge had been met.

Patrick stood frozen. He'd never seen anything like that before. Quite frankly, he never wanted to see anything like that again. He turned to Chastity slowly, "What just happened?"

"His sins caught up to him. The dead are very vengeful. Wherever he is, he will be tormented for all of time."

Patrick slowly smiled. "Good."

The intercom crackled. "T-minus one minute to laboratory cleansing. Please return subjects Six and Seven to containment to avoid this procedure."

"Shit!" Patrick screamed. "I forgot about that damned computer." He ran up to Mengele's remains and started sorting through his pockets. "Damn it! It's supposed to be here!"

"What is?" Chastity asked.

"A failsafe switch that will shut the computer down. It's supposed to be in his pocket, but it's not here."

Makayla pulled away from her mother. "Where is it?"

"I don't know," Patrick replied as he frantically kept searching. "Maybe it fell out of his pocket during all the chaos. Search on the floors, check every corner. If we don't find that switch, we're getting deep-fried."

"Makayla and I could always go back to a cell," Chastity said somberly.

"Fuck no!" Patrick said as he rummaged through the drawers in the office. "I am *not* leaving you two behind for more experiments. I'd rather die first."

"T-minus thirty seconds to laboratory cleansing."

Patrick started sweating profusely as he pulled useless gadget after useless gadget out of the drawers and cabinets. He tossed them to the floor like garbage and continued his search in a panic. Makayla, who was trying to help, raised her head, "What does it look like?"

"I don't freakin' know! It's not like the Nazi whipped it out and showed it to me, but it fit in his pocket, so probably about the size of a television remote."

"T-minus ten seconds to laboratory cleansing."

Patrick screamed in frustration, "Fuck!"

Suddenly, Makayla appeared out of the shadows carrying a black rectangular device. "Is this it?"

Patrick snatched it from her hands. "It better be or we're about to be toast."

He hit a large red button on the device and it promptly asked him for the access code. Patrick froze. "T-minus five seconds to laboratory cleansing."

He had to think of something fast.

"Four..."

Then it hit him, what else would a Nazi sympathizer use but Hitler's birthday?

"Three..."

He quickly punched in the numbers, "4, 20, 1889."

"Two..."

He braced himself for disaster, but the intercom buzzed. "Laboratory cleansing aborted. Lockdown protocols have ended. Please, have a nice day."

He couldn't believe it worked. Before he realized it, he had Makayla picked up in his arms, twirling her about and laughing. He ran to Chastity and hugged her tightly. He whispered, "Are you alright?"

She grimaced in pain but responded, "Nothing I can't live with. You did it, Patrick. You saved us all." She unclasped a necklace from around her neck and offered it to him. "Take this. It's my Vampire Clan's emblem, the sign of the Dark Sun. As long as you have this, no Vampire will ever attempt to harm you. From this day forward, you are part of our Clan, part of our family."

Patrick didn't know what to say. He took the necklace, awed at the craftsmanship. The dragon entangled around the sun was absolutely stunning. He eventually replied, "Thank you. I'm honored."

It sounded like thunder rolling above them. Patrick looked up and felt an uneasy feeling. "Shit! Sounds like as soon as Celine ended the lockdown, the cavalry came charging."

"How do we get out of here?" Chastity asked.

Patrick shook his head. "There's just the stairs and the elevator, and something tells me they're both about to be full. Wait! The air ducts, I completely forgot about them."

He cut his eyes at Makayla who blushed and bit her bottom lip as she swayed from side to side. She whispered, "Sorry."

Chastity seemed bewildered. "Sorry for what?"

Patrick hurried to the vent in the room and started attempting to pry it loose. "Your daughter tried to make a meal out of me earlier."

"Makayla!" Chastity said sternly.

Makayla hung her head. "I'm sorry, mamma. I didn't know him back then."

Patrick tugged with all his might but couldn't get the vent to budge as the roar of stomping boots got steadily closer. "I need a screwdriver or something to pry this free." Makayla calmly walked up and with one hand ripped the vent from the wall. "Or… that will work. Okay, everybody inside. Now that the lockdown's over, the bars blocking access to the surface should be gone. It's our ticket out of here."

Makayla climbed in first, fitting easily, but Patrick and Chastity were having issues. "Fuck!" Patrick grunted. "It's too damn small. We're going to have to figure another way out of here."

Chastity pulled Makayla to her and hugged her tightly. She whispered, "Baby, you go on without me."

"Mamma, no!" the child protested.

"You heard me. Get out of here. Patrick and I will catch up with you."

The child clung to her mother's neck tightly, but the sound of voices coming down the hallway put an end to that. Patrick pulled Makayla towards him and spun her around. "Look, there are woods all around this facility. You go and hide. Whatever you do, don't let them catch you again."

"I'm scared," Makayla whined.

"Me too, darlin', but we have to survive. Now get out of here before they find you. Go!"

The little girl placed a kiss on her mother's cheek and crawled into the air duct. Patrick placed the vent back over the hole, but that wouldn't fool anyone if they inspected it closely. He grabbed Mengele's gun, despite it being empty, and prepared to stall for as much time as he could.

With Chastity hanging on his arm, Patrick burst into the next room waving the pistol around like a character in a Quentin Tarrantino movie. "Alright, boys, everybody... *freeze?*" There were two dozen or so soldiers in full fatigues carrying M-16s, shotguns, and, quite disturbingly, a flamethrower, standing with their weapons pointed at Patrick and Chastity. Not being a fool, Patrick carefully laid his pistol on the ground and threw his hands up in the air.

"Where the hell is Mengele?" an officer dressed in blue demanded to know.

Patrick rolled his eyes. "Take a look around. He's like everyone else in this shithole. He's dead."

The officer elbowed a nervous little man beside him carrying a clipboard. "Who are these two?"

The little man flipped through several pages before answering. "I'd say that she is Subject Six, but I have no clue who he is."

"I'm a computer technician. They sent me down here to fix Colonel Mathew's printer."

The officer looked at the man with clipboard who continued flipping through paperwork until he said, "There was a technician scheduled to be here today, sir. His story checks out."

The officer grunted. "Fine. Now step aside, son. We're taking Subject Six back into custody."

Without thinking, Patrick stepped in between Chastity and the soldiers. "No! Do you have any clue what they were doing down here? She's been tortured; experimented on. She has rights. You can't do this to her!"

The officer laughed. "I don't know what she's told you, son, but she's not human. We can do whatever we want to her. She has no rights."

"That's the same things the Germans said about the Jews. What side of history do you want to stand on?"

Chastity placed her hand on Patrick's shoulder and pushed him to the side. "It's alright," she said. "There's nothing you can do."

The officer smiled, "Men, take the subject into custody."

Five men marched up with silver shackles, but they never saw what was coming. Chastity slammed one to the ground. Another she sliced his throat. She became a whirlwind of fangs and claws until not a single one of them was left standing. She smiled at the rest of the men in the room and screamed, "I swear to Lilith, I will kill you all before I'll let you take me!"

The officer calmly replied, "Men, light her up."

Every soldier began firing. Chastity dodged a few of the shots, but there were too many aimed at her. The shotgun blasts slammed into her and exploded into fire. Chastity fell to the ground, her clothes still smoldering. When the man with the flamethrower stepped forward, Patrick felt sick. He screamed, "No! Don't do it!"

It was too late. The soldier blazed the entire left side of the room as Chastity screamed at the top of her lungs. Totally engulfed in flames, she leaped forward only to be shot with another shotgun blast and sent flying backward into the wall. She convulsed for a moment and then fell silent. She was perfectly still; even an immortal can be killed.

Patrick had tears rolling down his cheeks. "Why? Why'd you do that?"

The little man looked up at the officer. "What should we do with *that one*?"

The officer looked at Patrick and smiled. "He knows too much. You know what to do."

Patrick slammed into the wall and slid down slowly as the two bullet holes in his chest started to bleed out. He thought about Makayla and wondered if she had made it out. He hoped they had bought her enough time.

Pain. Darkness. A voice calling out in the distance, "Wake up! Please, wake up!"

Patrick snapped awake, gasping for air. He was in total darkness. Something like a cocoon surrounded him and held him to the hard surface which he laid. He tore through it and sat up with a rush of adrenaline. He looked around and saw metal tables covered in body bags. The air was crisp and frigid. He knew exactly where he was; the morgue.

"How did I get here?"

He felt a tug on his pants leg and then a pair of tiny arms wrap around his neck. It was Makayla, and she was crying. "You're alive! I was so afraid you were dead."

Patrick was stunned. "I... I was dead. They shot me. How did I...?" He felt something grazing his bottom lip and he went numb. He ran his fingers along his teeth and noticed that he had grown a pair of fangs. He gasped, "Oh my God."

Makayla looked up at him. "Did you drink Mommy's blood?" Patrick slowly nodded, still in shock at his realization. "You drank enough that you've changed. You're one of us now; not a Pureblood, but a Vampire nonetheless." Then she asked the question he was terrified of hearing. "Where's my mommy?"

Patrick hung his head. "She… she didn't make it."

Makayla threw herself onto the floor and bloody tears started streaming down her face. She cried out, "I want my mommy! Where will I go? I don't have anyone else."

Patrick wasn't sure how it happened, but the monster he had been afraid of had become the child that he now pitied. He felt the cold medallion against his chest that Chastity had given him, and he suddenly knew what he should do. He picked Makayla up and sat her in his lap. He carefully wiped away her tears and spoke to her softly. "Do you remember your mother giving me this medallion?" Makayla slowly nodded her head. "She said this made me part of your Clan; that we were family. Family doesn't abandon each other. Would you like to come live with me?"

Makayla brightened up. "Are you serious? I can live with you?"

Patrick nodded. "Yes. You see, I lost my wife and daughter in a car accident several months ago. I don't have anyone either."

Makayla hugged Patrick tightly and slowly stepped away. She looked up at him with sad eyes and asked, "Can… can I call you 'daddy?'"

Patrick's eyes welled up. "I'd love if you called me that." They hugged again and the hole in Patrick's heart felt whole again. He looked at his new daughter and asked, "Are there any men here?"

She nodded slowly. "Yes, daddy. Two guards in a shack in front of the building."

"Are you hungry?" Again, she nodded. Patrick smiled. "Then let's stop and get a bite to eat and then I'll take you home and clean you up. How does that sound?"

"That sounds simply divine!"

They walked out of the morgue hand-in-hand. He didn't know where this new life would take him, but Patrick swore that he'd take care of this child no matter what the cost. He owed Chastity that much.

About the Author

Jay Michael Wright, II

Jay "Mikey Bookman" Wright is a horror/dark fantasy author living in Alabama. His interest in the genre started when he came across Bela Lugosi playing Dracula as a child. After that, he worked his way through the classic Frankenstein and Wolfman movies and made his way up to watching Tales from the Crypt (all behind his parents' backs). He is subservient to four cats who occasionally allow him time to pursue his love of writing. He won second place in Tell-Tale Publishing's 2017 "Scary Story Starters" contest.

Clowning Around

by

Janet Post

Clowning Around

By

Janet Post

Professor Smiley was nuts. The whole school knew it. He loved clowns. Who in their right mind loves clowns? Clowns are known to be evil killers. I've seen It. Never trust anyone who loves clowns. Smiley had photos of himself in costume on the wall behind his desk. None of us had ever looked at them or ever would. I mean they were pictures of clowns. And there he stood at the front of the class, waving his arms up and down ready for take-off, in all his insane, clown-loving glory, lecturing us, once again, on the evils of video games. I'll risk video games, Professor. Clowns are a definite NO.

"Everyone in this class," Professor Smiley's rant had reached the almost screaming stage. "Everyone in this class must know by now that video games suck your brains out. Everyone must know they make you stupid. They turn kids into killers." The entire rant was made even more ridiculous by Professor Smiley's looks. I mean, he couldn't help looking like a clown. It musta been the reason he started dressing like one to entertain kids. He had red frizzy hair sticking out like it had never been combed. He arrived every morning with it slicked down.

By second period, it had 'froed into the freaky mop he now wore. Then there was his nose. It was red. My mom told me it was red because he had a drinking problem. I didn't care. His face was white, his nose was red, his hair was red and then there were his feet. Professor Smiley had the biggest feet I'd ever seen on a human. Had to be seventeens at least. Mine were a decent size ten which went along with my very normal five-ten height, my completely normal brown hair, and my not good-looking, not ugly face. I was just a super normal looking sixteen-year-old named Josh Whitebread, yes really, but people I knew and who knew me, called me Joker.

"Video games will teach you to be violent. They teach you to ignore the real consequences of killing. They make killing easy. They teach you to solve your problems by killing."

The Professor finished his rant, took a deep breath, and stared at each one of us as though looking for that one kid who would lose it because of video games and become an insane killer. I hunched my shoulders. I've been known to enjoy playing games. What sixteen-year-old hasn't? Smiley turned around and looked at the clock. He hunched his shoulders and clumped to the back of the classroom where his project sat on a large table. None of us knew what it was. He tinkered on it when we had assignments or were taking tests. It was a large black box, sprouted wires, cords, and had the newest XBox inserted into a slot on the top. I personally preferred my PlayStation, mostly because that's the system I owned.

I glanced over at my best friend Charles, AKA Chucky, Dooley. He was sleeping with his eyes open. His father loved to lecture him on god. Chucky had learned the trick. I could tell he was asleep because his eyes were kinda glassed over and shiny and his breathing was deep and slow. Zonked out and with only five more minutes to the end of Chemistry class. I wadded a piece of paper in my mouth, chewed until it was well-moistened, spit it into my hand and made a ball. I zapped Chucky in the back of the head with it. His gaze sharpened, and he shot me the evil eye. I grinned and pointed at the clock.

Professor Smiley was winding down, talking and ranting on from the back of the classroom as he also watched the clock. I guess teachers look forward to the weekend as much as we do. "You all know there will be a quiz Monday. I don't care if Saturday night is Halloween. The quiz will be on Chapter Six in your Chem book. And no playing games all night. Night is for sleeping. Teenagers need more sleep than any other group of children. So, no gaming. Sleep."

He really hated video games and the kids he knew played them received crappy grades in his class. He couldn't help himself. His wife had been killed by a gamer who lost it in the local Walmart and shot the store up all because they didn't have the newest edition of Medal of Honor when they advertised its release. The bell rang and as one, the class rose and bolted for the door, thrilled to be escaping Professor Smiley and school for the weekend. He followed us out, clumping along in his enormous red sneakers. Fridays were casual at Mandarin High.

It was easy to find Chucky. He was about six-five and skinny. He could never get enough to eat. His weird parents were vegan. He always ate the school lunch, wolfing down meat like he'd never seen it before. Didn't matter what kind it was. Chicken, bacon, bologna, it was all good to Chucky. I punched him in the shoulder. "Are you going out trick-or-treating with your little brother Saturday?"

He groaned. "You know I am. It's my duty, dude. Mom makes me."

"He's in a wheelchair, man. What're you dressing him as?"

"Mom brought home one of those rolling stretchers from the hospital. We have a sheet with red blotches all over it. We'll cover most of him and make his face look like a corpse."

I shuddered. "That's just wrong."

"Mom's idea." Chucky's mom worked in the ER and aside from being vegan and thinking hospitals and doctors were dangerous, had a strange sense of humor.

We headed down the hallway, each of us lugging about fifty pounds of stuff in our backpacks. "Gonna dress up too?"

He shrugged. "I like to. And I might as well. Have to go out anyway. I'm going as a zombie."

"I'll come with you. I'll go as the Joker like always."

"Cool." We bumped fists. "Wanna go to Jane Morris's party after you haul Carlos around while he collects candy?"

He shrugged narrow shoulders. "Why not? We can walk or get my dad to drive us."

"When you getting your license?"

"Next month. I've had my Learner's since last year. Dad says I'm ready even though he's not."

We laughed.

"Why did your parents name your brother Carlos?" I asked. "You know it means Charles in Spanish and you're already Charles and so is your dad."

"It's part of their charm," Chucky said and snorted. "My sister's name is Charlotte and that's the girl version of Charles. When she went away to college last month, I went to church and thanked god. She made my life hell."

I nodded. I knew all about Char, as we called her. She was a big girl, kind of like Chucky, only not skinny. She played volleyball and softball, got a scholarship for softball. She could pitch crap no girl could hit and terrified every batter that stood in front of her. She'd bend over, roll the ball in the hand behind her back, and stare at them until they were ready to pee in their pants. When she stared at Chucky or Carlos like that, they ran, or Carlos rolled.

We walked home. Both of us lived in a gated condo community close to the school. We parted on the corner of Clark and Doris. He went home, and I walked on down Clark. His brother was lucky. Handicapped kids got door-to-door service on the short bus. Carlos would already be home.

When I got close to my house, I glanced at the neighbors' place. All the condos were townhouses. It was Florida, so they were painted pastel colors. Mine was turquoise and the one next door was pink. Samantha Braithwaite lived there, one of the hottest, meanest girls in school. I rarely saw her, but I dreamed about her a lot.

No girl or human should be that perfect. Her black hair hung precisely even to her waist. She had blue-green eyes and a cute little nose. Her Vietnamese mother was still drop-dead gorgeous at forty, and her dad was ex-military. The combo had created perfection. Her figure was made more perfect by her long-standing addiction to cheerleading. It was Friday night, she would be at the pep rally for the game. I did not do football, didn't like it, never played it, and didn't watch it on TV. However, if Samantha ever gave me a second look, spoke to me, or was ever sorta nice, I could develop an interest.

I pulled out my I-Phone and used the app on it to raise the garage door. As usual, no one was home. Mom worked as an administrative assistant for a big construction company and Dad was a closer for a title company. He worked long hours and sometimes had to work holidays and weekends. Mom would be home at six. Until then, I was alone. I grabbed a bag of chips and an apple, went into the den and flipped on my game console and the huge flat screen. Oh yeah, Professor Smiley. I am a gamer.

I woke with a start and glanced at the clock. It was two in the morning. Mom and Dad were sleeping. I was a little spoiled. I knew it. Only children get all the good things in life except experience at being social. I had zero social skills. I would go with Chucky to Jan's party and drink punch, prop up the wall, and wish I was at home gaming. No one would talk to me.

Chucky, on the other hand, had a wide and varied social life. Blessed with weirdo parents, siblings, and a carefree attitude. People liked him. Well not important, preppy, hot chicks, or jocks, or trendy kids, but us normal kids liked him. We could talk to him. I was always glad to go places with him because he never made a big deal about how awkward I was. And neither of us fit into any group in school. We weren't super smart, or band dorks, or into Sci-Fi. We didn't play sports, weren't skaters, goths, gay or emos. So, we hung with the outcasts. And as long as Chucky hung out there, too, I was good.

One of the best things my parents had given me was my super gaming system with the huge flat screen. I got out of bed and slipped downstairs to the den and booted up my game. I was making my way through the levels. I'd already ordered the newest version of The Art of War, so I had to hustle and get through the levels, so I'd be ready when the new one came. I eased my Skull Candy headphones over my ears, so the noise of the game wouldn't wake up my parents and got ready to kick some alien butt. I'd just hit play when the TV screen turned fuzzy. I checked the connection to the controller. The Wi-Fi must be out. Crap. I was about to shut it down when I heard a voice right into my head through the headphones, and the fuzzy picture sharpened to reveal the face, the hideous face, of a clown.

Then it laughed right into my ears. I screamed. I mean who wouldn't? Then I hit the off switch on my PlayStation. Nothing happened. The clown was still there and the light indicating the system was running was still on. The clown was hideous. Its face was white, blotched with red stains. Its mouth was wide open in an evil grin that revealed too many really sharp teeth. Most of its head was bald, but clumps of red hair stuck out in odd places. Its eyes were outlined with black lines and crisscrossed with red veins. Its nose was a red ball. Worst clown face ever.

The clown spoke. "It will avail you nothing. Turning off your infernal machine will not work. You're a very bad boy, Joker. You will be punished."

The clown's voice was deep and vibrated with evil. When he called me Joker, I whimpered. The game box shot blue and red sparks everywhere. The clown laughed. The controller was still in my hand. It was heating. I tried to drop it but couldn't open my hand. The cord to the box from the controller whipped wildly and climbed. My hand went with it. I helped the controller wrap the cord around my own neck and pull it tight. I heard the clown laughing. "Die, Joker! Die!"

I coughed and struggled but couldn't stop helping the clown kill me. Lights flashed behind my eyes as I gagged and coughed, and the cord tightened around my throat. There was only one thing I could do. The cord connecting the controller to the box was old. I needed a wireless.

The connection was loose. With one desperate lunge, I heaved myself backward, tipped over my chair, yanking the controller cord out of the box. Immediately, the cord loosened. I ripped it off my throat.

The clown screamed and groaned. I glanced at the hideous apparition out of the corner of my eye. It was tearing chunks of fake red hair out and if looks could kill, I'd be a flaming ruin. "I'll get you, you little punk," it screeched. "Don't think you've escaped me, Joker. You're dead. I'll get you someway, somehow." Then it was gone.

The game box started smoking. Flames shot out of it. I grabbed a throw off the couch and smothered them before they caught the curtains on fire. I lay there on top of the coffee table holding my system and sobbed. Chucky. I had to warn him. He was probably up playing Skyrim or Final Fantasy. He dug dragons and swords and stuff like that. I raced out of the house, closing the door quietly. No need for Mom and Dad to get involved in this. They'd only yell when they saw my PlayStation was a smoking meltdown and make me go to bed.

As I closed the door, I glanced at Samantha's house. The ground floor room, which I knew was the living room just like in my house, had a blue light flickering between the slats of her high-end wooden blinds. When the flickering suddenly began shooting off sparks, red and blue ones, I knew what was happening. Samantha was playing her weird fashion game. Everyone knew she did it. Even though real gamers didn't think of it as a legit game, it was a game. Or maybe she sometimes played something more exciting. I sure wouldn't know. But what I did know, was the clown was on Sam's TV right now trying to kill her.

I leapt the steps to her front door. It was locked. I rattled it, filled with helpless rage and frustration. "Sam," I screamed. "Tell Siri to open the garage door."

I yanked on her doorknob again. Nothing. Suddenly, I heard the whine of the garage door opener. The door was opening! I jumped off her doorstep and rolled under the partially opened garage door. The door connecting to her kitchen and laundry room was unlocked. I scrambled through her house to the living room and there she was. The clown must be talking into her headphones. I could see its awful face glowing on the seventy-inch flat screen like a demon straight from clown hell. Sam was sitting on a stool in front of the TV. The newest XBox sat on an end table. The controller was cordless, but the cord from the XBox had unplugged itself and was wrapped around her neck. Sam was slowly pulling it tight. Her terrified eyes stared at me pleading for help as she began choking and gagging. I knew the feeling.

I crossed the room in two strides, braving the horror of the insane clown magnified to an immense size on the giant TV, and pulled the end of the cord out of her hand. She tried to get it back, but I unwrapped her neck, holding the cord out of her reach. We wrestled briefly, and I tried to remain ignorant of the parts accidentally touching me, the vanilla-scented wonderfulness of her smooth skin, as we tussled for control of the cord.

I might not be a jock, but I was stronger than her. I yanked the cord away from her, XBox and all. It tried to turn on me, the cord like a snake, a living creature, evil and deadly. I held it away from me, ran through the kitchen and the laundry room into the garage. I tossed it through the open garage door onto her tiny square of front lawn and ran back inside. Samantha lay on her floor panting and sobbing. I gently removed her headphones, and smoothed her hair away from her forehead, a flawless forehead I had only dreamed of touching. "How did you know?" She sobbed.

"I just got away from it in my house." And then I remembered Chucky. "Gotta run. Chucky might be up."

"Call him," she said as she clambered to her feet and plopped on the stool.

"Why didn't I think of that?" I said feeling the usual stupefaction I always felt around beautiful girls creeping over me. I patted my pockets. "Crap, I left my phone in the house."

She thrust a pink phone encrusted with sequins at me. "Use mine."

"Okay," I said horrified to be touching something as sacred as her phone. I punched in Chucky's number and listened to it ring and ring. "He's not answering." Fear for my best friend quickly replaced the awkward feeling. "I have to get to his house."

"You're not leaving me here with that." She pointed at the gigantic screen.

"It's gone. You'll be fine."

She stood up and shook her head. "I may never be fine again. I was just sitting there playing," her face colored a beautiful rose as she blushed. "I was playing Halo. I know it's not in fashion, but I like it. And then there it was talking right into my head phones in that super-eerie voice. I. Hate. Clowns." She shuddered. "Really, clowns are so creepy."

"No kidding." I couldn't believe she played action games. "There's no need for you to come with me," I said even though the thought of her walking down the road beside me was intoxicating. "I mean the box is out in the yard. You're safe now."

"I know. I, uh, don't want to stay here by myself. I could wake Martha up, but she'd never understand. Mom and Dad are away at her sister-in-law's funeral in Des Moines. She's the only one here, and who would understand this if they hadn't actually seen it?" She fussed with her hair, brought a long strand around and began chewing on it. I'd never seen her do anything so human. "What if that hideous clown thing comes here in person? Like in It. I saw that movie." She shuddered again. "So, seriously, Joker, what if it's trying to kill other gamers, not just us or Chucky? I mean, we should do something, shouldn't we?"

I hadn't really progressed that far in my thinking, and for a minute, I couldn't breathe. Samantha Braithewaite knew my nickname. The knowledge was overwhelming my fear for Chucky. I shook my head to clear the vanilla fumes. "You're right, I guess. Let's check on Chucky and talk about it."

When we got outside I spotted the XBox on the lawn. It was slowly inching its way toward the garage. "Wait a minute," I said, turned and ran back in the garage. I found her dad's tool bench, grabbed a hammer, ran back out and demolished the system. It erupted in flames which were quickly doused by the rain.

Sam grabbed my arm. "That was brave."

My face heated. "Not really. It was necessary. You do what you got to in this world."

She nodded as we headed toward Clark Street. It started to rain harder. Late October in Florida. I was guessing we were due for a hurricane. I pulled the hood of my sweatshirt up. "I hate the rain. You can go back if you want. You don't need to get wet."

She was in her robe and pajamas. "Wait a minute," she said, and ran back into the house. She came out wearing a voluminous yellow slicker with slits up the side. "My dad was once a cowboy."

"I thought he was in the military?"

"Before, he lived on a ranch. The Boys Ranch." She flicked the rain coat revealing the slits. "This is so you can get on your horse."

The Boys Ranch wasn't far away. It was a rehab for bad boys without a family, but you had to be lucky to get picked. "No kidding?"

She pulled up the yellow hood and her beautiful face with its blue-green eyes glowed from inside the slicker. Who knew she could be this nice?

We jogged a block and suddenly, through the rain-drenched visibility of the dark cloud-covered sky, illuminated by the yellow glare of a streetlight, a figure stumbled out of an unlit garage another block up. Grabbing at his throat, the guy screamed in a horrible way.

We ran.

But we were too late. When we got there, the dude was dead. "Don't look," I said to Sam. I tried to shield her from the gruesome spectacle, but she insisted on seeing, even bending down to closely examine his face.

"Don't worry about me. I can take it. And this isn't a kid," she said.

I screwed up my courage and bent down beside her. "Wait. I know this guy. Eddie Donalds. He's going to UNF and living in his uncle's garage." We both glanced at the dark garage. The door was up, and you could make out a glowing TV screen on one wall. "Look," I said and I'm ashamed to say my voice quivered. The clown's hideous face was clearly visible, and it was laughing. Blood poured out of its mouth and my stomach churned.

"The more souls I consume, the stronger I get," the clown said. "Soon, I will walk the streets as a human and kill all you damn gamers." It giggled, a terrifying sound. "I know who you are."

As I stared at the screen, completely transfixed, a dog barked inside the garage. When the dog barked, the clown disappeared. Moments later a massive dog emerged from the garage wearing a studded collar. It was Duke, the Donalds's black mastiff.

"I thought he died," I mumbled.

"What?" Sam said.

I pointed. "Duke. I thought he was dead."

"Guess not," she said. "We need to call the cops. I mean there's a dead man in the middle of this street."

Duke walked over. He was massive. He sniffed Eddie, sat down and howled. I jumped up. "I don't care about Eddie. I mean I do, but it's too late for him. I have to save Chucky." I started running for the intersection of Doris and Clark.

Sam jogged along beside me. "Joker, we can't just leave him there."

"I'll call the cops when I know Chucky is safe."

She pulled out her bedazzled phone. "I'll do it."

"What are you gonna tell them?" All I could think was telling the cops about an insane killer clown would get us sent straight to the loony bin.

Her smile was grim. "Don't worry. I'm not stupid."

"Right," I said, and wondered why it was so easy to talk to her. Must be the emergency. Maybe my extreme unease and lack of social skills went away when I was scared shitless.

I glanced back at Eddie's body lying there in the flooding rain. Duke was following us. I shrugged. It couldn't matter. He would know how to get home. Sam called 911 while we jogged to the intersection, took Doris and headed for Chucky's cul-de-sac, Primrose Place. Halfway down Doris, I spotted a house with blue and red sparks flaring inside the big front window. I pointed. "Another one."

We ran. I pounded on the door just like I had done at Sam's. "Tell Siri to open the garage door," I screamed.

Nothing happened. Maybe we were too late, or they didn't have Siri. Suddenly, the garage door began to rise. We slid under and pushed through the kitchen door. "It's Margie," Sam said. "She goes to my church."

Margie was on the floor of the living room with the PlayStation cord wrapped around her throat. She wasn't struggling or choking. She lay flat on her back, just a little kid, maybe ten. Sam knelt beside her and tore away the cord. The clown was still on the huge flat screen. "You two!" It shrieked. "Go away. The child is evil. She's a gamer."

"Must be still alive or he wouldn't be pissed," I said to Sam.

Sam began chest compressions, bent, opened the girl's mouth and breathed in. She continued for six breaths. Suddenly, Margie coughed and began thrashing her arms and legs. Sam gathered the girl into her arms and rocked her as water from her wet slicker pooled on the hardwood floor. "Hush, hush, you're safe now."

A light appeared in the upstairs hallway. "Is someone there?"

I grabbed Sam's arm and whispered. "I can't be here. I have to get to Chucky."

Sam gently lay Margie down with her head on a throw pillow and put her finger in front of her lips to indicate the girl should be quiet. We sneaked out the garage door and started running down Doris, turned right onto Chucky's cul-de-sac and kept running. The best thing about Chucky's street was its lack of kids. We saw no more flickering lights and no more sparks as we ran toward the end of the cul-de-sac where Chucky lived with his brother.

Duke followed us. He was a huge black dog only visible when we were under streetlights. He trotted along looking like an animal with a purpose, glancing from side to side, eyes alert, massive nose sniffing.

The rain stopped flooding and turned into a miserable drizzle. I was soaked, but Sam was dry under the yellow rain coat. When I spotted Chucky's house I saw the dreaded red and blue sparks. "Back door," I snapped and started sprinting. "It's never locked," I called over my shoulder. I blew through the garden gate and into the back yard. The grass was neatly mowed. I crossed it and hit the patio. The sliding back door was, as always, unlocked. I'd told Chucky he needed to help his parents and lock it every night. They were way too trusting. This might be a gated community, but it was close to Jacksonville. You had to be careful. However, their terrible safety habits were proving to be a blessing. I yanked the door open and ran through a house I'd been in hundreds of times. Chucky would be in the den. That's where he gamed.

When I got close I heard the clown's hideous chuckle and prayed I wasn't too late. Sam and Duke followed. When Duke spotted the clown on the giant TV screen, he started barking. It wasn't Chucky on the floor being strangled by the controller cord. It was his little brother Carlos. Chucky was fighting to keep him from dying by unplugging the game box. "Won't work," I yelled and went for the controller cord.

I got it unwrapped and realized the clown was gone. Somehow, Duke's barking had made the insane clown go away. I looked around for Duke, but he must have gone outside. Sam knelt beside me. Together we got Carlos up and breathing. Chucky, all of him, had folded up and was sobbing. "Where's your mom and dad?" I asked.

"Tampa, visiting Gramps," he said through his sobs. "They'll be back tomorrow. I'm supposed to be watching Carlos. What if he'd died? Oh my god," and he started bawling again.

Sam patted his arm. "It'll be okay, Chuck," she said.

He suddenly realized Miss Perfection, head cheerleader for Mandarin High, was in his den touching his arm. "How did you get here?"

"I came with Joker," she said. "The clown thing attacked both of us. It killed poor Eddie Donalds."

His eyes seemed to focus. "That was his mastiff, Duke. I thought he died."

I had Carlos up and sitting in his wheelchair. "Guess not."

"Chuck," Sam said. "We have to do something. I called 911 for Eddie, but I don't think we can tell the police an insane killer clown is attacking gamers through their TVs."

"Nope, very bad idea," Chucky said. "Uh, maybe I'm being a little slow here, but what can we do?"

Sam sat on the couch. "We stop it."

I stared down at her. She was so lovely even in a soaking wet yellow slicker. Her black hair, exposed to the rain in the front where the hood had slipped, was slicked tight to her perfectly shaped head and her heart-shaped face. At that moment, I would have fought the clown hand to hand for her if that's what she wanted. "Got any ideas?"

"Yeah," she said. "We figure out who it is. I mean, there has to be a real person somewhere pulling the strings, making this happen. The clown didn't just come out of hell and start killing gamers. There's a plan, there's always a plan."

"We need a plan," Chucky said.

"Tomorrow night, well since it's four in the morning now, tonight, is Halloween," I said. "All Hallows Eve, the night the dead rise out of their graves and walk the street."

"I don't think the clown is ah, you know, other-worldly, a ghost thing," Sam said. "I think there's someone making it happen. A real human who hates gamers."

"Professor Smiley," we all said at once.

"That machine," Chucky said. "The one in the back of the classroom. It has an XBox stuck in the slot on top."

"We can't get into school over the weekend," I said. "It's locked down because of Halloween. The gates'll be locked, the building locked up and guarded. Every year kids try to get in and toilet paper the place or egg it on Halloween. There's no way to get inside."

"Can you imagine how terrible it will be if it eats enough souls to become real?" I shook my head. "Sam's right. We can't let that happen."

"What do you mean become human?" Chucky asked.

"When we were at Eddie's I could see the clown on the TV in the garage. It said if it ate enough souls, it would become real and kill all gamers. It said it knows who we are."

Sam made a scoffing sound. "Unhuh, it's already human. It's Professor Smiley. He's gonna dress up in his clown suit and come after us."

Suddenly Carlos spoke. He'd been sitting quietly in his chair trying to return his breathing to normal. Carlos was a typical fourteen-year-old. He'd been in a bad car wreck with his dad when he was three and was partially paralyzed. His legs wouldn't work from the knee down. He had braces but was still learning how to use them. "Uh, guys, I know how to get into school.

"Exactly how?" Chucky rolled his eyes.

"Hey, you don't know half the people in school I know. I need help to use the bathroom. You should try a day in my shoes, or my chair, I should say."

Carlos was really smart. Chucky and I figured it was overcompensation because of his disability. He managed to get around school as a freshman, get help whenever he needed it from almost anyone. I mean even jocks and mean girls helped Carlos. "Don't knock him, Chucky. He knows people. You know he does. Who, Carlos? Who can get us into school on Halloween weekend?"

"Mr. Sharts."

Chucky and I both burst out laughing. "No teacher at Mandarin High is named Sharts. You're making it up."

"He's real and he's not a teacher. I even know where he lives. He's the janitor."

"No! Not the old man who practically lives in the school basement. That's Mr. Sharts?"

Carlos nodded. "Yep. And he lives right outside the gates. That old house next to the vacant lot."

"No way," Sam said. "Everyone says the old man who lives there eats children."

"You know that's a load of crap," Carlos said. "Nobody eats kids. Except maybe the clown. He could eat children."

"The house is supposed to be haunted, too," Chucky said.

"Well, if you want to get into school on the weekend Sharts is your man. He has a key to the gates, the school and every classroom."

"Why do you know him?" Chucky asked.

"I told you. I need help to do the simplest things. You never take that into consideration. Mr. Sharts is a very nice person. I'm sure if his house is haunted, it's not his fault and he would fix it if he could."

"I thought he spent all his time in the basement fooling around with the water heaters and stuff like that," I said. "No one ever goes down there but him."

"He fixes everything and cleans the school, mops and polishes the floor. He's a very busy man, but he's always available when I need him. I might be a freshman, but I know my way around the school and I know a lot of people." Carlos's smile reeked of satisfaction.

We all groaned. "I guess we're making a visit to Mr. Sharts," I said. "But not until daylight. No way I'm knocking on that door in the dark."

"It's almost light," Sam said. She looked at her phone. "It's five-thirty. We could all go home and get some sleep or go get pancakes at IHOP."

"How?" I asked. "IHOP is five miles away."

Sam tilted her head coyly. "I have a car and a driver's license."

"I have to take Carlos," Chucky said.

"I drive an SUV. Throw his wheelchair in the back."

So, we walked to Sam's house followed by Duke-the-mastiff. When we reached Eddie's, Duke stopped and sat down where Eddie's body had been. The cops were everywhere in the house and tape was strung all over the street. Cop cars and a white city van were parked down both sides. Neighbors either stood on the lawn staring or peeked out of curtains while they remained safely inside. We carefully skirted the clusters of police and crime-scene people dressed in hazmat suits, eyes down, trying to be invisible.

Sam opened her garage door when we got there, and we loaded into her SUV and went to IHOP. None of us had much to say. The mood was somber as we got to the restaurant, trooped inside, pushing Carlos, and go a big corner booth.

"That was weird," Chucky finally said. "I've never actually seen a crime scene before."

"I've never seen a dead person before," I said. "It's not what I thought it would be like. It was awful. Maybe Smiley's got something with that video games make killing, blood, and dead people seem too easy."

"Professor Smiley is insane, Joker," Chucky said. "Period."

"Yes, he is," Sam said. "No sane person dresses up like a clown. Clowns're gross, hideous and disgusting."

We all nodded. None of us had. We ordered from the elderly waitress and ate pancakes. When we were finished, the restaurant was just beginning to get busy. Sam checked her phone. It had been pinging constantly with messages. "Eddie wasn't the only one who got it," she said in a hushed voice. "Kailie says her neighbor, Dallas Simpson was killed."

"Kailie Perkins?" I knew they were friends.

Sam nodded and kept scrolling through her texts. "Tori Cagle says a gamer on her block was killed last night. The police are there."

The waitress used a remote from the cashier's stand and flicked on the TVs. The news was blasting the rash of murders committed during the night. Twelve teens and young people had been killed in an odd way, strangled by the cords from their video game systems. The reporter said the police were mystified, but an unknown group of teens had been seen running away from one murder scene in the Mayfield Gardens gated community. Sam covered her mouth with her hand. "They're talking about you and me, Joker. We're wanted."

"No, we're not," I said. "They just wanna talk to us. There's no way we could kill all those kids, all over town. But talking to the cops would be a really bad idea. What could we even tell them they would actually believe?"

Sam glanced at her watch again. "It's almost nine. We should go visit Carlos's Mr. Sharts."

When we got to the huge old house, Sam pulled into the driveway behind Mr. Sharts old white Chrysler van. We sat there for a minute. I could hear everyone breathing. Finally, Chucky spoke. "Who's gonna knock on the door?"

"It's not haunted," Carlos said.

It looked haunted, the huge windows like blank eyes staring out at the street. The house was two stories and badly in need of a paint job. The front porch sagged on the far end. A garage sat next to the house with two doors chained with a giant padlock. I pointed to the padlock. "See, Chucky, Mr. Sharts knows about locks."

Sam opened her door and got out. "If you guys are too chicken to knock on this nice man's door, I will."

"Get me my chair," Carlos said. "I'll go with you."

Motivated by the word chicken, which I was, cluck, cluck, I climbed out my side. "I'll go with Sam. You guys wait here."

Sam and I cautiously approached the porch. "It looks like it's ready to fall down," she said.

The blank floor-to-ceiling windows lined the porch. The panes were sparkling clean. I looked through one and saw wood floors, an old couch and Mr. Sharts sitting on it watching TV and drinking something in a mug, probably coffee. I backed away, but not before he spotted me. We could hear him clumping across the floor. I knocked. Better late than never. Mr. Sharts yanked it open and Sam and I gave him our best smiles. I was suddenly afflicted with doubt. We'd forgotten to discuss what to say to him.

Perfectly at ease, Sam stuck out her hand. "Hi, Mr. Sharts, we need your help."

I heard the car door slam, looked and saw Chucky pushing Carlos up the walkway. "You know him?" Mr. Sharts asked as he pointed at Carlos.

"Yes," we both answered.

Mr. Sharts went down the steps and patted Carlos on the shoulder. "You need something, son?"

I was so relieved. Carlos, the handicapped guy, would handle everything.

Mr. Sharts and Chucky got Carlos and his wheelchair onto the porch and we all followed him into his house. Inside, there was little furniture which made it easy for Carlos to wheel around. The house was clean and smelled like furniture polish. Mr. Sharts resumed his seat on the couch and said, "Give. Tell me what's brought you to my house. I thought I was untouchable, the old man in the basement who scared all the kids."

"I know better," Carlos said. "You help me every day."

Emboldened by Mr. Sharts' benevolent attitude, I spoke up. "It's Professor Smiley."

Mr. Sharts frowned. "I knew he would go off his rocker one day. That clown is a loose cannon. What's he done?"

I sighed with relief. Sharts knew. "He's invented a machine that's killing gamers."

Sharts nodded. "So that's what happened last night. I saw it on the news."

"He almost got me," Carlos said. "He's insane."

"Yup, it was his wife. Gamer killed her, you know." Sharts sipped his coffee. "So, what do you want from me?"

I tried to hide my disbelief. Sharts, probably because Carlos was telling him and he apparently trusted and liked Carlos, hadn't even blinked when told one of the teachers invented a machine capable of killing gamers. I had seen it and still couldn't believe it was possible. Not for real. And yet I knew it was true. Horrible, terrifying, and real.

"He says he's eating the souls of the kids he's killed and wants to get strong enough to come to life and kill all the gamers," Carlos said. "We think if we destroy the machine, he'll stop."

"No way we can tell all this to the cops," I said. "They'll never believe us."

"News said they're lookin' for a bunch of kids seen leaving one of the murder scenes. Didn't happen to be you guys, did it?"

"It was me and Joker," Sam said. "We saw Eddie die, but we didn't kill him. The clown made him strangle himself with his controller cord. We called it in, but we had to run for Chucky's house. We saved Margie Wannamaker on the way and just got there in the nick of time to save Carlos."

"You really think destroying the machine will stop Smiley?" Sharts asked. "You really sure it's him?"

I shrugged. "It's all we can think to do. I mean, it's gotta be him. I mean clowns, plus hating gamers, equals Professor Smiley. There's no one else it could be."

Sam smiled at me and bubbles formed in my stomach. Or maybe it was just the huge pile of pancakes I'd consumed, but I'd never felt anything like it before.

"I have an idea," Carlos said to Mr. Sharts. "Why don't you go into the building and destroy the machine for us. That way we don't have to."

"I'd love to help you, son," Sharts said to Carlos, "but Professor Smiley put his own lock on the lab's door. He had it installed after he told Dean Fallows kids were breaking into his lab and snorting his chemicals. And anyway, Smiley hates me. We got into it after one of the kids blew up table six and I had to install new Bunsen burners and clean up the biggest mess you've ever seen. Smiley watched over me like a hawk and wouldn't lift a finger to help. Treated me like I was some peon."

"I can see why you'd dislike him," Sam said. "But not why he'd dislike you."

Sharts snorted. "I punched him in his big red nose. He was yelling and pointing his finger at some imaginary spot on the floor I supposedly missed, and I lost it. He reported me, but Fallows has known me for twenty-five years. And he knows what Smiley is, but chem teachers are hard to find, especially ones who used to be professors."

Chucky laughed. "You punched old Smiley?" Chucky stuck out his hand. "Shake bro, you're awesome."

Sharts shook Chucky's hand, then fist-bumped. Carlos was right. Sharts was okay. "So, you can't get into the lab, but you can get us into the school and you don't care how we get into the lab, right?" I asked.

"If that's what you want," Sharts said. He glanced at his watch, an ancient chrome thing with hands on the face. Who wore watches anymore?

"It's almost eleven. The guards will take a lunch break in an hour. You guys can load into my van and we'll get into the school then."

"You're taking me," Carlos said.

Chucky frowned. "Dude, Mom would kill me, literally kill me, if I let anything happen to you."

I knew Chucky was really thinking about what a pain dealing with the chair would be. One look at Carlos's face and I knew the kid was coming no matter what Chucky said. Carlos might have a weak body, but the Force was strong in that one.

"Bring him along," Sharts said. "He knows a lot about the school, and he can handle himself."

"That's right. I know stuff," Carlos said.

"Like what?" Chucky scoffed.

"Like which locker is Smiley's in the teacher's lounge, and that Smiley keeps the key to the lab in there."

Sam walked over and hugged Carlos. "You rock." She fist-bumped Carlos.

"All the lockers have combo locks on them," Sharts said. He patted Carlos's shoulder. "Got any ideas what Smiley's combo might be?"

"What's his wife's birthday?" I asked.

Sharts shrugged. "Don't know her birthday, but I do know the day she died."

Carlos nodded. "Might be the right numbers. What day?"

"I guess he doesn't know everything," Chucky said to me.

"Shut up," Carlos said. "At least I know which locker is his. There's a hundred of them."

"Stop fighting," Sharts said. "She died on ten, thirty-one, ten."

"Holy crap," I gasped. "His wife died on Halloween."

"That's wild, dude," Chucky said.

Sam stood up and headed for the door. She glanced back. "No wonder he's nuts. You guys coming?"

We loaded Carlos and the chair into Sharts' van and headed to the school. We got there just after noon and like Sharts said, there was no guard at the gate. He got out of the van, unlocked the gate, got back in and drove through. He relocked the gate and tooled behind the school close to the cafeteria and the Dumpster area. He looked around. "Guards probably went off campus for lunch. We're clear."

There was a ramp for Carlos's wheelchair behind the cafeteria, probably put there for big garbage cans to roll down. He let us all in and turned around to leave. "My van can't be here," he said. "I'd have to think of some lie to tell when the guards come back and find it, and I ain't lying." He glanced at that old watch again and I wondered if he had a phone. He pulled a set of keys, there had to be fifty on it, out of his pocket, took one off and dropped the remaining wad in Carlos's lap. "Keys. Guard them with your life." He held up the one key. "I gotta keep this one. It opens everything and the gate."

"Can we text you when we need a pickup?" I asked.

He pulled a flip phone out of his pocket. It looked like a burner, a disposable. "Give me all your numbers."

"He added us to his contact list. "I'll be back in exactly one hour." He looked at that old watch again. "That's one-fifteen. If you need me before, you have to call. Texting on this thing is hard." He started down the ramp heading for the van and stopped. "Now you kids be careful, watch after Carlos, stay low, and try not to destroy anything I'll have to clean up."

The school was creepy, empty like this. No kids, no noise, just the sound of our breathing and a tiny squeak from one of the wheels on Carlos's chair. "You need to oil that," I hissed to Chucky. He waggled his eyebrows as an answer. Sam held a finger over her lips. "Shhh."

The science labs were in their own wing of the school. As we approached, my stomach started doing flipflops. What if old Smiley was in there? What would we do? We had to walk by the doors to the labs to get to the teacher's lounge, which was by itself at the end of the hall where it intersected with a hall going to the admin offices.

The door to the lounge would no doubt be locked. Too many teachers came and went on the weekends, planning, bringing in props and supplies, and using the school-provided computers. They had personal stuff in their lockers and sometimes, they kept tests in those lockers and the answers. Teachers were totally afraid kids would break in and steal them.

For the most part, kids were terrified of the place. It was full of teachers, and the vice principal, Mrs. Stringfellow, the meanest woman on the planet, rumored to have once been a prison guard at Starke Federal Prison, sometimes hung out in there.

We crept up to the door. There was a window at the top. I peeked over the edge. "Looks empty."

"Only one of us should go in," Carlos said. "I'll go. I know which locker it is."

"How you gonna reach it meals-on-wheels?" Chucky asked.

Carlos smirked. "There are two rows of lockers, one high one low, Smiley's is low."

"Try the door," Sam said.

It was locked. Carlos handed me the ball of keys. "This could take a while," I said as I filed through the keys. They were all brass and they all looked alike. But I quickly discovered Sharts had a piece of white tape on each with a number. I had to assume they were classroom numbers, so all the numbered keys, I shuffled to one side of the gigantic ring. There were keys with the letter A on them and a number. I hoped that meant admin offices.

"What are you doing?" Chucky hissed. "Hurry the hell up."

I gave him the evil eye and shook the keys. "Wanna look for yourself?"

"No," he mumbled. "Just hurry. I feel naked standing out here in the hall."

I found two keys with T's on them. I tried T-1. It must be for a teachers' lounge, right? And there were two of them. The key didn't work. I held my breath and stuck T-2 into the doorknob. It turned, and I breathed out a sigh of relief as I pushed the door open. Carlos rolled by me and entered the room. We stood out in the hall, watching both ways, listening, freaking out quietly. Carlos emerged moments later. He held a small ring in his hand with one key dangling from it. "The lock worked on her death date. Sharts nailed it. I left it open, so we can return the key fast."

We left the lounge door open, too. Unlocking doors was time consuming. We wanted to get the key back and get out as quickly as possible. With the key to the chem lab in our hands, we fast-walked as quietly as possible down the hall and back to the lab. Carlos used the key and the lab was ours.

We ran inside. There on the table in the back of the room was the machine. It was lit up like Fourth of July. Lights flashed. The XBox was on and it hummed. It was the first thing you heard when you entered the room. There was an odd odor in the lab as well, odder than usual anyway. Rising above the stench of formaldehyde, chemicals, and kid funk was a weird burning electrical wire smell.

"Grab it," I said to Chucky. "I'll check his desk."

"You're gonna look in Smiley's desk. You nuts?"

I grinned. "Well we're here. Might as well see what grade I'm getting. And check for other incriminating evidence."

He snorted softly. "Well hurry. Smiley could show up at any minute. I'm grabbing this machine and running."

Sam glanced at her phone. "We only have eleven minutes left until Sharts returns. Hurry."

I went for the desk but kept an eye on Chucky and the machine. I started pulling open drawers. Ugh, first drawer held clown makeup and a red wig. I glanced up and saw Chucky unplug the machine. As soon as he yanked the plug out of the socket, a siren sounded. It was so loud and so terrible we all freaked. Even though it was unplugged, the machine didn't die. It began flashing red lights from four spots on the top. Chucky ignored the siren and the flashing lights, picked up the machine and raced out the door with Sam right behind him. I opened another drawer and found a tablet with a charger. I snagged that and raced after Chucky, pulling the door shut behind me and locking it.

Sam was waiting. "I'll take the key back," I said. "You go with Chucky."

"I'll go with you."

I pushed her gently in the direction Chucky had gone. "You go with him, find Sharts and stay safe. I'll be right behind you."

She reluctantly headed after Chucky and I ran back down the hall to the teachers' lounge. I found the open locker, hung the key on a hook in the door, slammed it shut, and spun the lock to make it look good.

I locked the lounge behind me and ran for the cafeteria. We had the machine and Smiley's tablet. Things were looking up. I got to the cafeteria, ran out the back door and jumped in the van. First thing I noticed. We were missing Carlos. "Where's your brother?" I grabbed Chucky's shirt and shook him. "Where's Carlos?"

Sam's phone rang. When she answered, the evil-clown voice was clearly heard. "Missing something?" The voice asked sweetly. Then it screamed. "Well so am I. Where's my machine?"

"We have it," Sam said.

"Well I have Carlos. Bring that machine to my house at eight tonight and it better be in mint condition. You can have Carlos if I get my machine." Then the clown giggled insanely. "Carlos will be fine, Carlos will be fine, Carlos will be fine."

I grabbed the phone. "We need to see proof of life." I'd heard that term used on a movie and in my game.

"Check your inbox, Samantha, my dear," Smiley said.

I glanced at her screen. The hideous clown was still there. Ugh. Sam zeroed out the clown and checked her email. Nothing was there so she checked instant messaging. There was a video downloading into her phone. She opened it and held the phone out, so we could all see. Carlos was sitting in his chair in a dark room with one lightbulb hanging over his head. He was still alive.

Evil clown voice spoke. "Tell your brother you're okay, Carlos."

Carlos began blinking rapidly, sequences. I looked at Chucky. "What's he doing?"

"Right after his accident, he was totally paralyzed. We made up a code. It was so long ago," he grabbed his head and moaned. "Of course, he wouldn't forget it." Chucky concentrated on Carlos's eyes. "I'm in the basement," Chucky said. "Clown is nuts." No kidding. "Be careful will try to get out on my own."

Chucky groaned. "How's he gonna do that? Gee-freaking-whiz, my parents are going to kill me when they find out."

Carlos spoke. "Bring him the machine, Chuck. Or he says he will kill me."

Chucky sobbed.

Samantha put her arm around Chucky's shoulder and patted him. "We'll get him back, Chuck," Samantha said. "Stop stressing."

Sharts spoke up. "So, you lost your brother, Chuck. After I specifically told you not to." He spun the van around and headed back to his house.

"It's all of our faults, Mr. Sharts," I said. "We had the machine, ran out, I had to lock up, I don't know how Smiley got him."

"He must have been in the back of the lab, in Smiley's office," Sam said. "I saw Carlos go in there."

"We have to go," Sharts said. "You guys go on home. I'll pick you up at seven."

"What about the machine?" I asked. "What do we do with it?"

Sharts pursed his lips like he was thinking as he pulled into his driveway, and then smiled. "Leave it with me. I know some stuff about fixing machines. Maybe I can "fix" this one."

Chucky gasped. "But we need it to get Carlos back."

"Don't worry," Sharts said. "I'll make whatever I do to it, happen after we get him back."

Chucky started to cry. "I am so screwed. My parents are gonna kill me."

The screaming siren had stopped. The flashing lights on the machine were gone, but the XBox still glowed with the blue power light. It must have a battery pack inside.

Sam punched Chucky. "Is that all you're worried about? What about your brother? I wish I had a brother."

Chucky scrubbed his wet eyes. "I know. I do care about him, but my dad can be so mean."

I patted Chucky's shoulder. "We'll get him back before they get home. They'll never know."

He nodded as tough not convinced but stopped sniffling as we all piled from the van and headed over to where Sam had parked her SUV at the curb to let Mr. Starks out of the driveway.

Sam dropped poor Chucky first, then we went home. When we got out of her SUV, I glanced up the street at the Donalds' house. Duke was still sitting on the spot where Eddie's body had laid. Poor dog. He was probably broken-hearted.

Sam took my hand. "You were great in there," she said shyly. "What're you gonna do with the tablet?"

I looked at it. "I don't know. I'm kind of afraid to turn it on."

She nodded. "I would be, too. But, I mean, you have to look. Don't you?"

"Yeah, I do. Then I noticed there were two cars in my driveway. "Oh god, my parents are home. I'm screwed."

Sam laughed. "Can't be that bad."

"You have no idea. My PlayStation is a burnt ruin. They'll blame me."

"Joker, tell them to watch the news and tell them about Eddie. That should get their attention."

I brightened. "Good idea."

She squeezed my hand and I felt like my heart would explode. Was she playing with me? Were we just friends? She'd taken my hand. Should I say something? I wanted to grab my head. Why did I have to be such an idiot with girls? "See you at seven," was all I could think of to say.

She laughed and walked up her driveway. I turned and walked up mine with my face burning. Was she laughing at me or with me? Was it like the shared adventure kind of laugh or you're stupid kind of laugh? I was thinking this when I walked straight into hell. Both my parents were sitting at the island in the kitchen.

"Where have you been?" My father demanded.

"We've been worried sick," Mom said.

Dad held up the ruined PlayStation. "What happened?"

I tried to play it cool. "Have you seen the news?"

"Are you talking about all those murdered kids?" Mom asked. "That's why we were so worried. Where did you go?"

So, I explained about the PlayStation trying to kill me, left out a lot of weird stuff, especially the breaking into the school stuff, played up Eddie's death, and ended by saying Samantha from next door had been with me. I decided to leave out the part about Carlos. They would've called the police and that would ruin everything.

"You saw him die?" Mom said and gave me a hug.

I nodded. Mom hugging me was different. We weren't the hugging kind of family. Dad put his arm around my shoulder which was even stranger. "You probably should go lie down, son. It must have been very hard for you."

"Yeah, it was pretty terrible," I managed to say. Wow! Sam had nailed it. Telling them about Eddie had completely derailed their planned rant. I hung my head like I was devastated and went to my room. Mom called after me.

"We'll get you an XBox this time."

I turned on the stairs. "Please, just a PlayStation. No XBoxes." An XBox was the last thing I needed. I took Professor Smiley's tablet into my room and shut the door. I laid it on the bed and stared at it. I was curious and terrified at the same time. I hit the power button and held my breath.

The screen flickered and then there he was. Professor Smiley in his terrifying clown suit. "You. Stole. My. Tablet." Smiley snarled. He opened his mouth and blood poured out from between his sharpened teeth. "Bring it to me at eight or no Carlos." Then he laughed that insane clown giggle.

For a minute, I was frozen with horror, then I grabbed the tablet and pushed the power button switching it off. He knew I had it. I fell back on my bed and whimpered. What a terrible Halloween. It would never be the same for me again.

I must have fallen asleep because the next thing I knew, was my mom banging on my bedroom door. "Wake up Josh. There's a girl here for you."

I sat bolt upright, stared at the clock and then myself in the mirror. I was just a normal looking kid usually, now I looked demented and totally not normal. My hair stuck up in all directions and when I sniffed my armpits, I stunk. "Imma jump in the shower and I'll be right down."

I tossed the drawers looking for a clean shirt and jeans, then raced for the shower. I was in and out in two minutes, using a ton of Axe shower gel, pulled on jeans over wet skin, dancing on one foot then the other like an idiot. Sam was down there waiting for me. I was freaking. I ran back into my room, thought about cologne, decided no, grabbed the tablet and bolted downstairs, praying I smelled good.

Mom saw me and lifted one eyebrow. I almost giggled. Sam was sitting at the island in clean clothes. "Sorry I took so long," I mumbled. "I fell asleep."

Sam had her phone in her hand. "Mr. Sharts should be here any minute."

"Where are you two going?" Mom asked. She was dressed as a mermaid. The gigantic candy bowl for the trick-or-treaters was on a table by the front door. I was glad Dad was nowhere in sight. He always hid on Halloween.

"We're taking Chuck and Carlos trick-or-treating," Sam said with a straight face. She was not only hot and athletic, she was smart. I could never have spit out a clanker like that. I'm a terrible liar.

"Where's your costume?" Mom asked.

My turn. "We're not going to dress up this year. Uh, we're getting too old for that."

My mother rolled her eyes and pointedly stared at Sam. I smiled with lots of teeth as we bolted out the door. When we got out on the street, Sam grabbed my hand. "Your mother is nice, but she asks a lot of questions."

"I know. Hey, I opened Smiley's tablet."

"You did? How'd it go?"

"You don't wanna know?"

"Yes, I do, tell me."

Sharts pulled up then so I didn't have to tell her. Chucky jumped out as a group of six kids in goofy costumes and an adult walked toward my house. "Hurry, dude, we gotta get Carlos. My parents are driving back from Tampa right now."

I climbed into the van and noticed Duke right away. "You're bringing Eddie's dog?"

"He got in, so I guess so. Besides, the clown doesn't like him. Remember when he barked at Smiley and Smiley disappeared?"

I shrugged. "Where does Smiley live?"

"Don't freak when I tell you."

"I won't. Where?"

"He lives down by the river in an abandoned restaurant. It's got a dock and there used to be feral cats everywhere."

"Good thing you brought Duke. Do we have a plan?"

"Mr. Sharts did something to the machine. It will work for exactly an hour, then catch on fire. We give it to Smiley, grab Carlos, and then haul butt."

I held up the tablet. "He wants this, too."

Chucky took it and examined it. "You turned it on, didn't you?"

"I hung my head. "Yeah. He wasn't pleased."

Sharts laughed. "I guess not."

We drove toward the river, then turned down a dark road. All the houses on it were old and creepy. It was prime trick-or-treating time, and no one was doing it on this road. Giant oaks lined the road. Their branches hung over the street making a tunnel. It was dark, the streetlights were not working. Tree branches hung so low, they scraped the roof of the van. I saw a porchlight on two houses, other than them, it was dark. The moon must be behind clouds.

Sharts rolled down his window and the smell of the river wafted in. It was a wet, algae and dead-fish kind of smell. We pulled into the parking lot of the old restaurant. Smiley's car, a 1989 Buick LeSabre, was parked as close to the old building as it could get. The parking lot was overgrown with weeds. One track was worn into them leading to the LeSabre which might have been silver rather than gray at one time but was faded and covered with blotches of rust. There was one light. It was on the porch hanging out in the river. The yellow light illuminated an old John boat tied to the dock and three skinny, moth-eaten cats eating something out of a bowl. I thought sure Duke would chase them when we opened the door, but he seemed to have no interest in cats. The huge dog climbed out of the van one foot at a time and followed us as we grouped at the edge of an old board walkway leading to the building.

"Think he knows we're here?" I asked.

"I have no doubt," Sharts said.

"Smiley, we have your machine," Sharts yelled.

"Bring me my brother," Chucky screamed.

Suddenly, Smiley, dressed in the insane clown costume, lunged out of the shadows. His hideous face glowed white with the evil red stains. He opened his mouth revealing long, pointed teeth and Sam screamed.

We were cut off. He was between us and the van. Sharts stood strong which was a good thing because I was crapping in my pants and I could see from the expression on Chucky's face he was, too. Sharts held the machine close to his body. "Where's Carlos?"

Smiley pulled a machete out of a pocket on his baggy clown suit and advanced toward us. "Give me my machine. All of you are gamers. Nasty, killers, all of you. Give it to me or I'll chop you up and feed you to the gators."

I tried not to look. We all did, but I had to. I glanced at the black, oily water slopping against the dock and saw the red eyes of at least four gators. "Where's Carlos?" I squeaked. "You promised to give him to us."

'I fed his crippled carcass to the gators," Smiley giggled. "I love to feed them. They leap out of the water to grab cats when I hold them out far enough."

Chucky screamed. "No!" Then he turned away from Smiley and ran into the building. I stayed to support Sharts.

"Now give me my machine. Put it on the ground where I can see it, and back away, or I'll cut you in two." He swung the machete.

"Not until we get Carlos," Sharts snarled.

Smiley waved the machete and I thought I saw blood stains on the blade. The full moon came out from behind the clouds and I could see the dock, the door to the building, Sam, Sharts, and the old car clearly.

Smiley's white head glowed in the light, the sprouts of orange hair like fire. Everything felt like it was moving in slow motion. Moonlight glinted off the blade of the machete. Smiley swung it at Sam and I lunged for his arm.

Suddenly Duke was there. The big dog had been watching from the shadows, not barking, not acting like a dog at all, but like a person waiting. The dog opened his huge choppers, Duke was big, at least two-hundred pounds of muscle, and grabbed Smiley by the throat. Blood spurted everywhere, and Smiley's scream was gut-wrenching. The clown dropped the machete as Duke shook Smiley back and forth, blood and dog slobber flying in all directions. Smiley's struggles grew weaker, then Duke clamped his massive jaws on one of Smiley's arms and dragged the insane clown slowly down the dock toward the water leaving a wide trail of clown suit parts and blood.

We just stared as Duke lifted Smiley over the water and held the clown there, his huge jaws clamped over Smiley's right arm. Suddenly, a gator leaped out of the water, grabbed a floppy clown foot, and dragged Smiley under. The clown's final shriek was gargled as he disappeared beneath the water's oily-black surface.

Duke turned and looked back at us. I saw his eyes glow, and for a minute, I could swear I saw Eddie looking out through the dog's eyes Then he just disappeared. Duke and Smiley were gone. The machete lay where it had fallen on the ground with the moonlight still glinting off its blade.

Sharts stepped forward, looking into the dark bushes and out over the river. "Where'd the dog go?"

Sam turned and hugged me. "Duke was dead, wasn't he? He came for Smiley from the grave because he loved Eddie."

I didn't know what to say. "So, All Hallows Eve is true? Wow, I think you must be right."

Sharts stared at me. "You're saying the dog was a ghost?"

"Everyone knew when Duke died. Eddie cried for days and he was in college."

"Well, that's a hell of a thing," Sharts said. "Guess we better go look for Chucky. No telling what kind of booby traps are inside."

"I found him," Chucky suddenly yelled from the building. Chucky opened the door to the building and backed out dragging Carlos in a wheelchair. It wasn't Carlos's nice, state-of-the-art chair. It was an old cane-back chair with wheels. I ran to help and together we got Carlos out to the van. "What'd you do?" I asked Carlos. "Escape?"

Carlos grinned, and I was proud of him. "I crawled out of my chair and hid in a closet full of rotting paper products. The old clown couldn't find me. Man, there were rats and roaches in there. It was gross."

"What do we do with his machine?" Sam asked.

Sharts walked out on the dock and dropped it into the water. "Feed it to the gators."

"How'd you get rid of Smiley?" Chucky asked.

"Duke," I said. "Turned out he was dead after all."

About the Author

Janet Post

Daughter of a Colonel, Janet lived the military life until she got out of high school. At that point she was a self-described wild child. She got married and moved to Canada where she lived up the Sechelt Inlet, the scene for her YA novel, Spellcast Waters. She lived in Hawaii and worked as a polo groom for fifteen years, then moved to Florida where she became a reporter. Janet loves kids and horses, and she paints and writes. Now she lives in the swampland of Florida with too many dogs and her fifteen-year-old granddaughter.

She writes young adult fiction with her son, Gabe Thompson, who teaches middle school. Together they wrote a young adult science fiction novel which will eventually be a series, and have a middle grade book out, Voodoo Child, another, My BFF is an Alien, and one she wrote solo, Spellcast Waters. Vagrant was named a Finalist in the International Book Awards contest and was a Green Apple Special Selection winner. She's a veteran Tell-Tale author, and has coauthored and illustrated a how-to book, The Young Adult Writer's Journey, with acquisition editor, Elizabeth Fortin-Hinds.

Hans and Greta

by

Elizabeth Alsobrooks

Hans and Greta

By

Elizabeth Alsobrooks

She snatched the puppet by the arm and jerked the stiletto from its grasp. "Knock it off, Mother. You deserved it, you know you did. Did you think you could make me live like your slave forever? You told me if I helped you kill your husband I would finally get to live as your daughter."

"How dare you lecture me?" the puppet snarled. "What kind of DAUGHTER kills her own mother? I was working on it. You know I was. I bought us a chalet in France. The passports were being created. We could have lived there under new names and you could have gotten a rich husband of your own."

"Shut up, Mother. You know you would never have left. You only cared about yourself, your prestige, your charity functions. What a joke. You didn't give a damn about any of those people your charities were helping. You used to call orphans useless brats, a suck on humanity. Yet you treated your own daughter as though you were ashamed of her. Was it my fault you were raped and your parents threw you out onto the streets once it became apparent that you were pregnant?"

"Did I abort you? Did I abandon you? No! I have always taken care of you, and this is the thanks I got?"

"I'm sorry, okay? I was angry. You kept putting me off until I no longer believed you."

The puppet jerked its hand away and ran over to the dresser. Its movements were awkward and disjointed, limbs jerking as though seized and released. Clearly it wasn't used to pulling its own strings. It pressed a button and a secret drawer opened on the bottom of a jewelry box from which it extracted a key. Running to the closet, the jerky movement more pronounced when hurrying, it threw open the door and hurried to the back. Prying up a floorboard, it reached in and took out a book. The key fit snugly into the lock and the puppet opened it, flipping through until it found what it sought.

"Yes, yes, I thought I remembered this. Kill the girl first. I can use this spell to switch bodies and we can burn this puppet in the furnace after she's trapped inside. Then I'll inherit the estate again, after I kill the boy, and we can finally move to France, but this time as sisters. We can both get rich husbands, not that we'll need them."

"If I help you again, do you promise to do it this time, Mother?"

"How can you doubt me? Haven't I gotten us this far, despite your screwups? My husband would have survived that car crash if I hadn't given him that injection and left him in the ruination of his precious sports car for the authorities to find him."

* * * *

"It doesn't make any sense that everything was left to us. She hated us. There's no way she would have allowed father to leave us so much," I insist.

"Maybe she felt guilty and regretted sending us off to school. Maybe she didn't know what was in father's will."

"No way, Greta. Didn't you read it? You didn't, did you?" I throw my hands up and push back my chair. Taking a calming breath, I say, "It was a joint will. She had to know."

"Now you listen to me, both of you. Hans, I agree with you. There's no way Gretchen would have wanted you to have a single thing of your father's let alone anything belonging to her. Something is just not right about this inheritance," Aunt Gwen interjects.

Greta studies Aunt Gwen's face a moment, sees the conviction and turns away. With a defiant toss of her long, golden curls, she clicketyclomps to the window on impractical heels I told her, to no avail, would end in a broken leg.

I know my twin too well, and that means I should have known she couldn't make sense of the thick wad of papers I thrust into her hand just that morning. She purposely ignores me and looks out at the gray London sky through the fogged window pane and declares, "I'm going. With or without you, Hans."

"Just like that? You won't even discuss it or listen to reason? You don't know what you may find there. We haven't been back since we were five, Greta."

She turns away from the window and I regret my harsh words. Tears glisten in her expressive blue eyes and she sucks in a little sob. "Which is why I must. Don't you see that? I thought you of all people would understand that I need to go home. I need to visit Father's grave. Put flowers on Mummy's grave. Please, Hans."

I rise with such haste I nearly topple the chair. Rushing to her side, I wrap my arms around my sister. "Hush. I'll take you. Don't cry." Older by only minutes, I have always felt a duty to be her champion. It was the last task my father whispered to me on a stolen visit to our school. That rare visit had been a ray of hope in a cold dank manor filled with strict school masters and bitter loneliness.

Take care of your sister, Hans. She may need you more than you need her, but you need each other. You're twins. A special bond, like the one your mother had with her sister, Gwen, he said softly.

My promise had been a bond, too. Greta wasn't slow, but she was too optimistic, too forgiving, too trusting. Of course, she wouldn't question a will that left us the sole heirs of an enormous estate and several million pounds of various other assets. The investigation would be up to me. I would have to make the arrangements and schedule the appointment with the solicitor and obtain the keys and whatever else we would need to just "go home" as my sister insisted. Shoving my hand through hair as thick and fair as my sister's I resign myself to the coming trials.

I am reminded of a silly American movie as I pull the car to a stop outside the gate and put it into park. It took over an hour by plane to get to Stuttgart, and then the train ride to Neustadt took an hour and a half. Now, a glance at my watch and I see that it took us twenty-five minutes to arrive home, but that isn't counting the hour with the solicitor, or the additional hour spent shopping for a few staples, at the solicitor's suggestion.

Greta sighed. "I thought I would feel happier to be here, but suddenly I'm a little frightened, Hans."

"You're just tired and hungry," I assure her and reach to squeeze her hand before fidgeting for the switch location to down the window in the rental car. Greta reaches over to the center of the dash and helps me out. I remind myself from the back of the Solicitor's business card and punch the code into the box. The gates swing inward, and I drive forward, feeling every bit as anxious as my sister, despite my false assurances to the contrary.

Dense pine boughs encroach on the long driveway, forbidden admission by select pruning. We approach the circle car park at the house and the small tires bump across cobblestones, centered by an impressive fountain which no one bothered to shut down. I slow to take in the first view we've had of our childhood home in fifteen years.

"It's even more beautiful than I remembered," Greta says softly, clearly moved by the tall stone façade, with its steepled turret and angled roofline. "It's so big. I thought I just recalled it as castle-like because I was so little the last time we were here."

"Did you forget the hours we used to spend playing hide-and-seek through all three floors and the attics and cellars, until the nanny finally quit because she was so tired of trying to find us all the time?"

Greta joins in my laughter, and I pull forward, around to the side door, under the carport used for deliveries and almost always by us when we were little.

"Do you suppose she kept any of Father's work?"

"Why wouldn't she? Some of it must be rather valuable," I say, trying to keep the bitterness from my voice. I am the one who never forgave Father for abandoning us, for caving to the demands of an evil witch of a stepmother. Though young and undeniably beautiful, she was too preoccupied with being the Baroness to a family fortune, to have time for an actual family.

We get out of the car and I open the boot to pull out our luggage. Greta reaches for her carryon and a small bag. "I forgot how dark it is here," she says, shrugging her shoulders as if from a sudden chill.

"Schwarzwald is dense, and we're right in the middle of it."

"Do you remember how frightened the children were when we told them we lived in the Black Forest?"

I laugh, remembering. "They asked me if witches and monsters lived in the forest." *They certainly used to*, I remind myself, shouldering the bags and digging the ring of keys the solicitor gave me from my pocket.

Finding the one I want, I shove it into the lock and it turns easily.

Greta breezes past me, excited to be home, at last. She flicks on the lights as she sweeps forward, like a breath of sunshine in a dark cave.

I follow, dutifully carting the luggage and closing the door. The dark panels of wood from the surrounding forests take on a warm glow with the overhead lighting. Brushed aside, the foreboding impression that froze my entrance dissipates, but doesn't vanish.

My sister chirps on, like a happy finch, childhood remembrances flitting through her head and into the warm embrace of home. I smile to see her so happy, happier than she's been in many years. It's almost as if she has been reborn, as if taking her from the heart of Germany broke her somehow. I know I never took the place of Father, and certainly not

Mother, but I do feel I've been as good a big brother as I was capable, feeling cast aside and forgotten myself.

I turn from the mudroom to the kitchen, where Greta is opening and closing cabinets. "I'll just set these bags down and pop out for the sundries," I say, turning back to the foyer.

"I'll help," she says cheerfully, all but skipping across the room to catch up.

With her help, we get the entire lot in one go, and she begins putting them away as I heft the luggage once more, heading toward our rooms.

I surprise myself by reaching with automatic familiarity for the switches that flood the main hall, and then the sweeping grand staircase, with light. A less pleasant surprise awaits me on the first landing. Larger than life, a humungous painting of the evil one herself stares at me with bitter accusation. I can only stare back, open mouthed.

The artist captured her true to life. The bluish gleam of her raven hair, a triumphant nest for the diamond and sapphire tiara that once graced mother's fairer tresses. Her lips tip upward, ever so slightly, as if she is privy to an insidious secret. Eyes, black as her heart, appear to have little or no pupil. The whites are shadowed by sooty lashes, giving them a grayish cast. The black wrap of Ostrich feathers she intends as chic make her look like a raven of death from my perspective. "Witch or demon?" I ask the silent bitch before turning to trudge up another flight of stairs.

My dark mood is back. I push the door to Greta's room open, walk across thick carpet that cushions the hardwood floors, and deposit her bag on the small bench at the end of her canopy bed. The cleaning woman, alerted by the solicitor's office, dusted and vacuumed and furnished fresh linens. The bed is turned down invitingly, a fire, I note, set out in the grate, awaiting a match.

I don't linger, but hurry past the adjoining room that was once our nanny's and into the room in which I spent the first five years of my life.

My bag drops unheeded to the floor as I stare at the large bookcase that dominates the wall between the floor to ceiling windows. Nestled on the bottom shelf, upright and columned in rigid military style are the wooden soldiers my father caved with intricate precision for my fourth birthday. Thirty centimeters tall, their uniforms are still brightly painted and authentic looking. Though their limbs are jointed and moveable, they appear stiff and abandoned, like I was. I reach down and pick up a miniature cannon, so real it looks able to fire. Why didn't my father send them to me?

Why didn't I ask for them?

I set it back down and swipe a hand across my eyes, chew my bottom lip and reach for the nearest soldier. I slip my finger along the silver bayonet of his rifle, then jerk it back. "Ouch!" A small slice begins oozing blood. I turn my back on the renewed pain and head for the adjoining loo. I run cool water over the wound, then flick my attention to the mirror above the sink. Something, or someone, flashes out of sight, having just crossed the doorway.

"Greta?" I call. No answer.

I turn off the faucet and rush into my empty bed chamber.

"What the hell? Where's Mummy's painting?"

Greta has arrived at the landing. So, who or what was just in my room? I step back and grab a hand towel, then seeing that the bleeding has stopped, I toss it on the counter and walk out to the hallway.

Greta arrives on the third-floor landing. "You don't suppose they destroyed it, do you, Hans?"

"Unlikely. Don't worry, it's probably delegated to an attic room under a tarp. We'll have it returned to its rightful home."

"Well, if we can't find it, that one still has to come down."

"As soon as possible. I swear. Come on, I'll light the fire in your room and you can take a nice hot bath before supper. You'll feel so much better if you get into some fresh, warm clothes. I think I can manage to hop into a quick shower and put together some sandwiches and tea. I'll have it all ready by the time you're done."

She reaches to give me a one-arm hug, lugging her carryon and bag with the other. "You're the best brother ever," she says, all smiles again.

I have no intention of telling her I'm imagining things. No need for her to be unsettled too. The matches are atop the mantle, and I strike one against the brick and bend to ignite the fire. Well-laid, it catches quickly. I stand and turn. "Never tell me that's what you've had in that bag all this time?"

"Of course," she says simply. The puppet jingles as she perches it against a lace-fringed pillow at the head of her bed. Strings held in hand, the medieval jester stands as tall as Greta had been at four, when my father gave it to her. A magnificent puppet, the features are almost lifelike, and he is dressed in a satin black and gold jester's uniform, complete with three-pointed hat, each one sporting a jingle bell. In his right hand he holds a mock scepter with another jester's head carved at the top of the bauble. Somehow, my father managed to bring it to Greta at school, and she is never without it. Even now, apparently.

 "Okay, get comfy," I say. "I'll see you in around an hour."

I'm rather proud of the feast I've prepared. Hard sausage, cheese, fruit and dark beer. Tea can wait until morning. I want to relax and get to bed, not wake up. It'll tide us over until the cook arrives in the morning. The solicitor's office is arranging to have the staff return, if they are still available, and if not, he will have the agency send someone, he assured us.

"This looks perfect! I'm famished," Greta says, pulling out a chair and reaching for a strawberry, her favorite.

We settle in to a nice meal around the kitchen table, reminding us both of what life used to be here at Leiderhosen Hall. It's pleasant and familiar, but I still have a nagging feeling that something isn't right.

"You feel it too," Greta says sudden-like. Gazing into my eyes with intense focus, she adds, "I knew it. What have I done? I shouldn't have made you come, but I-I just feel like I have missed Mummy and Daddy all my life and the only way I can be close to them is to come home."

"I think we're just too tired and too sad to even think rationally. We need a good night's sleep. Things always seem better in the morning. We will go to the crypt and place flowers from the gardens. Did you notice how wonderful Mummy's roses looked when we drove in?"

"Oh, yes, she would love that," Greta says softly. Then, "Hans?"

"What is it?"

"I know this is going to sound mad, but I feel like someone is here. I-I think I saw someone, heard someone, in my room, when I was taking a bath."

I glance away for a moment, so she won't see the shock in my eyes, the fear. "Nonsense, a cleaning staff was here today, but they're gone now. The regular staff is to return tomorrow. Tell me, what exactly did you see?"

"I told you it would sound mad. I saw a shadow, a silhouette really, like someone was spying on me. I left the door open to the bed chamber when I was taking a bath, and I thought I saw someone move away from the door, just out of sight, in my peripheral."

"The fire was burning. You probably just saw flickering shadows from the flames."

She nods, looking thoughtful. "Yes, you're probably right," she agrees, sounding relieved.

I wish I shared her relief.

"Hey, I have an idea, Sis. How about we lock the hallway doors and leave the doors to the nanny's room open. That way, if you need me for anything during the night I can hear you straight away. Will that make you feel better until we have staff sleeping in again?"

"Oh yes, let's do. I know it's foolish, but I'd feel so much better. Thanks, big brother."

Unknown by my sister, I'm unnerved enough to leave the hallway lights on, despite the fact that I carefully locked and removed the keys from all three outer doors to our connected suites.

So much for getting a good night's sleep, but I'm determined to make sure Greta sleeps peacefully. At least one of us should.

The clocks in the house, many of them Cuckoo clocks from before my father opened the factory and hired dozens of other artisans to help with his woodworking, chime or coo-coo or play music, alerting me that it is now midnight. I sigh and reach to shove the financials from the lawyer, that I stared at for the past hour without reading a single word, onto the nightstand. That's when I see it. A shadow, two shadows, feet, pausing outside my door as though someone listened, before moving on down the hallway.

Sliding out of bed, I run on soundless bare feet across the carpets to the nanny's room, then through the other open door to Greta's. The slow rise and fall of her breathing tells me she is asleep. I watch the band of light beneath her hallway door.

I don't have long to wait. Again, the shadows appear, but this time the doorknob turns, just enough to let the intruder realize the door is locked. I hold my breath, waiting to see what they will do. The knob turns back slowly as though they fear being heard. Then, the shadows move away.

Back to my room for a pillow and blanket, I camp out in front of the fire in Greta's room.

"What are you doing there? Did something happen?"

I wake with a start and look around, getting my bearings. Rubbing my eyes, I roll over and look at my sister. "Morning. Nothing wrong, just wanted you to feel safe it you woke to a strange room in the middle of the night. I remember how bad your nightmares used to be."

"Ew, me too. Thanks, Hans. I'm glad I haven't had one of those in a couple years."

"No reason that you should," I say as a stand and tug my blanket up around my pillow. "See you at breakfast. I'm sure Frau Lutze will be here by now. I can already taste the strudel."

Half an hour later, I smell strudel as I race down the stairs, freshly showered, and shaved. By the time I hit the first-floor foyer, I can hear Frau Lutze singing and making wonderful cooking noises in the kitchen. The oven door closes just as I stride into the room.

"Streuselkuchen, fresh from the oven, just for die Kleinen, Hans and Greta. Where is your sister?"

I catch my breath after she releases me from a bear-hug, and say, "She'll be here any minute. It's so good to see you, Frau Lutze."

"It broke my heart when they sent you angels away. But here you are, all grown up and you sound like a British citizen rather than the good strong German nobleman that you are. You are a Freiherr now, a Baron, Hans. Finally, you have come home, where you belong. Maybe now the curse will be lifted."

"What curse," says Greta, walking straight to the strudel.

"We may not be staying," I say, figuring we better be truthful with Frau Lutze, so she doesn't get her hopes up. "We've lived most of our lives in London, and we live with Aunt Gwen now."

"Your aunt should come here, to you," Frau Lutze insists. "Here, sit, eat, you are both too skinny," she says in German, grabbing Greta up into a smothering hug.

I'm not used to the rich coffee, but I pour a generous serving of cream into it and find it goes great with the breakfast strudel. The eggs and ham went equally well with the homemade bread, dripping with fresh butter and marmalade. *Frau Lutze is going to make me fat, but I'm sure not going to complain.*

"So, tell me about this curse."

"Obvious, no? First your father dies in that terrible motor crash, then just five years later, your stepmother dies in much the same way, in almost the same spot. Why they must drive those sports cars so fast on these mountainous roads, I never understand this."

She's interrupted by a knock on the door, which she hurries off to answer. I hear another female, this one sounding much younger, but arrogant and demanding. When Frau Lutze reappears, she no longer looks happy or animated. She nods toward the young woman following her and says, "This is Fräulein Anna. She was personal maid to your stepmother and now is maid for Greta."

"How do you do," we both say in German.

The woman nods to us each in turn. She smiles, but the expression never reaches her eyes and for some unknown reason, she makes me feel anxiety. Something is wrong with her eyes. They are nearly black and seem filled with hatred. I give myself a mental shake. What nonsense. I am imagining things.

"I don't really need a personal maid, but we do need to have someone help around the house. A few someone's it's so large," Greta says.

"Happy to help however I am needed."

"That's settled then," Frau Lutze says. "You know where everything is. Why don't you get started on making up the beds and cleaning the baths?"

"Of course," the newcomer says, but the look I think I see her give Frau Lutze is murderous. But why, I wonder. If she came here looking for a position as a maid, why be angry because she obtained one and is expected to perform these duties? *There is something odd about this young woman,* I tell myself.

I finish my coffee, and Greta says, "Let's go see Father's workshop."

"Sure," I say with artificial enthusiasm, for I am not sure my heart is yet ready to see my father's lifetime work laying alone and forlorn without him.

"Yes, enjoy yourselves, my little ones," Frau Lutze says, but then adds, "Just don't go into the back room. It's not safe. The tools have not yet been put away. I'll have Fritz come in and put the room to rights later this afternoon."

I nod, frown my confusion to Greta and join her as she gets up to leave the kitchen.

When we reach the entrance foyer, about to head to the other wing where Father's workroom resides, I stop. I look at the closed front door with confusion. Greta turns to question my hesitation and stops as she notes the plumes of frost from her breathing.

The ovens kept the kitchen warm, but here, so close to the front doors, it became obvious that the furnace isn't working. But wait. It isn't cold enough to freeze the fountain and it isn't cold enough to frost the windows of mother's rose greenhouse, which would have prevented us from seeing the first spring blooms.

"Why is it so cold in here, Hans?" Greta says and rubs her hands up and down her arms.

"No idea. I'll go check the furnace," I say, as I turn to walk toward the back of the stairway and the cellar door. "Wait here. I'll only be a minute. If it's not a quick easy fix, we'll have to ring someone."

I don't mention that the further I get from the front hall, the warmer it feels. *Maybe the door was left open. No, it wouldn't be cold enough to see your breath, even if it was open all night.*

The light switch works. The steep stone steps are pitted and worn. They're wide enough to feel stable. There's a handrail, which I use. It doesn't feel damp, but a definite sense of neglect and disuse is created by the clutter of cloth-draped furniture that comes into view as I near the bottom.

Nothing is changed. Except for a deeper layer of dust, I know every cranny and hiding nook among and under these cast-off items. Greta and I played here for hours.

A metallic rattle pulls my attention to the furnace at the far side of the cellar. There's no flame in the glass window of the doors across the front. The cellar has ceilings capable of housing the three-meter high monstrosity large enough to heat a manor this size. An industrial unit, it's older than me, and I hope it doesn't need extensive repair. Who knew how long it would take to replace, and the house would be colder than the crypt even with the fireplaces stoked.

I pull open the heavy iron doors and they groan in protest. One look tells me there is no fire and even the doors are cold to the touch. A lean forward into the furnace reveals little more than if I'd looked in as a child. I knew nothing about mechanical equipment, but perhaps there was a pilot to light or a switch to turn.

A hard shove reels me forward. My hands flail at the open space before me. The knuckles of my right hand slam into the metal grill and I try to grab hold to keep myself from summersaulting into the open fire box.

I hear it and cry out in alarm. The ignition, the hiss and the swoosh of the explosion. I watch hopeless as the flames rush toward my face. Then I am tumbling backward. Swift and sudden. Flat on my back, but not on the floor.

"Get off me, Hans! I can't breathe."

A quick roll and scramble lands me on my feet, shaky but alive. I run my fingers across my brittle eyebrows. "Why did you push me, Greta? I could have been killed."

"Push you? I pulled you, Hans. I heard the furnace start up and jerked as hard as I could, pulling you away from the fire. What were you doing with your head in there anyway? You were almost cremated."

I give her a quick side-hug and say, "Thanks, little sister. You saved my life." *If not Greta, who?* "Did you see anyone? Anyone run past you on the stairs?"

"No one. Why? Oh! Your hand." She reaches for my wrist and pulls my hand closer. "You're bleeding all over the place. Is it burned?"

"What?" I lift my hand and remember the punch against the grid. A nasty wound, ragged and wide, runs across the top of my knuckles. The cut on my middle finger looks deep. Blood flows down my hand and drips on the floor. I cup it with my left hand. "No, cut."

"We need to clean this up and take a better look before you get an infection. You might need stitches," Greta says, reaching to slam the furnace door shut.

I shove the one on the right closed, twist the handle to lock them in place and let her lead me toward the stairs.

Something white flitters behind a stack of chairs. I fly after it. The chairs teeter and collapse behind me. Around another cloth-draped pile, under a tarp and shoving and pushing my way through stacks of tables and bookcases, I reach out to grab hold of the fleeing figure, a woman, black hair pulled into a ponytail.

She dodges to the right, slams into Greta and bolts for the stairs.

I stop just long enough to help my sister stand, make sure she's okay, then sprint after the would-be assassin. Adrenaline gives me speed I've never known before. Who wants to kill me? Why? I wonder. I open the door at the top of the stairs and run full-out toward the foyer where I'm sure the culprit headed.

The front doors stand open, so I run through them into the car park.

Nothing. A quick spin. Still nothing. No one could have disappeared that quickly. I run back inside. Greta shakes her head.

I lost her. What now?

"Come to the kitchen. Let's take a look at that. We need to call the police, too."

I shut the front door and throw the bolts. My heartbeat slows, and I head to the kitchen. Frau Lutze will have a fit.

The *Stadtpolizei* finish questioning the staff, which numbers eight now that the gardeners, driver and housekeeper are back. Two maids and a cooking apprentice for Frau Lutze round out the nervous group of locals. The police know them all by name and their questions seem routine. They search the grounds and find nothing. They search the house and find the same.

They leave.

"What now?" I say softly.

Let's start by you telling me the truth," Greta says.

I sip my coffee and study her frown. She's not going to relent. My intent is always to keep her safe, but my sister has a hot-wired intuition and knows both when I'm fudging my answers to shelter her and outright lying.

She raises her eyebrow but remains silent as she waits.

"Do you know, I just realized Gretchen's maid wasn't here for questioning. Frau Lutze," I call out, so she can hear me in the pantry, "Do you know where Fräulein Anna was during the police interrogation?"

The plump woman exits the pantry, her arms full of flour and other ingredients for a baking frenzy. "Ja, she is in town getting me poppy seeds and a few other items I needed. Is there a problem?"

"Fräulein Anna wasn't here to speak to the police. How long has she been gone?"

"An hour and a half, no more."

Just then, Fräulein Anna bursts into the kitchen, her arms laden with groceries. She's followed by Fritz, the local handyman and Frau Lutze's husband. He sets a bundle on the counter and says, "I fixed the broken fence in the back as you asked."

"Ja? Good then. Have some strudel and a cup of coffee to warm you," Frau Lutze says.

I notice that Anna's blue-black hair, so like that of the assailant is in a neat bun at the back of her neck and her uniform is black under her tan coat.

She glances toward me and says, "Good morning, Baron. I saw the police leaving as I drove up. Is anything wrong?"

Not interested in explaining, I shake my head and look at Greta. "You ready to finish what we started?"

"Are you up to it?"

"Let's go."

Father's workshop is much as we remember, except that it's clean. Missing are the curls of wood piled near his workbench and the sawdust around his table saw. We smell it though. The faint cow manure scent of the walnut is made earthy and appealing by the grassy, flowery scent of the linden wood. Both are douched with a more petroleum-based scent of the finishing oil Father always used to rub the wood to a lustrous sheen. To my senses, it smells like home. I feel that any moment he's going to walk in from the storage room, and say, "Mind you keep away from the saw, meine Kinder."

I join Greta, who stands next to a grandfather clock case Father created, but never finished. Her finger trails the vines and leaves that frame the prominent stag, lifelike in its every detail. The forest scenes are unique and intricate, a custom order from the master himself. I will need to visit the factories, the clockworks, the woodworks and the porcelain factory our stepmother purchased when it became available a few years ago, to accommodate the figure-topped clocks.

Greta will be a huge asset with her eye for detail, beauty, and organization, her kind and honest nature which affords her splendid people skills, but I know the financial end of the businesses will fall to me. I was the logic first, mathematician at prep school, after which I considered a career as a barrister, or was, before all this. *All this. What is this, exactly? Whatever it is, it is changing our lives forever. Again.*

I swipe the tear trickling down my sister's cheek with my finger and say, "Let's get to that storage room we're supposed to avoid."

She sniffs, then laughs at me, her unconventional brother, and grabs my hand, tugging me across the room toward the sliding barn-like door of the huge storage room that houses my father's wood and finishing supplies, along with his completed projects awaiting delivery.

There's a huge garage door at the back that opens to a ramp where deliveries and pickups are made, out of sight behind the house. He didn't need to accept orders financially but had done so to the end out of love for his craft. The house is bulging with his handiwork, most priceless to us. And now they are ours and we no longer have to worry about our stepmother selling them at auction.

We walk into the enormous room that runs half the length at the back of the first floor, past the storage bins and shelves of containers and then stop when we come to the finished pieces. For the most part the storage area here is empty, deliveries having been made of the pieces my father completed before his death.

"What's this?" Greta says, and drops my hand to run to the back where shelves line the wall. She tugs at a tarp of plastic and it slides to the floor.

I hurry behind her and stare as she stares at a row of marionettes, standing, their crutches slipped into a notched board above them. It's as if they were just completed and placed here. The carving of their faces is so realistic, the painting so natural, I feel their moveable eyeballs are tilted a bit as I gain their attention and they stare back at me. The fine hairs at the nap of my neck lift, as does my heartrate.

Greta, whose stringed puppet has slept with her since she was four, its crutch tucked into the little slot in its back Father created to keep the removeable strings out of the way when not in use, says reverently, "Oh, how beautiful. I wonder who *Vati* made them for?"

"No idea, but why wouldn't they have requested delivery? After his death, these would have been even more valuable. Father never made puppets for anyone other than the children of friends and, well, yours, and those soldiers he made for me are like puppets, though they've no strings and their bodies are wood, not fabric."

"You're right. They were more a hobby than a business item. He always said they were only made with special purposes for special children because they were magic."

I forgot that. Father insisted that when he carved a human-like figure from the wood of the Black Forest, it had magical powers. It would protect and cheer its owner for their entire lives. I smile and remember how sober Greta was when Father gave her the marionette, telling her it was a jester like the ones who entertained kings and queens. She was his little princess, so it was fitting and would always entertain her and keep her happy, but that it would also always protect her if ever Father wasn't around. Neither of us knew at the time what Father already did, that he would never be around because they were sending us away as soon as we were old enough for the school to accept us.

I push the melancholy thoughts aside and study the figures before me. A woodcutter with an axe, a field worker, complete with pitchfork, a baker with a rolling pin, a hunter with a rifle, a barmaid with a stein, and a seamstress, I suppose, as she has a giant needle in one hand and a swatch of fabric in the other. "What an odd assortment," I observe.

"That's what I was thinking. Perhaps there were more, and these ones weren't chosen?"

"Yes, they're eerily beautiful, but they don't seem the regular sort of characters one uses for a marionette show, and I doubt most folks would special order these for children."

"For children?" Greta says, laughing. "They have weapons in their hands, and they're not attached like your soldiers'. They move. That axe almost looks like it's been sharpened."

I laugh and reach for the tarp. "Here, help me cover them back up. I'm sure we'll find out about them once we go over Father's books."

"So, what do you think was in here that made Frau Lutze tell us to stay away?"

"No idea, but by now perhaps Fritz cleaned up whatever was broken or spilled or whatever. Let's get going, I want to go into town and speak with a private investigator I spoke to earlier. Have you phoned Aunt Gwen?"

"What?" She spins around and hands on hips says, "You called a private investigator and didn't even tell me? What for? Why do we need one?"

"Because the police struck me as incompetent, and I want to hire some bodyguards until the would-be murderer is found. I also want to find out why anyone would wish us harm, now that Gretchen is dead."

"I still don't understand why she hated us. I always tried to be very good whenever we were in her presence, and to always follow all her rules. The only thing we ever did that was naughty is play hide-and-seek in the attics and cellars, but that was so we wouldn't run into her or disturb her with our laughing and running."

"I don't think it had anything to do with us, Sis."

"Do you really think we need bodyguards?"

"Maybe not, but you'd feel safer, wouldn't you? The alternative is to send you back to Aunt Gwen until this is over."

"You can't make me go back to London and leave you here alone. If not for me, you'd be a pile of ashes right now!" she snapped.

I already knew she wouldn't return to London alone, which is why I'd called the investigator.

"And the businesses. Do you know if there are any problems there?"

"I've been over the financials and they're all doing very well. My father monitored them carefully and made an appearance at each of the factories several times a week. He trusted his managers explicitly, according to his solicitor. When he died, my stepmother, who loved money far more than stepchildren, stepped in and even added to the family fortune."

"We'll do some preliminary checking there then but won't spend the bulk of our manpower in that direction. You say your stepmother wasn't fond of children, or of you in particular?"

"To be honest, we thought she hated us, though there were never any confrontations and she always smiled and said the right things in our father's presence, which is the only time she spoke to us at all."

"She conveyed her rather numerous rules to us via our nanny," Greta adds.

"They were gone a lot. Father worked all day and she attended charity meetings or shopped for all the parties and galas they attended."

"I overheard them arguing about us, and soon after our fifth birthday we were shipped off to England."

I study Greta's face. She spoke as though merely conveying facts, as if she hadn't come running into my room, sobbing and hugging me, sputtering that Gretchen hated us and wanted us gone. The mean lady told Father that we were ruining her life and if he didn't send us off for a good education, so we weren't such heathens, she would leave him because she didn't want people saying she was a bad influence on our manners and deportment. Neither of us knew what deportment meant at the time, but we soon learned what it was to be deported. Father's clocks, thus treated, received better care and appreciation than we had.

I sigh, deep, and resigned. We must only move forward. No looking back.

"So, your father didn't want you to go, but your stepmother convinced him to send you away to boarding school?" Mr. Heinrich asks. Greta nods and he says, "How were things when you came home for holidays?"

"We never did," I supply. "Our Aunt Gwen, mother's twin sister and a widow, moved to London to be near us and we spent our holidays with her there."

He's quick to mask the surprise on his white-whiskered face, pushes his spectacles up his nose and says, "Did you ever see your Father or stepmother again?"

"We saw Father, perhaps seven or eight times before he died, when he managed to sneak away from a business trip, but we never saw our stepmother again."

"Ten, we saw him exactly ten times," Greta says, a faraway look in her eyes, and I know she's remembering the last tearful time she kissed our father goodbye, just before we turned fifteen. She begged him to take her home, promising to be good and assuring him she had the very best of deportment now. He told her he couldn't, she was safer where she was. My heart broke for her then as now. Hard as it is, it seems easier than acknowledging my own heartache.

"There seems to be an issue with the stepmother. We'll focus there. I think I have enough to go on for now." The door opens, and he stands. "Ah, good. Your bodyguards have arrived."

* * * *

"Where have you been, Fräulein Anna? It doesn't take that long to fetch the supplies. I ordered ahead and they were ready and waiting for you," Frau Lutze said with authority.

"It snowed last night, and the roads were difficult," the young woman replied with a defiant shake of her head.

"No need to take that attitude with me. The Baroness isn't here to protect you anymore. I don't know why she kept you on, but I'm assuming you had something on her. You never did anything and were constantly surly, even to her, so what other reason could she have? I'm not sure why the solicitor hired you, other than your name was on the list of previous employees. Know this, if you don't do your duties with a better attitude from now on, you will be looking for other employment. I have already spoken to the housekeeper, Frau Schmidt, and we are in full agreement."

The young woman lowered her head and nodded. "Ja, forgive me, Frau Lutze. I will do better."

* * * *

"I'm so exhausted, Hans."

"It's been an eventful day. Add that to Frau Lutze's wonderful cooking and it's amazing that I can keep my eyes open. A hot shower and bed for me. Do you need anything?"

"No, just sleep," she says, hugs me and heads down the hall to her bed chamber, bodyguard in tow. It had taken a bit of arm pulling for that one. I'm going to sleep much better tonight, though, with security on all three floors, three walking the grounds and each of us with our own bodyguard.

"Hans!"

I turn away from my door and race to Greta's room.

Nothing seems wrong, just Greta and her bodyguard standing next to the bed. "What is it?"

"He's gone! Mr. Jangles is gone!"

"Where did you leave him?"

"He was right there," Greta says and jabs a finger toward her bed.

"Calm down. One of the maids probably just put him away. Have you looked for him?" I ask and bend down to shove my head under the bed, empty space except for Greta's fluffy slippers.

Greta and the bodyguards, mine having followed me, begin searching the room, opening drawers, searching the closets, the bathing chamber. Nothing.

Hands clasped, Greta addresses her bodyguard, "Please ask the housekeeper to question the staff."

I know better than to suggest she wait for morning. Instead I help her toss the nanny's old room, for now to be used by our burly, former military bodyguards, and then mine.

By then the staff has been assembled and tasked with searching the entire house. Greta, a grown but sorely neglected child, was given that puppet by a father who promised it would keep her safe. She will not sleep without it.

I consider and discard the idea of asking the staff for a sleeping pill. Last resort. "How about the workshop, Greta? Want to help me look there? Maybe someone thought it belonged there, with the others." *Or maybe it scared someone on the staff as puppets often do, and they put it under tarp with the rest of them, and don't want to admit it.*

We head straight for the storage room, Greta often having the same idea I do. It might be a twin thing, but our intuitions are deadly accurate. This time I pull the tarp, and suck in my breath.

Greta's Mr. Jangles is there all right. Only all the marionettes are just puppets, their crutches having been tucked away, strings removed. Just like Mr. Jangles now, they are independent entities.

"Mr. Jangles!" she cries, reaching up to pull him down and crush him to her chest in a warm embrace.

There's something else, too. They're out of order. And they're not just sitting leaned against the back wall. They are sitting up in a semi-circle, as if they've been having a conversation. It's a foolish thought, I know, but I can't shake it. Their moveable eyes, no matter how they are sitting, seem focused on Greta, and their expressions seem pleased. For this, at least I am happy. Better to have them for us than against us. I shake my head. More tired than I'd thought, obviously.

"Come on, Greta. I'm glad you found your bud, now let's tell the staff they can go to bed, and let's join them in getting some well-deserved rest."

It was the scream that woke me. Woke everyone.

I run into the hall and nearly collide with my bodyguard, and Greta's comes running out of her room, having sought his client's wellbeing.

"What is it?" my bodyguard, Mr. Withers, yells down to the security guard in the foyer, guarding admission to the stairwell, and us.

"Not sure yet. Scream came from the kitchen."

I look at my watch. 6 am, only Frau Lutze and her apprentice would be up this early.

Greta hurries to my side, still dressed in her pajamas too, though she's taken the time to don a robe. "What now?" she whispers.

I put my arm around her. "Not sure yet, Sis."

Another security guard joins the one at the base of the stairs, says something too soft for us to hear, and they both start up.

This isn't going to be good, I think, and instinct makes me draw Greta closer as though I can protect her from even bad news.

They reach the landing and the taller one says, "I'm sorry to have to tell you this, but Frau Lutze has been murdered."

Greta cries out, fists her hands and smothers a sob against them.

"I'm sorry," he repeats. "The police have been called. The husband, Fritz, seems inconsolable, do you know of anyone we might call for him?"

"Who found her?" I ask, hoping it wasn't Fritz.

"Her assistant, a young girl by the name of Johanna, I believe, Freiherren."

"Oh, I must go to them. Who could have done such a terrible thing, Hans?" Greta says.

"I can't imagine. I thought someone was after me, but who would possibly have a motive for killing such a kindly old woman?"

Greta shakes her head and hurries back to her room to dress. I do the same, considering how I might get her from a car ride to a train and then to a plane, all against her will.

Their son arrives at last from a nearby town and bundles Fritz off to the Inn, away from the crime scene the police have finally vacated. I thrust a cup of coffee into Greta's hand and note the circles beneath her eyes.

 The phone rings. I'm standing beside it, so I answer. It's the head investigator, Mr. Heinrich. He says he's found something, and wanting a change of scenery, I agree to meet him in his office, where it's more private.

Greta insists on coming. I don't want her in the house until the staff has finished cleaning the blood that spilled from the butcher knife in Frau Lutze's back all over the white kitchen tiles, so I let her, without argument.

* * * *

We walk into the kitchen and Johanna says, "I'm sorry dinner's not ready. They were busy cleaning, but I'll get at it right away."

"Nonsense," I say. "We ordered enough dinner for everyone from a restaurant in town that caters, and it will be delivered shortly. We've also called an agency to send over some candidates for the housekeeper to start interviewing. We'll have a new cook before you know it, Johanna. You've been through enough for one day." We all had.

"Thank you, Freiherren," she says, then curtsies and disappears down the hallway to the servants' quarters.

The bodyguards wander into the hall to discuss how things went with the security team, and Greta joins me at the kitchen table. The formal dining room is elegant but stuffy, and we grew up here, in the kitchen. We feel comfortable here.

"Coffee?"

"You really like that now, don't you? Is the kettle hot?"

I flip the spout cover and steam rises. "Yes, and yes. I'll get you a cup of tea. Cream and sugar?"

"Heaven."

I slip a bag into a cup of hot water, snag a cup of coffee from the pot on the counter and set them on the table before reaching into the refrigerator for the little container of cream. The sugar's already on the table, so I add a dollop to my coffee and set the cream in front of Greta, joining her at the table.

"Where do you think the girl is hiding?"

"She'd be a woman by now. Who knows? Must be nearby. Heinrich said he'll have a picture by tomorrow, from that guy who has a computer program that updates how people look as they age. Maybe we'll recognize her."

"I don't see how, but maybe one of the staff will recognize her from town or something."

The housekeeper walks in and freezes. "Oh, sorry. I didn't realize you were back. I was going to help Johanna with dinner."

"That's very kind of you," Greta says, "but my brother ordered dinner for us all from the restaurant in town. It should be—" she turns her head as the back-doorbell sounds. "That would be them now. We'll go get freshened up."

I take my half-full cup of coffee with me. Recent events have made me grateful for the newfound pick-me-up. It feels smoother than tea, and the caffeine packs a much more powerful zing.

As I approach my nursery-attached bed chamber, it occurs to me that I no longer need to sleep in the nursery on the third floor. Neither of us do. I spin on my heels, apologize for nearly colliding with my bodyguard, and head back down to the second floor. Gretchen, liar that she was, and her possibly murderous daughter have no business here, but Greta and I do.

I pull open the door to the suite that was once my mother's, more recently Gretchen's, and stride into the room as though I own it, because I do. The investigator revealed something the solicitor felt unnecessary to mention, and that is that our father's will contains a codicil, apparently the reason Gretchen didn't mind signing. If anything happens to Greta and me, the estate passes to Gretchen's heirs. At first I thought that was to cut out Aunt Gwen, but the investigator provided us with the truth. Gretchen had a bastard daughter, one she kept hidden, apparently her entire life.

"No wonder you didn't want us around, Gretchen," I say to the empty room. "Two little children running through the house would eventually bump into a little girl who didn't belong to anyone and would have asked questions about her identity. You couldn't chance that!"

The room is chill, with dark green velvet drapes that hang heavy over the floor to ceiling windows. They match the bed-curtains tied back with gold-tasseled ropes around the massive canopy bed, thick with elaborate carvings whose lifelike mastery proclaim themselves my father's handiwork. He made the bed for my mother, though the gauzy white bedcurtains she chose flirted with rather than overpowering the craftmanship.

The beautiful rugs are still here, warm and cushy underfoot. I glance around once more, intending to head toward the sitting room that separates this suite from my father's, when something catches my attention.

A puppet.

Sitting against the headboard, watching me, is a large puppet that looks disturbingly like my stepmother, Gretchen.

"What the hell," I whisper.

The door flies open, Greta says, "What are you doing?" and I yelp, fly into the air half a meter, land and pivot to face her.

"What the hell are you doing?" I screech.

Greta laughs, amused she startled me.

Until I point to the bed and she sees Gretchen wannabe.

"No," she whispers softly. "Just no."

She marches to the bed, grabs the puppet, fast-walks to the closet, tosses the doll inside and slams the door shut. "Let's go eat," she says, turning to exit.

I hurry to catch up. *The rooms will have to be cleaned and emptied before we can switch,* I tell myself.

"Hans, are you awake?"

"I am now that you've awakened me."

"He's gone again."

"Mr. Jangles? Was he there when you went to bed?" She nods affirmatively, and I sit up, awake enough to realize the implication of that. Someone was in her bed chamber while we slept.

"The bodyguards too, both of them. Gone."

"What?" I jump from bed, and into my slippers, grab my robe and motion her behind me as I enter the hall.

The lights are on in the foyer. I look over the banister and spot our bodyguards, along with one of the security guys, laying on the cold parquet floor. "Stay here," I whisper, and head down the stairs, wishing I'd gotten the gun from the bottom drawer of my father's office desk. The security team is armed, so I didn't feel a need. Until now.

Having of course ignored me, Greta bumps into me when I stop at the bottom of the stairs to reach down and check for a pulse. Alive. I move to the next guard, and then the security guy. All alive. One of them snorts out a snore and I realize they're asleep, probably drugged. I look at my watch and remember it's on the nightstand.

The clocks announce the time in an explosion of chirps, chimes, dongs and music. I count. Midnight. Of course.

"Are they dead?" Greta whispers.

I shake her bodyguard. Hard. Harder. He doesn't react.

"No, dear, sleeping. I think they've been drugged. That means someone is in here with us. Please try to stay close and do as I say from now on."

"Drugged? Was it poison?"

"I don't think poison makes you snore. So no, just put to sleep to get them out of the way."

"So they can get to us. It must be her daughter, here in the house with us," Greta articulates my thoughts and grabs my hand, a habit from childhood, whenever she's scared. It reassures me.

"We need to get to Father's study."

"His gun. Good idea."

"What was that?" A tap. A jingle.

She stops talking and listens, then turns to follow my line of attention. "Mr. Jangles?"

She says what I don't dare. Can't. My heart's in my throat.

Mr. Jangles isn't smiling. He is walking though, his movements rather stiff and robotic, but each hinged joint bending and moving with the sequential precision of a master clockwork. He walks to the cellar door with surprising speed, his footfalls creating the soft tap-taping sound that first caught my attention. The solemn jester turns to look at us and holds his finger against his lips for us to be quiet, then opens the door and disappears down the stairway.

"Oh my god, what's going on, Hans? It's true isn't it? Daddy told me Mr. Jangles would always protect me and it's true."

"I-I, yes, that must be it," I say in a rush, willing my knees to unlock. *Is this why Father sent us away? Was he protecting us?* I head toward the cellar. The time for hiding has passed. No sense telling Greta not to follow her knight in jester's clothing either.

We get almost to the bottom of the stairs, having seen nothing, even Mr. Jangles, from over the railing, when the lights go out. *Naturally.*

Greta squeals and I feel her raise the hand not breaking my fingers to clamp it over her mouth.

The furnace rages and provides dim but adequate visibility. I use my free hand on the guardrail and edge downward until I'm on the cellar floor, Greta too. I squint against the oppressive darkness, but only see shadows of clumped furniture. Then I hear something. Greta squeezes my hand. She hears it too. I nod, remember she can't see me, and squeeze her hand back.

Little click-clacks sound from somewhere behind the stacks of cloaked furniture. I frown as I try to figure out the source. The sounds are faint but discordant, as though not originating from the same source. The noises get closer together, faster somehow. Then they stop.

I inch forward. Greta inches forward. Again. Again. Once more. There's an aisle down the center of the stacks. It goes all the way to the shelves on the far wall. I need to see if there's anyone, or anything, there.

Mr. Jangles came down here for a reason, and I feel certain that we need to know what it is if we are to survive. The desperate sense of determination increases when we reach the aisle and find it empty.

More clatter. This time I squeeze Greta's hand. She squeezes back. The sound is uniform in pattern. Click-clack, click-clack, click-clack. It's like hearing little echoes of the same sound, over and over. Then there's a soft patterned squeak, like something needs to be oiled, something that's rolling. Somewhere in the back of my mind is this nagging feeling that I recognize the sounds. Know them. Should remember them.

I hear a jingle. A shadow darts across the aisle. Then another. About the size and shape of Mr. Jangles chasing . . . dear god, no. Not that.

We squeeze hands simultaneously.

I rush forward, with a plan to intercept who or whatever ran behind the stacks, thinking they will probably chase each other up this far side, just past the furnace. I can see better here, so I dart around the corner.

Something flies at my face and bashes me. I fall to one knee, wobbling. Greta screams, and I feel her kneel behind me, holding me up. I try to shake my head, to clear my vision, to stop the spinning.

I hear a groan. Realize it's mine. Fade to black.

Tug, tug. Someone is tugging at my arm. "Get up! Get up now and save Greta!"

I don't' recognize the voice. Greta? In danger? My head hurts.

"They're going to kill Greta!"

That wakes me. Memory returns in a rush. I stumble to my feet, look down at Mr. Jangles and emerge from behind the stacks.

Greta is fighting with someone. Even in the dimness of the cellar and the pounding of my head I can see they struggle for possession of a large kitchen knife that gleams each time the firelight hits it. Grunting and gasping with their efforts the women focus on survival, spinning and twisting back and forth.

I wonder why the furnace doors are open but focus on helping Greta. I reach out to grab the dark-haired woman's hair, to distract her, to pull her away, and help Greta overpower her.

"Aaagh!" I reach down and clasp my injured calf. Something stabs through the bandages into my already injured hand, and I scream in pain, but preservation makes me twist around to see what I feared. Gretchen, or rather the Gretchen puppet.

"Why wouldn't you just die when you fell out of that window?" she snarls.

She paid someone to push him out that second-story window when he was a boy? If not for the heavy shrubs underneath, he might have been more injured than just a broken arm.

Pulling the knife out of my hand, she drew back her arm to shove it into another location but was punched in the face with the jester's scepter, knocking her across the floor.

"Help Greta," I yell at Mr. Jangles, and limp toward Gretchen.

"Get her! Get her!" Gretchen screeches.

I hear them coming toward me, Mr. Jangles beating the dark-haired woman with his scepter. But she's human, and tall, and he's just hitting her legs.

"Her knees!" I grab Gretchen just before she manages to retrieve the knife she dropped during her flight, pinning her arms against her torso.

A shriek sounds. Mr. Jangles is zeroed in on the woman's knees. They spin and she crashes against me. I manage to hold onto the puppet, despite its thrashing.

Until it sinks spiked teeth into my injured hand. I shake it, pry it, anything to get its teeth out of my flesh.

"Hahahaha," it gurgles past my blood. "You can't win. Give up." It made a mistake. Opened its mouth to gloat. It turns its head down to reattach itself, but I throw it like a home run out, straight into the fires of the furnace.

The woman pulls her hand free, the knife flashes downward, into Greta's arm, and she spins toward me.

"Anna!" I shout in surprise.

She stabs me and lunges for the furnace, grabs hold of the door. I clasp my hand to my stomach to slow the bleed. An earsplitting wail erupts from the furnace. Anna reaches out to save Gretchen from the flames. A roar sounds, then another and another. Something whizzes past me and into the back of Anna's neck.

The uniform click-clacks run past. My soldiers run past. They jab their bayonets into Anna's calves. She clutches the cannon ball holes at the base of her neck. Her knees buckle in their failed attempt to hold her up despite the pain in her calves.

I see it coming, and reach out to stop them, unable to speak from the shock.

Too late. Mr. Jangles and his odd crew of comrades jump up and shove, bludgeon, pierce, stab, fork, and axe Anna from behind. She tumbles into the furnace, and Mr. Jangles pushes the doors shut, twisting them into a locked position.

A melting face accompanies the anguished cries for help. Then, it falls ack, and disappears along with the screams.

"Hans?" It's Greta. She presses her hand against the wound in my stomach.

"Are you down here?" I hear called from the stairwell before beams from a half-dozen torches dart about the room.

My ears buzz, the sound drowning out all others. I note Mr. Jangles and crew, lying silent beside the furnace. My soldiers are lined up next to him, in rigid formation.

Inanimate.

Just toys, carved wood cut with love from the Black Forest.

About the Author

Elizabeth Alsobrooks

Since retiring from her "day" jobs, Elizabeth lives with her personal social media editor, Hudson (AKA Maltese), and husband, Kenton, (AKA Irish-Scotsman) at the foot of the beautiful Santa Catalina Mountain Range in AZ. She loves to sit on her patio sipping coffee (or wine) and reading or brainstorming plots and enjoys the grandeur of her mountain views.

These days, she divides her writing time between urban fantasy, horror, and nonfiction. Work on her Illuminati series continues, but she loves throwing out a horror short on occasion. She grew up with a love for Shakespeare, Chaucer, Poe, Dickens, the Bronte sisters and Koontz, so her taste is as eclectic as her range. That creative range reaches to art and sculpting, as well as learning to play the piano, now that she has time to pursue more interests she always loved.

When Pumpkins Go Bad

by

Janet Post

When Pumpkins Go Bad

by

Janet Post

Mary Ann McGinty stretched and shoved the wooden slat over her head out of the way. It knocked dirt everywhere. When she sat up, she finished pushing the top of her ancient coffin to the side. Dirt fell into her face and she brushed it off. It seemed she'd been asleep forever. Her bones creaked. She was in her coffin in the middle of a large green grassy space. The grass was cut short and strangely smooth. The hole she was in was right in the middle of this space, and there was a flag sticking up out of the center of the kidney-shaped area with the number sixteen on it.

"This be well and truly strange," Mary Ann said as she rose out of the coffin and glanced at the sky. It was blue and there was a bite to the air. Late autumn, close to Samhain, she speculated. The dead would soon be walking. She reached out her hand and pointed at the ground. It must be fertile. Mary Ann remembered she'd been a midwife and she'd had the best pumpkin patch in all of Salem before they'd hung her on Leach's Hill for being a witch. Which she was, but only part time. She should never have cursed Henrietta Shapp's garden. She giggled. Henceforth, the old bag could only grow pumpkins.

When Mary Ann pointed her finger at the ground, pumpkin vines sprouted and began growing. She mumbled a spell under her breath. "Pumpkins rise, pumpkins grow, from now until doomsday only pumpkins will thou know." That had been the curse she'd died for. Yawning hugely, Mary Ann lay down in her grave and pulled the coffin lid closed. Time to go back to sleep. Her work was done.

* * * *

I really hate Halloween. Aside from the fact school is closed, Halloween In Danvers Massachusetts is a nightmare. See, Danvers is really old Salem Village. Salem itself is on the east side of town. On Halloween, weirdos from all over the freaking world converged on Salem and Danvers for strange and bizarre rituals that had zero base in reality.

As I listened to Mrs. Crookshank go on and on in a rapt voice about all the events taking place tomorrow in a location my friends and I wish we could avoid, I glanced over at my best friend, Calvin Johnson. He is staring with his usual intensity at Mary Ann McGinty, a girl so beautiful every boy in Beverly High School stared at her. I wondered as usual why some people are blessed with luxurious red hair, milk-white skin, eyes the color of the summer sky, and a tall willowy figure, while some, like me, not so much. I mean, I was all right, I did my best with thin brown hair, big brown eyes, a flat chest, unlike Mary Ann's blossoming mounds, and a small body. Yes, I was short.

I glanced at the clock. Ten more minutes and we could escape to our various homes where Halloween would arrive, and as usual, we would dress in costumes, go to the annual party at the Johnson's apartment across the street from ours, and then go watch the fireworks in Salem. It was a tradition I loathed.

When the bell rang, Cal waited for me. His eyes were still glued to the perfection of Mary Ann's derriere as she walked out of class with the quarterback of the Panthers, our football team. His name was Lee Folly, known as the L-Train, and he lived on Folly Hill Farm. Everyone knew Folly Hill Farm. It was on a hill, Leach's Hill in the sixteen hundreds. We'd all heard the story a million times. That's what living in Danvers did to you. History was fed to you with your pablum. I planned to leave Massachusetts and go to college in California the minute I graduated. USC had already accepted me. I wasn't a genius, but my grades were great, and I played the clarinet in the marching band. If you're good at any instrument in a marching band, getting into college was a cinch.

"Joe," Cal said as he bumped his meaty shoulder into me. Calvin was pretty heavy. He was also in the marching band. He played the tuba. Both of us were labeled band dorks. I'd carried that label since middle school and no longer cared. I mean, if you play in the band, own it. That was my opinion.

"What Joe?"

My name is Jolean Crenshaw, but everyone, and I mean everyone, even my grandmother, called me Joe.

"I think she looked at me."

I rolled my eyes. "Cal, if she did it was because you were blocking her view of the L."

"You think?"

I shook my head. He was a sad case. "I know."

We caught the bus outside and rolled to our houses. We both lived in Apple Village Apartments. My unit was on the edge of thick woods that ended at the Beverly Hills Country Club, a huge eighteen-hole golf course. Cal lived across Manor Road on the other side of the complex. The bus dumped us all out on Trask Road and we walked. I noticed some weird vines in the woods. "Look, Cal, are they pumpkins?"

"Who would plant pumpkins in the woods around here? It's stupid."

I walked over to get a closer look. It was pumpkin spice everything season. I kind of liked pumpkin pie, but pumpkin spice should never be included in donuts, coffee or cupcakes. Sure enough, the vines were everywhere in the woods. "Doesn't this chunk of woods cross all the way to the golf course? Maybe some golfer cleaned a pumpkin and tossed the seeds in the woods."

Calvin stared into the dense oaks and underbrush. "That's a lot of pumpkins for a handful of seeds."

He was right. The vines were everywhere and seemed to be spreading as we spoke. "Do they look like they're growing to you?"

Cal glanced at his foot where a vine had thrown a feeler and was quickly covering his huge, flat sneaker-covered foot. "Holy shit. It's gonna eat me."

A flower sprouted on top of his sneaker, rapidly morphed into a budding fruit which turned orange and swelled. "This is not right," I said backing onto the asphalt.

"No kidding. We need to tell someone."

We ran home, me to my apartment, Cal to his. I went out on the balcony and stared into the woods. I thought I saw movement and sure enough, a tendril crept out of the forest and began growing in the direction of the Murphey's apartment on the bottom floor. I pulled out my phone and called my mother. She was divorced from my deadbeat dad and managed a car dealership in Salem. "Mom, pumpkins are growing out of the woods."

Probably not the cleverest thing I'd ever said.

Mom laughed. "Joe, you have the funniest sense of humor."

"I'm not joking. There's a pumpkin on Mrs. Murphey's railing."

Mom laughed some more. "You are such a jokester. Though I did wonder why my coffee this morning was pumpkin spice when I clearly ordered my usual, half-caf, soy latte with a squirt of caramel." She laughed again. "The pumpkins must be taking over."

I glanced out the window at the woods, and saw the vines were now climbing the trees. I took a quick picture and zapped it to her. "Check your inbox. I sent a picture."

A few seconds later she said. "If that's our woods, I better call the golf course. This has to be due to some weird fertilizer they're using on the greens. I keep calling and complaining the crap is going to get into our water."

"Better hurry," I said and clicked off.

The next person I called was Cal. He answered but I could hear him playing the tuba in the background. I had to scream over the noise. "Talk to me!"

So, he picked up his phone. "I gotta practice, Joe," he said. "Big game this Friday and I have to learn the new song."

I rolled my eyes. I had to learn it too and on a clarinet. All he had to do was learn oompa noises. How hard could it be? "The pumpkin thing is worse than I thought. Did you try your lunch?" Now Cal was big-boned as his mother loved to say because she was big-boned, too. He was actually pretty over-weight, so I knew he'd eaten his lunch. "What'd it taste like?"

He paused. "You know, it was weird. Everything was like pumpkin flavored, even the spaghetti, the bread and the green beans, though I didn't eat them, well maybe I nibbled, I hate green beans."

"Mom's coffee was pumpkin spice. She never drinks anything but a soy latte with caramel."

I could hear the noise of the fridge in Cal's apartment opening. He screamed. "There's nothing in here but pumpkins."

"I'll be right over," I said. "We have to go to the golf course. Mom thinks it's the fertilizer they use on the greens."

I jumped in my Corolla. My own car was one of the only perks Mom received for managing Trellawny's Cadillac Dealership. And she'd only got that because Marlena Johnson, Calvin's mom, was her lead saleswoman. Marlena took the Corolla in on a trade deal and called Mom right away because she knew we could get it for practically nothing. It was a good little car and I was glad to have it. I rarely drove it to school because next year it was going to take me all the way to SoCal where I was going to live forever. I was babying it. When Cal climbed in, I winced. The springs on that side would have to be replaced before I left. If Mom could afford it.

"Use the County Way Extension road," Cal said. "The other way around takes forever, and I need to get back to my tuba."

The Extension Road cut through the woods, met up with Elliot and you could get right around the course that way to the clubhouse. I spotted the vines as soon as I got into the woods. They filled the road and were a moving mass. Calvin stared. "Holy shit, Joe. Would you look at that?"

The vines were growing in our direction. I put the car in reverse and looked behind me. "They're trying to cut us off," I said in the calmest voice I could muster.

"Put the pedal to the metal!" Calvin screamed as one of the vines climbed his side of the car and tried to poke in through the window.

I stomped on it and the car shot backwards. It ran over a huge pumpkin. The gigantic orange globe smacked into the bumper and exploded. Orange, slimy goop, seeds and pieces of pumpkin slapped into the rear window. I couldn't see a thing. "I risked rolling the window down, peeked out and got whacked in the face with a vicious vine. It already had flowers and baby pumpkins. One of the pumpkins hit me in the forehead. I ignored the pain and accelerated. We shot out of the Extension into the apartment complex. Both of us were gasping and panting.

"I thought we were goners," Calvin said.

"We almost were. I think those vines were trying to kill us."

I turned the car around and drove to the golf course. We got out and I examined my car. Pumpkin crud had dried on the back window. I scraped at it with a nail. "This is going to take scrubbing."

"Stop worrying about your precious car" Calvin said. "We need to find the greenskeeper. He'll know about any fertilizer."

I walked to the putting green and stared out over the course. I thought I saw movement on the far side. It was hard to tell from this distance. Howard Berndock, a fellow senior from Beverly, walked over to us. He caddied here evenings and weekends and sometimes worked on the course to help put money in his college fund. He wanted out of Danvers as much as I did. You had to understand. Right now, this very minute, every hotel room and boardinghouse room, every bed and breakfast, was filled to overflowing with the wanna-be witches, perhaps-real witches, psychics, mediums, freaks, weirdos and tourists from all over the world. It was hell every Halloween.

"Hey Howard," I said. He turned an alarming shade of red. Teenaged boys.

"Uh, hi," he croaked.

"Seen anything weird lately?"

He laughed. "We live in Salem Massachusetts. At Halloween it's all we see."

"I know, but I'm talking about something else, something different, something real, like pumpkins taking over everything."

He scratched his shock of wheat-colored hair and gazed off into the distance as though searching for something in the depths of his memory. "You know, I seen two things. First, one of the greens was dug all up the other day. It looked like a grave. I had to spend three hours putting the sod back and making it perfect for Mr. Buttertub."

Calvin guffawed. "Buttertub? Seriously?"

"Yeah," Howard said. "Richard Buttertub. He's the greenskeeper."

I sighed. So juvenile.

"He had to go to high school as Dick Buttertub?" Calvin laughed again, big loud snorts.

Howard laughed, too. "I know."

"Hey, when you two are through we kind of have a problem."

"Right," Howard said. "So aside from the grave on sixteen's green and the pumpkin vines, I ain't seen much."

I latched onto the vines. "Checked on them lately? The vines."

"Wanna ride out there now? We can take a cart. Buttertub won't mind."

So we jumped in a golf cart. I had to sit in the back where the clubs go because Calvin took up most of the seat. When we drove by the sixteenth green, Howard stopped. We all got out because Howard wanted to check on his work. He pointed at a thin line in the grass where he'd repaired the hole. "They're gonna bitch me out about that, but it was the best I could do."

You could see the line went about six feet, crossed over two feet, then went six feet the other way making a perfect rectangle. "This does look like it was a grave," I said.

"I know," Howard answered. "And when I was digging, I thought my shovel scraped against wood."

Calvin snorted. He did that a lot. "If it's a grave, and ya know this is Salem so it could be, the last thing we need to do is uncover it. Can you imagine the stir? The fuss? We'd be in the middle of it all. The mediums would be trying to commune with the ghost. The witches would be performing rituals on Howard's green. The tourists would be everywhere taking pictures. The grass'd be all tore up. Uh, bad idea. Very bad."

"Cal is right," I said and shuddered. "Too horrible to consider."

We climbed back into the cart and Howard took us to the edge of the forest, or what used to be the edge. Pumpkin vines had grown onto the fairway and were covering the ninth tee. A huge pumpkin sat on the bench beside the tee like a sentry. Howard leapt out of the cart and grabbed the enormous orange fruit. He hefted it, grunting, and shot-putted it across the tee. It promptly exploded. Howard screamed as orange glop, seeds, stringy stuff and chunks of pumpkin skin smacked into him. The force of the blast knocked him over. He lay moaning under the goop. Cal and I ran to save him. A seed had landed in his mouth and a green sprout was growing over his face. Howard choked and plucked at it, but his hands were securely vined to the ground. "Save him," I yelled to Calvin.

Cal snatched the plant in Howard's mouth out and it turned on him, throwing a feeler and a vine around his head. Cal ripped it off and threw it away as I scraped as many vines as I could off Howard. They grew back as fast as I grabbed them. Cal fought with the plant trying to wind around his thick arm and won. He threw it off and snorted. We managed to clear Howard enough to help him to his feet. The three of us ran to the golf cart. The vines had begun to wind around the cart. A huge orange pumpkin sat on the seat and I swear it had eyes and a mouth. It looked like an insane jack-o-lantern. "You grab it," I said to Calvin.

"Unhuh," he shook his head violently. "You saw what happened to the last one."

Howard was mad. His yellow hair was covered with orange goo. Glop dripped down his face and a seed had sprouted under his shirt and was growing up his chin. He yanked it out, reached for the pumpkin on the seat and, I swear, it attacked him. Its jack-o-lantern mouth opened, and it spewed orange glop everywhere. It got on me and Calvin and drenched Howard who ignored it, grabbed the thing and flung it as far as he could. It immediately exploded. More goo flew everywhere.

"In," Howard gasped. "Get into the cart."

We clambered in. I threw myself in the back as Howard released the clutch and the cart shot forward. He weaved and swerved to avoid hitting any more exploding globes, punched it, and we tore off across the fairway as fast as the cart would go.

When we felt like we were a safe distance away, I said. "Well, that was gross."

"You're not kidding," Howard said. "Wait till I tell Buttertub what's happened to the course."

He drove straight to the cart barn where a man much larger than even Calvin was sitting in a small office. He nearly filled it. I was guessing that was the Dick Buttertub. He'd grown into the name. Howard stopped and ran to talk to his boss. Calvin and I followed. Buttertub got up and came out of the office probably because there wasn't room for anyone else in there. "Why are you covered in orange slime?" He had a thick Southern accent. I tried not to giggle. We didn't hear it much up here in Massachusetts.

Howard started stuttering. "Pu-pu-pu-punkins," he finally got out.

Buttertub patted Howard's shoulder. "Slow down Howie and tell me what's going on."

"There's punkin vines all over the ninth tee and the punkins are everywhere. One exploded on me."

Buttertub noticed me and Calvin. "Did you two see this?"

I nodded and pointed at the cart. "The cart's covered in it, too."

Buttertub lumbered over to the biggest cart in the barn. It had a backseat. "Take me out there." I did not want to go, but neither did Howard or Calvin, so it was up to me to man up. "Let's go," I said. "I knew being a short little chick would challenge their masculinity. I learned that in psychology.

So we climbed into the cart and Buttertub drove across the fairways, crossed close to the sixteenth green and then through the woods to the other fairway. When he got out of the woods, it was plain to see where the vines had originated. They were spreading from the woods behind the sixteenth green, across the seventh tee and into the woods on the other side where they went wild. The ninth tee was now covered. Huge orange pumpkins dotted the fairway.

Buttertub stopped the cart and stared with his mouth hanging open.

"My mom thinks this is from some fertilizer you guys are using," I said.

"We stop putting nitrogen fertilizer out after July. The growing season this far north stops about then. We'll put down a top dressing in November, but we haven't used any new fertilizers. Mostly we manage the course by mowing and watering. Your mom's just wrong. It ain't us."

"What could it be?" Howard asked.

Buttertub moved the cart closer to he vines. They'd already spread into the distant ninth fairway. "I wouldn't go any farther," I said.

Buttertub scoffed and moved the cart to the edge of the growth. A long stringer seemed to sense us and headed our way. I pointed. "You better move, or it'll get us."

Buttertub scoffed again. "I doubt that, missy."

The vine sprouted flowers, quickly followed by small, baseball-sized fruit that swelled rapidly. Before Buttertub could move the cart, one had wrapped around the tire and was growing up the front of the cart. Buttertub stepped out.

"I wouldn't do that," Calvin said.

"Really, sir," Howard started stuttering again. "Ssttopp, d-d-d-don't do do do it."

Buttertub turned to look at Howard, the vine sprouted over the top of him and quickly wrapped him in its coils. "Help!" He screamed as he toppled over backwards. A huge pumpkin was on his chest and getting bigger.

Howard and Calvin tried to move it, but it just kept growing. Buttertub squirmed helplessly in the coils of vine. Another pumpkin broke loose of its vine and rolled toward us. "Look out!" I screamed.

Calvin glanced at me and I pointed. He and Howard saw the huge orange fruit rolling, picking up speed. It had to weigh five hundred pounds. "Run!" Calvin stopped trying to save Buttertub, turned and ran for the cart. It was too late for the cart. The vines had claimed it. I grabbed Calvin's hand. "We gotta run," I screamed.

The huge pumpkin rolling for us was actually growling. I could hear it. Howard was refusing to leave Buttertub who had stopped moving. "Come on, Howie." I pulled his hand as a vine reached for Howard's foot.

"But Mr. Buttertub."

"He's done for," Calvin said. "Run."

So, we took off over the fairway toward the clubhouse and away from the pumpkin's worst infestation. Howard was crying and kept stopping to look over his shoulder. "Poor Mr. Buttertub. We gotta get him some help."

We were whipped when we got back to the clubhouse. Calvin's usually brown face was purple. He never ran. He fell into a chair, it broke under him, and he sat on the deck sobbing. "This is crazy. We're caught in a terrible nightmare."

I helped him up and onto a solid-looking bench. "It's because we live here," I snarled. "Frigging Salem. It must be a curse or something. The place is overrun with witches and weirdos. One of them cursed us with the attack of the killer pumpkins. We have to figure out who and get them to make it stop."

Howard had gone into the clubhouse. He emerged with a woman dressed in a gray business suit. "Howard can barely talk," she said. "I'm Aurelia Melkinthorp, the club manager. "Can any of you explain what's going on here?"

I stood up and took a deep breath. "This is gonna sound weird," I started. "But pumpkin vines and killer pumpkins have Mr. Butterbean, I mean Buttertub, pinned down somewhere near the sixteenth green. He needs help, or he could die. I think."

"Well, take me out there to look."

"No, call 911, call the fire department," I said. "He needs rescuing right now."

She backed up with her hand over her mouth and looked from me to Howard and then focused on Calvin. "Who *are* you two?"

"We're Howie's friends," Cal said. "And Joe is right. You need to call the fire department. Right away or Mr. Buttertub is a goner."

"I took a picture," I said and pulled it up on my phone. It was of the fairway and the lump that used to be Mr. Buttertub.

She glanced at it. "All I see are vines and pumpkins. Are you sure this is our golf course?"

"It is," Howie squeaked out. "And that lump is Mr. Buttertub."

She backed another step. Indecision played across her aristocratic features, thin, sculptured nose, perfect makeup. "I'll call, but there better be a real emergency. If this is some Halloween prank ."

"I hate Halloween!" I screamed. "Call."

"All right, all right," she said and disappeared into her office.

Ten minutes later we were all headed out onto the course riding in the cab of a big, red, fire truck. When we got to the sixteenth green, I saw the vines had surrounded it. "What is all this green viney shit?" The fireman, whose name was Randy Wainwright, said. Then he seemed to remember we were kids and said, "Excuse my French."

"It's okay," Calvin said. He was enjoying the ride like he was a five-year old. He had his elbow stuck out the window. I was squished between him and Fireman Randy. "It's those vines like we told you. They ate Mr. Buttertub."

We arrived at the spot where we thought Buttertub might be. We'd driven over the vines and squished a lot of pumpkins. Every time we hit one, it exploded. The firetruck was covered in pumpkin goop. "This is some weird shit, excuse my French," Fireman Randy said. "Where's your greenskeeper fellow anyway?"

I pointed. "I think that lump is him."

Fireman Randy pushed the door of the truck open. Vines immediately began growing in through the opening. Randy yanked it shut. "This shit is evil."

"You got that right," Calvin said.

Randy reached behind the seat and pulled an axe off the wall. He pushed open the door again and began hacking vines. I took out my phone and began videoing the whole episode. I figured it might be worth something one day. You never knew.

As Fireman Randy climbed out, a huge orange pumpkin, one of the four-hundred-pounders, headed for the truck. It was growling. Randy squared his broad shoulders, hacked more vines and approached the growling orange fruit. It had eyes. I could see them. Triangles of black glaring out of the pumpkin's sides. It opened its huge mouth and orange goop shot at Fireman Randy. He fended it off and attacked the pumpkin, slime dripping from the brim of his red fireman hat. He hacked a chunk out of the pumpkin and it exploded. Vines wrapped around him. He screamed and whacked vines with the axe handle and hacked into more with the blade, backing rapidly toward the truck as another gigantic pumpkin rolled into view headed straight for him. I got it all recorded on my phone.

He leapt into the truck and slammed the door. It cut some vines off and the ends withered where they dropped onto the truck floor. He picked up the radio. "We got us a big problem out here at the Beverly Country Club," he said into the radio.

"Did I hear that right?" The voice asked. "What kind of trouble?"

"Killer pumpkins," Fireman Randy said. "The vines are alive, and the pumpkins are attacking. There's a man down out here and I can't get to him. Call forestry and get a bulldozer, maybe some flame-throwers or a bazooka might help."

The man on the other end burst out laughing. "This another one of your Halloween pranks, right, Randy?"

"No, dammit all, there's killer pumpkins out here. I need help." Vines had grown over the top of the truck. They were trying to get into the windows. "I'm gonna have to make a run for it. Meet me at the clubhouse. Bring everything we got."

He hung the radio back in its holster and revved the truck engine. The engine roared, he slammed the big truck into reverse, and took off.

When we got back to the clubhouse, Howie was waiting. He'd washed off most of the pumpkin goo. "I have an idea," he said.

Cal and I climbed out of the truck as in the distance, sirens sounded. "I should really call my Mom," I said. "But what're you thinking?"

"It's the grave."

"It's the what?" Calvin asked.

"That grave on the sixteenth green. You know, the one I covered up. The vines start on the other side of the green and go into the woods from there and across the fairway into the woods on the other side. The pumpkin infestation must have started there."

"I bet you're right," I said. "Curses and stuff like that are the whole problem with Salem. It's like we can never escape them. We need to go dig up that grave. Find out who's in it and what we can do to get rid of the curse."

"We need a witch," Calvin said. "A good one who can reverse the curse."

I rolled my eyes. "Seriously, Cal, you really think we should go hunt down a witch to help us?"

"Yeah," Calvin said. "There's more witches per square inch in this town right now than in the entire world. We hunt down the best one and get her to reverse the curse."

I shook my head. "I really hate this town."

Howard left for a minute and came back with Buttertub's two-seater golf cart. "I have to save Mr. Buttertub. If it means digging up that grave, I'll do it. If it means hunting down the best witch in Salem, I'll do it. We can't leave him out there."

"Howie," I said as gently as I could. "Mr. Buttertub is gone. The pumpkins ate him."

"You don't know that!" Howie's screeched. "D-d-d-d don't even think it."

"Okay, okay," Calvin soothed Howie. "We'll go dig up the grave. But we really can't go out on that fairway. The vines have covered your boss and if we go anywhere near him, they'll get us too."

"I'll just drive by," Howie said. "I won't get too close."

I glared at Calvin. "This is a stupid idea. We should let the fire department handle the vines and the exploding pumpkins."

Howie drove the cart down the eighteenth fairway, crossed to the seventeenth and then cut through the woods to the ninth which ran parallel to the sixteenth fairway which is where Buttertub was. Or where he used to be. We popped out of the woods and spotted the massive patch of writhing vines slowly working their way toward the eighth hole. Suddenly, a huge lump of vines lifted off the ground. "Stop," I yelled. "Look."

Howie started crying. "No! It can't be."

"It's Buttertub," Calvin said in a voice dripping with terror. "He's a pumpkin. Run for it."

Sure enough, Mr. Buttertub's head was now a jack-o-lantern. The pumpkin rode on top of Buttertub's shoulders where his head should be. Buttertub was now Pumpkin Man. It lurched like Frankenstein down the fairway. Vines retreated before him as he headed straight toward us.

"Run, Howie," I screamed. "Drive this thing."

Howie was frozen with fear and horror. He couldn't move. I took out my phone and snapped some pictures while Calvin got out of the cart, went around to the driver's side, shoved Howie over, climbed in and spun the cart around, racing away from Pumpkin Man.

I hung onto the rail beside the seat, tapped Calvin's shoulder. "Go to the grave site. Let's dig it up."

Howie was moaning. Drool ran down his chin and tears flooded his face. He looked at me. "Buttertub is dead."

"Most likely," I said. "Maybe if we lift the curse, he'll come back."

Howie brightened. "Yeah, let's go dig up that grave."

When we got to the green, Howie was the first one out of the cart. He grabbed his shovel and started digging like a mad man. Sod and dirt flew as he shoveled. It didn't take long to reach the old wooden coffin. While Howie cleared around it, Calvin and I scraped the remaining dirt off the top. There was an inscription. I read it aloud. "Here lies Mary Ann McGinty, convicted of witchcraft and hung on October 30, 1693."

My mouth fell open and I took my trusty phone out and snapped more pictures.

Calvin shouted. "This must be Mary Ann's ancestor. Maybe Mary Ann can reverse the curse."

"She won't do it," Howie said. "She's the most popular girl in school, the queen of tonight's parade, and she's mean. She'll never even try. She probably doesn't even know this relative existed, and she's not gonna believe us if we tell her." He sobbed. "Mary Ann doesn't give a crap about Mr. Buttertub. She won't help."

"Do you want to open this coffin?" Calvin asked.

"No," I said. "I really don't."

Howie insisted. "Maybe there's an amulet, or a charm, or something in there we can use to save Buttertub."

So, we pried open the lid with Howie's shovel. One of the slats on top broke as the lid rose. All of us gasped at once. There, totally preserved, was the body of an elderly woman. She wore the black waistcoat common to the seventeenth century, a close-fitting white cap over filthy red hair and a white apron over a dark skirt. It was impossible to see her shoes. Aside from the dirt, dust and general filth, she could have been buried yesterday. I looked away but pulled my phone and snapped more pictures. I was collecting quite a file. I backed away rapidly. "Close it. Quick."

Howie looked over his shoulder at me and snarled. "I got it open. I'm looking for something to save Buttertub."

Calvin gasped and lumbered to his feet. "I ain't touching that."

Howie found pockets in the apron. He pulled out a lock of red hair tied with a ribbon that might have been pink a long time ago. "Here," he said to Calvin who was closest. "You hold it."

"No," Calvin said and backed further away.

"Neither of you are any help at all," Howie said. I stepped closer, averting my eyes so I didn't have to see the body, and stuck out my hand. Howie dropped the lock of hair into it. My hand was shaking so badly, I almost dropped it, but drew a deep breath and didn't. Howie continued to search the corpse. He came up with a tiny gold cross on a piece of rotting string,a cloth bag and something wrapped in black cloth. "That's it," he said. "Let's shut her up and go find Mary Ann McGinty. This shit belongs to her anyway, and there's nothing here that's yelling curse-breaking amulet at me."

I didn't want to visit Mary Ann now, next week or ever. Just the thought made me want to barf. When we got back to the clubhouse, Howie dragged us to my car. The fire department and the forestry service had arrived. They were unloading massive amounts of equipment including Fireman Randy's requested bulldozer. Howie stopped and stared at it. "Buttertub would freak if he saw that thing on his golf course. It's gonna tear up all the grass."

Calvin climbed into the back of my Corolla, Howie rode shotgun and I, reluctantly, got into the driver's seat. "I have no idea where she lives," I said hoping they didn't either.

"She lives at six Ardmore Drive right behind Folly Hill Farm," Calvin said.

I turned and glared at him. "You would know. I don't want to go to Mary Ann's house, not now, not ever. I'm only doing this because Howie thinks Mary Ann can somehow help get Buttertub back and right now, it's all we got. But I think she'll laugh at us and we'll be horribly embarrassed and then she'll go to school and tell everyone."

"She's not that bad," Calvin said.

"She is," I said as I slammed the car into reverse, pulled out onto Elliot and headed for Ardmore. It was almost seven. The parade was due to start at nine. We'd been dealing with this pumpkin crap since we got home from school. I was getting pretty tired of it. "I really don't want to do this," I said again as I pulled into the driveway of one of the biggest homes in Danvers. "I'm not going to the door."

"Stay in the car then. You'll just look stupid."

I groaned. Mary Ann McGinty didn't even know I was alive. She certainly didn't know Calvin or Howie though she'd probably gone to school with us her entire life. She'd been breathing the rarified air of the super popular, amazingly beautiful, uber rich child since she'd entered the school system. I followed them up the stairs, literally ready to barf. For some reason, I could watch Buttertub get eaten by pumpkin vines and arise with a pumpkin for a head, stare at a not-rotting corpse and feel just fine. But the mere thought of facing Mary Ann had me ready to power hurl.

Calvin squared his shoulders and knocked on the door. We all waited, my stomach rolling. Nothing was worse than being put down by the prettiest girl in school. Nothing. And then she answered the door.

"Hello," she said in her sweet-girl voice. "How can I help you?"

Calvin and Howie, you know, the guys who demanded we come here, could not utter word one. They stood there like giant goobers. After thirty of the most awkward moments of my life, I stepped forward and stuck out my hand. She took it. "Hi, Mary Ann, we have a problem you might be able to help us with," I said. She stared at me like she'd never seen me before. "I'm Joe from seventh period. We go to school together." Her eyes were glassing over. "Can we come in and talk?"

She did a slight eye roll which I caught. "I'm getting ready for the parade right now. Can you come back later?"

I found the video of Fireman Randy on my phone, clicked it open and hit play. I turned my Android's screen in her direction. She stared at Fireman Randy hacking away at vines and then the exploding pumpkins. "There's more," I said, searched the phone and found the picture of the coffin lid. "We think your ancestor is the cause of the, uh, the whole pumpkins gone bad at the golf course thing."

"That's my name on the coffin."

Howie finally woke from his stuper. "No shit," he said.

Calvin punched Howie's arm. "Don't curse in front of the lady."

I rolled my eyes. Mary Ann caught it and sighed. "Come in, I guess."

Her mother was in the living room fussing with a long gown on a dress form. She stood up and I saw the resemblance. "Hello, are you kids in the parade, too?"

"I'm sorry to bother you, Mrs. McGinty," I said. "But there's a problem at the golf course and we found the, uh, the corpse of someone named Mary Ann McGinty." I thrust the phone with the picture in her direction. "And, well pumpkins have gone insane down at the golf course, and I, uh, I think they murdered Mr. Buttertub, the greenskeeper."

I nudged Howie. Why was I doing all the talking when they were the ones who wanted to come here?

Mary Ann's mother took my phone and stared at the photo of the inscription. "This is my great, great, great a bunch of times grandmother. She was wrongfully accused of witchcraft and hung. We never knew where she was buried."

I looked confused. "I figured it would be your husband's relative and Mary Ann's."

"I'm divorced," she said. "McGinty is my maiden name. Mary Ann was born after the divorce."

"Okay, but we still have this pumpkin problem and then your ancestor, who looks quite fresh, if I may say so, is in a coffin on the sixteenth green." I indicated the goober twins. "We've all seen it. I have pictures of the corpse if you'd like to view them We think she cursed the golf course and we were hoping you'd know how to reverse itHowie handed Ms. McGinty the lock of hair, the bag and the cross."

Ms. McGinty stared at the objects in her hand like they were going to bite her. She finally picked up the bag. "What's in this?"

"We didn't open it," Howie said.

Ms. McGinty opened the drawstring holding it closed and dumped something into her hand. It was round and shiny. She gingerly picked it up between her thumb and forefinger. Mary Ann screamed. I gasped and Calvin oofed. "It's an eyeball, a crystal one," I said. "I'm thinking this Mary Ann relative of yours was either really a witch or trying to be one."

Ms. McGinty closed her hand around the eye. "I guess I better help you. It appears my relative has done something I might be responsible for in a way."

Mary Ann stomped her perfect foot. "This is going to ruin the parade, isn't it?"

I turned on her. "Hey, Mr. Buttertub is a freaking pumpkin. I bet he's not going to any parades either."

"That's enough, Mary Ann. You'll have to call Laura and tell her to take your place."

"Let Laura Skelton take my place? Are you insane?" Mary Ann's perfect features were screwed into an ugly snarl and her milk-white complexion had turned a hideous mottled red. Tears swelled in her blue eyes turning them red as the tears traced paths through her makeup closely followed by the black streaks of mascara and eyeliner.

"This is more important than the parade, Mary Ann," Ms. McGinty snapped. She pulled a cellphone out of her jeans' pocket and sent off a text. "I've called some . . . some friends to come help. Why don't you, uh, you three have a seat while I gather some things."

Calvin, Howie and I plopped on a vast dark-blue sectional in the living room. "What's she doing?" Calvin hissed.

"She's a freaking witch," Howie said. "She's gathering her coven or something like that."

"I think you might be right," I said. "The eyeball thing sure said something to her."

"It said something to me, too," Calvin whispered. "It said welcome to weirdville."

Ms. McGinty came back into the room and sat next to me. "Do you have any more pictures you could show me?"

I showed her the video of Fireman Randy and the pictures of her relative and Mr. Buttertub as a pumpkin, and all the other pumpkin pictures I'd taken. She gave me back my phone after watching Fireman

Randy a couple of times. I lifted an eyebrow and she shrugged. "He's kind of cute."

"He was being attacked by killer pumpkins created by your relative."

"I believe it's the old pumpkin curse. Mary Ann was hung for it. I need some help, but I think I can reverse it."

While we waited, Mary Ann threw two more tantrums. Ms. McGinty brought us a tray of sodas and snacks. Mary Ann started screaming, grabbed her beautiful dress and tore it into shreds. Ms. McGinty then ordered her to her room. Mary Ann promptly burst into hysterical sobs. Ms. McGinty put her arm around the bawling girl and helped her to the stairs talking to her in a soothing voice. I could hear every word. She was promising Mary Ann everything but the kitchen sink for this serious disruption of her child's planned evening. Calvin and Howie watched all this with their mouths open.

"What a freaking bitch," Howie whispered. "Can you say spoiled?"

"She's too beautiful," Calvin said, and I rolled my eyes.

"She's horrible, Calvin. Get over it. She acts like she always gets her way and the slightest obstacle to her plans sends her into hysterics."

"I know," Calvin said. "But when your child is that perfect, I guess you give her all she wants. I mean, I sure would, you know, give her anything she wanted if she would just look at me."

Howie smacked Calvin in the shoulder hard. "Dude, you have issues."

"What he has is the biggest crush on Mary Ann I've ever seen."

Howie reached into his pocket and pulled out a piece of black cloth. He unwrapped it and took out a porcelain heart. It was really old. "This came out of the witch's pocket. Maybe it's a love potion. It was a locket. He clicked it open. Inside, was finely ground greenish powder. He clicked it shut and handed the faded red heart to Calvin.

"What do I do with it?"

"Nothing," I hissed. "You're not a witch and neither is Howie."

Mary Ann's open can of soda sat on the end table next to Calvin. "Put the powder in her drink," Howie whispered.

"You're nuts," I said. "You could poison her. You have no idea what's in that."

They both ignored me. "Imma do it," Calvin said. He opened the heart and poured the powder into her drink just as Mary Ann flounced back down the stairs.

First thing the beautiful girl spotted was her soda. She held her cell phone in her other hand. "I'll call Laura," she said followed by a deep sigh and an eyeroll. Her mother came into the room followed by two other women, one I recognized as the most famous witch in Salem, Agnes Taverner. Agnes led the biggest coven of witches in Salem, and tonight she should be leading them in the magic circle which contained hundreds of witches from all over the world. For Ms. McGinty to get her here, must have taken a lot of pull, and or money.

For a moment, I forgot about the powder in Mary Ann's soda and stared at Agnes. She was old, I knew that, but it was hard to tell. She looked like she was in her forties or maybe fifties. She was thin and vibrated with energy. It oozed out of her pores.

"Let's go," she said. "I need to see these pumpkin creatures myself."

Meanwhile, Mary Ann took a long pull off her soda. I grabbed Howie and got him out of the way. If the charm was a love charm, she would fall for the first guy she saw, and I really wanted that to be Calvin. If she died, I wanted all of us somewhere else.

Calvin hadn't spent his life in Salem for nothing. He clambered out of the sectional and parked right in front of her, the heart clutched in his meaty fist.

"Why didn't you use it on yourself?" I whispered to Howie.

"Going to college. W-w-w-want out of this h-h-ho-horrible town, and besides, not in l-l-l-love." Then he turned bright red and looked away. "With her, anyway."

I grabbed his hand. "What does that mean?" His face turned even redder.

Mary Ann lifted her gorgeous head, face scrubbed clean of makeup smears and mascara and stared at Calvin. I held my breath. "Who are you?" She said to Cal in a breathy voice.

"Calvin Johnson, Miss Mary Ann. I'm in your seventh-period class."

Mary Ann touched his heavy jowls with a white hand and stoked his cheek. "You're cute," then she giggled. "Why haven't I ever met you before?"

Calvin looked over his shoulder at me and mouthed holy shit. Ms. McGinty pointed at the three of us. "Let's go. Mrs. Taverner has a busy schedule."

"I want to go, too, Mother," Mary Ann said and pouted adorably. A gesture I felt sure she practiced in front of a mirror.

"Then let's go." They piled into Ms. McGinty's Escalade, one I was sure she'd bought from Calvin's mother, and we got into the Corolla. I smothered laughter when Mary Ann blindly followed Calvin and climbed in beside him. It was touching and truly freaky. She sat as close to him as she could and clutched his meaty forearm. I glanced into the rearview and saw her whisper something in his ear. If Calvin hadn't been a black guy, he would probably be beet red.

We followed the Escalade to Beverly Country Club and climbed out. It was a scene from Dante's Inferno. Flames shot into the air from somewhere out on the course, fire engines raced back and forth, bumping over curbs, crossing the practice sand trap and the putting green. Firemen raced everywhere and right in the middle of the parking lot, with her bun askew and soot on her face stood Aurelia Melkinthorpe who looked like she was having a real meltdown.

There was no place to park. Howie bolted from the car groaning and swearing. "Oh my god, my golf course. Mr. Buttertub will kill me. This is all my fault. Shit, damn, fudge!" Only he didn't say fudge he said the real F word, the mother of all swear words.

Aurelia Melkinthorpe spotted Howie and ran to him. "They're destroying the course," she screamed. "I know," he replied and they hugged each other.

Fireman Randy emerged from a cloud of smoke and ran to us. "You kids see the pumpkin guy run by?"

Ms. McGinty stepped in front of me and wrapped one hand around Fireman Randy's enormous bicep. "We came to fix this."

He stared down, he was at least six-five, into her lovely face. "Who're you?"

"I brought Agnes," she said.

Well the witch's name acted like magic on Fireman Randy. I guess everyone knew who she was. "Oh," he said. "Come with me."

We trooped along behind Fireman Randy leaving Calvin and Mary Ann canoodling, cuddling, and I think even kissing, in the back of my car. Calvin was going to regret feeding her that potion.

The Fireman led us to a bank of golf carts waiting in a row. They got into one. Ms. McGinty made sure she found a seat next to Fireman Randy. Agnes sat on her other side. I got in a different one with Howie.

Where to?" I heard Fireman Randy ask McGinty.

"Follow me," Howie yelled.

The pumpkins had grown over the first hole. Flamethrowers had cleared a pathway through it, across the woods and into the back nine. We followed a burned pathway in the vines to the sixteenth hole. The police or the fire department or someone had put up a fence around the green where Mary Ann McGinty's coffin now lay exposed.

The witches climbed out. Ms. McGinty had a capacious crocheted bag with her. She took out candles, salt, a sage bundle, and some other items I couldn't see and proceeded to draw a pentagram in the middle of Howie's precious green using the shovel we'd left on top of the coffin. The witches laid out the candles, one on each point of the pentagram and lit them. Then they sat around it. Ms. McGinty stole another look in the coffin on her way around the edge, stopped, and reached into the top of the dead woman's bodice. She removed what Howie had been looking for, an old leather-bound book. It was small and thin. She handed the book to Agnes and took her seat.

Agnes opened the book and smiled. "This should be quick." And it might have been, but a pumpkin man, from the look of him it was Buttertub, ran across the green, grabbed Agnes in a bearhug, vines quickly wound around her tying her to Buttertub. He bolted into the night with Agnes and disappeared.

We all stared into the darkness for a few seconds. Ms. McGinty screamed. Her friend screamed and then the pumpkin vines took over the green, growing across the carefully gouged pentagram and covering the coffin. "Run!" I screamed, grabbed McGinty's arm and dragged her to the golf carts. Fireman Randy scooped her into his arms and set her on the seat, a wholly unnecessary gesture in my opinion. The other witch scrambled in and we took off back the way we came. Pumpkin vines were growing at an even faster pace, pumpkins were sprouting in bigger numbers and I saw three more pumpkin people lurching around the course.

McGinty climbed up in the seat and pointed. "Go get them. They have Agnes."

Fireman Randy patted her rump. "Sit down. Ms. McGinty, we can't go over there, the pumpkins will get us."

McGinty started crying, leaning heavily on Fireman Randy's broad shoulder. The other witch was in our cart. "Where do you think they would take Agnes?" She asked Howie. "You seem to know this course."

"It depends on why they want her, Ms. Uh, Ms...."

"Call me Carol," she said. "I'm here from Canada. I come down for the gathering and the Circle every year."

She pulled out her cellphone. "I think we need more witches. This thing is huge. The pumpkin element alone is massive. I mean the vines are spreading like wildfire."

"I still have the eye," McGinty said from the other cart. Fireman Randy now had his arm around her shoulders. No need for a charm there. She held up the eye Howie had taken from the coffin. "And the lock of hair and the book."

We got back to the scene from hell at the clubhouse. McGinty and Carol put their heads together. They went to my car and dragged Mary Ann out. She didn't want to leave Calvin, so he followed. "She's her namesake," McGinty said to Carol. "My first name is Serena. Mary Ann has all the power." She handed the lock of hair and the eyeball to Mary Ann who looked confused.

"This lock of hair came from the head of your great, great great, great grandmother. She was burned at the stake in England. The Mary Ann in the coffin on the golf course is her granddaughter. I knew the book and the hair were supposed to exist but didn't know where they were. So, you take these two items, and sit in a circle with me and Carol and you concentrate on that eye."

"It's gross," she said.

"Mary Ann," her mother's voice held an iron note.

"Whatever."

Carol had drawn an enormous pentagram in the parking lot. Two vans pulled in and dozens of witches and warlocks emerged. Mary Ann sat in the middle holding the eye. Her mother handed her the old book and pointed. "Concentrate on the eye and read this three times."

The witches began to hum. It was a high note. Fireman Randy and I backed up. I could see Calvin wanted to hover. "Pumpkin men are coming!" Howie screamed. "There's five of them."

I followed his pointing finger. Over the crest of the second hole, five figures with pumpkin heads galloped awkwardly toward the circle. I didn't want to interrupt the witches, so I said nothing as the pumpkin men closed in. Vines trailed from their behinds, spreading as they ran. Rolling mammoth pumpkins followed in their wake heading straight for the circle.

The humming increased in volume and Mary Ann began to read. "Doomsday is gone, pumpkins beware, the giant wood carver will soon be here. He's sharpened his blade, he's readied his knife, to take from each pumpkin all signs of life."

A huge shadow rose from the smoke. It grew bigger and bigger until I could make out the image of a giant carrying an equally big knife. The pumpkin men were almost on us. Firemen moved into position holding the flame throwers used by forestry personnel to burn back underbrush. They lit their flames. The pumpkin men ran faster. I heard the whoosh of the flames igniting. The pumpkin men opened their mouths and an eerie howl erupted from them. One crashed into a fireman, vines covered him, he sprouted a pumpkin head, rose and ran for the witches. Now there were six.

The firemen toasted two but the other three got through and followed the new one and the old one I thought was Buttertub. The witches broke their circle. Some threw spells of protection over themselves. Sparks flew, and pumpkin vines burned. It wasn't enough. Suddenly, the black shadow that had risen from the smoke began to chop vines and pumpkins. They exploded and caught fire. The shadow advanced on the pumpkin men.

"Not Buttertub," Howie screamed. He raced for his former boss, now a man with a jack-o-lantern head. The shadow creature hacked into the pumpkin men. Witches scattered. Only Mary Ann sat in the center of the pentagram focusing on the eye. She held it up, pointed at Buttertub who was almost on her and screamed, *"Reditus ut hominum,"* three times.

"That means return to human," Howie translated.

"I know. I live in freaking Salem," I snarled.

"Look," he said. Buttertub was writhing on the ground. The jack-o-lantern was shrinking and melting. Orange goo ran down Buttertub's now-recognizable face. It took only minutes. Buttertub was a man again.

Mary Ann seemed to have discovered her power. "Be gone," she said to the shadow creature. All the vines were dead or dying. Every pumpkin had exploded, and the remaining pumpkin men were now normal people. Sadly, one looked dead. The firemen dragged the unconscious one toward Mary Ann and the clutch of witches. "He's still breathing," Fireman Randy said. "Can you fix him? He's one of our guys."

Carol touched him on the forehead and he started moaning. Ms. McGinty screamed. "Agnes, oh my god."

Agnes Taverner wobbled out of the woods covered in orange slime from head to toe. McGinty ran to help her along with every other witch. "What happened?" She asked. "I thought I was supposed to run the circle. How did I get here?"

When I finally got home, my mom was waiting. "Where have you been. It's time to go to the party."

I thought about explaining, but after all that happened what could I say? We dressed in our costumes. I was a witch, of course, and Mom always wore her scarecrow costume. As we headed out the door, Calvin walked up dressed like a huge orange jack-o-lantern. And trailing behind him was Mary Ann in an elf costume. My mother looked at me with one eyebrow raised.

"Calvin and Mary Ann McGinty are in love," I said.

"Joe!"

I ignored her. After all, it was Halloween and some secrets were better left untold.

Thank you for your purchase. If you would like to read more from these or other find TT authors, please visit our website:

www.tell-talepublishing.com